A
Special
Kind of
Advent

By
S J Crabb

Contents

More books by S J Crabb

Romantic Comedy:

sjcrabb.com

1

Today is going to be a good day. Finally, all of my hard work is about to pay off and everything I've ever dreamed about is heading my way.

I check my reflection and smile with satisfaction. The person looking back at me shouts success. She looks the part that I'm about to play and I'm pleased with how things have worked out.

Victoria Matthews has come a long way since she was known as Vicky Matthews from flat 23 Roundshaw Towers.

The girl who against all the odds managed to claw her way through school and rise above the expectations of her peers.

As I gaze at myself critically in the mirror, I take a moment to remember the child I once was. The child with a loving single mother, struggling to make ends meet on the council estate everybody feared to visit. The child who made do with hand-me-downs from her older sister and Maria Dawes from number 35. The child who shrank with embarrassment as she joined the line for free school meals and watched with envy the other kids opening their packed lunches made by their perfect mothers, who made sure their children wanted for nothing.

Well, I wanted it all too. Every last felt-tip pen and glittery notebook. I vowed to make something of myself and here I am on the verge of making my dream come true. Finally, Victoria Matthews is about to have it all and I can't wait.

With a small triumphant smile, I grab my designer handbag and keys from the hall table. With one last critical look in the mirror,
I head purposefully towards the door. Today is the day I make senior partner in the law firm I have struggled to rise to the top of. The hours of study and sacrifice are about to pay off and there will be no looking back. This is it. My moment of triumph and I can't get there fast enough.

I start the familiar walk to the railway station. Fifteen minutes is all it takes, and I set off with a spring in my step. For once the rain has held off as I march briskly along the dusty pavements. The building site lies ahead and I prepare myself for the first ritual of the day.

As I near the scaffolding, I brace myself for the inevitable greeting. I see the builders working away and set my mood accordingly. However, today something happens that takes me by surprise. *Nothing*.

Not a sound or a whisper. Not even a shout or a wolf whistle of appreciation. Just stony cold silence which makes me think they haven't seen me. That's strange, I always get a cheery call and a request for a date. Normally, I get a whistle signifying their unbridled lust for me as I sashay past. Usually, I gaze around with irritation as the feminist in me tosses her head and throws a disapproving glance in their direction.

However, it's the woman in me that craves their attention. The girl that feels the flutter of excitement and revels in the knowledge that she is desirable and attractive.

Not today though. Today they carry on with their work and act as if I'm invisible. I frown and look at my watch. It must be my outfit. I always thought my figure-hugging black dress showed off my feminine side while showcasing a successful businesswoman. I've even worn my hair down and still *nothing*.

Maybe it's my make-up. The red lipstick is a sure-fire winner and usually has the desired effect.

I make it past the site and wonder if I have time to head back and change. Today of all days I can't be found lacking in any department. However, I can see that I only have ten minutes before the next ritual and sigh to myself. Bother, this is not turning out to be a good day and I've only just started.

Feeling somewhat unsettled I try to brush it off as just one of those things.

By the time I reach the station I have left it behind me. It's what happens today that counts and nothing can possibly stand in my way.

I join the queue for the usual coffee at 'grab and go' and check my appearance again in the window beside me. Nothing looks out of place and I think I look great. I took extra time this morning to get things just right. When I step inside Mr Rowanson's office at 9 am, I intend on stepping out of it as his new senior partner.

Five minutes before the train arrives I reach the front of the line. As I stare at the woman waiting to serve me, for the second time today I feel irritated. *She's new.* Not my usual server and now I'll have to explain what I want. She smiles sweetly as I sigh inside. "What can I get you, love?"

Quickly, I say clearly, "Triple, Venti, half sweet, non-fat, caramel Macchiato."

She looks at me blankly. "Sorry hun, can you repeat that I didn't quite get it?"

I try again and she holds up her hand as she starts to write every instruction on the outside of the cup.

The line starts shifting impatiently behind me as she struggles to understand my basic request.

By the time she hands me my coffee, I feel like downing it in one but have to settle for running at full speed towards platform one where my train is waiting to leave imminently.

I think I make it on the whistle of the guard - at least that's one whistle I can count on - and the doors close behind me as I stumble breathlessly into the carriage.

The train lurches away and I stumble and watch with dismay as the coffee splashes onto the floor. Bother!

I recover remarkably quickly and look towards my usual seat. Then, for the third time today, something is wrong. *There is someone sitting in my seat.*

This isn't right. I always sit on the seat nearest the door in the aisle facing forward. I'd think I was in the wrong carriage but my usual companions are seated firmly in their places. Yes, there's raincoat man clutching his briefcase on his lap and looking down at the Daily Telegraph. Next to him is student Sam, wired to his music with his eyes shut and just the steady tap of his toe to the beat of the music to signify he is still alive. Then there's Kim Kardashian. Not the real one of course but the one who always looks as if she's trowelled on her make-up and slept with her hair under an iron. Throughout the journey she flicks through the latest Cosmo and texts her friends continuously.

Then there is my seat. The last one available before the train reaches Raynes Park and is always empty waiting for me to take my rightful place. Not today though. Today there is a person squatting in my space. Daring to look like they have a right to be there and looking at their iPad with an air of boredom.

I catch the eye of raincoat man and almost see a flash of sympathy in his eyes before he looks down again. Five years I have sat in that seat with these very people. Everybody knows where to sit and at what time. They are only excused on sick and leave days, of which I never have any. This man is in my seat and doesn't even have the decency to look embarrassed about it.

The train gathers speed along with my heart rate and if I could haul him up by the scruff of his neck and toss him from the train like Superwoman, I would. In fact, in my mind, I do just that.

As I cling onto the pole like an exotic dancer on her first day, I seethe inside. This is not how my perfect day is meant to start. This is a bad omen and I try not to think about what this could mean for my future.

Then I reason with myself, after all it's what I do. I can argue a case against the best of them and win. Yes, this is all merely an inconvenience and when I step foot inside the pristine office block in Canary Wharf, my world will right itself.

2

"Morning, Ms Matthews."

I nod at Diana the receptionist as I head through the revolving doors into the world where I feel most comfortable.

Here I count for something and here I am respected and my word is law. This is my home and I make sure that every hour I'm here counts and stands for something.

There are no long lunch breaks and no days off for frivolous things such as holidays and dental appointments. I arrange any personal appointments in my own time, so they don't interfere with my work. I've never gone sick and feel irritated by those who do and I work hard and there's no time for play. I live alone and wouldn't want it any other way because families and partners are for people who don't want to succeed. There are no distractions in my life away from my goal and it is all about to pay dividends today.

I head to my office on the third floor and note that, as usual, I'm alone. Apart from Diana and the security guys, I'm always the first one in at 7 am and ready to start the day. Diana job shares with another member of staff and likes to do the early shift. By the time her replacement finishes at 7 pm,

I'm still here. I work 12 hours a day and use every minute of it. Life is just how I want it to be and I feel a shiver of excitement as I think about the conversation I'll be having in just two hours' time.

As I make my way to my office I think about Mr Rowanson. He formed this company with his brother and they built it up to be one of the most respected law firms in London. I always aspired to work here and begged and hounded them until they gave me a break as an Intern after I graduated from university. Then I worked my way up the ladder making myself indispensable to them and now I run the department responsible for their most prestigious accounts.

Then it all changed when his brother, Simon Rowanson died last month. Suddenly, Mr Rowanson lost interest. He started late and left early. He actually took holidays and weekends away and left myself and Charlie to man the ship.

Now he wants to step back from the business and take more of a back seat and I'm the perfect candidate to step up to the plate. In fact, there are really only two of us who could, unless he brings someone in from the outside.

Just for a second, I feel a flash of fear as I think about that possibility. Then I think of Charlie Monroe and roll my eyes.

Charlie is my counterpart who runs the corporate side of the business. Where I had nothing to help me in life, he had everything. Born with a silver spoon in his mouth he had his future mapped out for him from an early age. He was born to wealthy parents and lived the life I could only dream of. He went to Eton and then Oxford and hasn't ever had to try for anything because where his brain fails, his looks win. He has everything and I couldn't hate him any more than I do.

We are chalk and cheese and work in very different ways. I like to think that I am a professional where he is not. I am organised, he is not. I rule my department with precision and he does not. However, despite it all, he always gets what he wants. Somehow fate shines down on him and everything comes right in the end. He's my main competition and I can only hope that Mr Rowanson realises he shouldn't leave his beloved company in the hands of the frivolous. He needs an Iron Lady, and that is me.

I push away all thoughts of the meeting and reach for my usual folder. My assistant Sarah prepares this for the day ahead and I like to spend half an hour going though it with a fine-tooth comb before the office fills up and the day takes over.

By the time she starts at 9am, I am usually a third of the way through the list.

So, it's with surprise that I look up as she enters my office with a cheery, "Morning, Ms Matthews."

She sets my usual coffee down on the desk accompanied by a huge file and smiles.

"It's a wet one today. I must say, I hate these winter nights and mornings. The rain is seriously messing with my mind and I find myself watching reruns of Benidorm to raise my cheery levels."

She grins as I fix her with one of my exasperated looks as she rolls her eyes.

"Ok, I know you don't approve of such frivolous programmes but they keep me sane."

I shake my head and wonder again at the people who work here. They may do a valuable job but I sometimes wonder about their sanity. Surely, any television should be kept to the news channels with the odd documentary on a worthwhile subject thrown in. What a waste of time to watch something that has no benefit on one's future goals in the slightest.

However, I forgive her frivolous nature as I reach for the coffee. For all her flaws she's a great assistant and very good at what she does and I can't function properly without her.

She makes to leave and then turns as if she's forgotten something.

"Oh, I forgot to mention, Annie's not in today, her son's sick and home from school."

She smiles apologetically and I feel the irritation flooding through my veins as I say roughly, "But I need her here. The Mackenzie's are scheduled for their intervention meeting. She's been working on their case and I need her knowledge."

Sarah shrugs. "Sorry, there's nothing I can do."

I exhale in exasperation. "Phone her and tell her to get here ASAP. If she has to bring the kid with her, so be it. He can colour in a few photocopies until the meeting's over."

Sarah looks worried. "I'm not sure she'll be happy with that. You know how stressed she gets where it concerns her son."

Shrugging, I wave her from my office dismissively. "That's not my problem it's hers. She should have a support network in place for such occasions."

Sarah frowns and heads out of the room and I immediately forget about it. Annie will be here, she needs this job and won't want to jeopardise it so near to Christmas.

One thing I always drill into my staff - loyalty.

Loyalty to me and the company that pays their wages which enables them to enjoy the finer things in life. A sick kid just doesn't cut it as an excuse to miss an important meeting.

By the time the meeting with Mr Rowanson comes around I've worked my way through half of my morning list. I've briefed Sarah about the day ahead and walk with excitement towards his office. I can't help but feel the smug sense of inevitability accompanying me as I walk. This is my destiny. I just know it.

It doesn't take long to reach Mr Rowanson's office. It's a familiar path and I relish the opportunity waiting for me inside.

Smoothing down my dress, I lick my lips and check my reflection in the window nearby. I feel confident and sure that when I leave his office, it's with the senior partner role firmly in my grasp.

Sandra his assistant smiles as I walk past and waves towards the door.

"You can go straight in, Ms Matthews, he's expecting you."

I just nod and walk confidently inside.

3

As soon as I set foot inside the room, I take a deep breath. I savour the aroma of the wood panelling and the tangy citrus smell of the polished wood and faint trace of whisky and cigar smoke.

Health and safety have no place inside these walls. Mr Rowanson flouts every rule set in place by the government in private and abides by every word in his professional capacity. He is a rule breaker when it suits him and it is that side of him that interests me the most. He is a charismatic role model and I've learned a lot from him over the years.

I, on the other hand, break no rules inside or out of the office. I have a clear set of professional and personal ethics that I live and breathe by.

As I enter, he stands and smiles as I approach his desk.

"Victoria. Bang on time as usual. If I may say you are looking particularly lovely today."

I stifle the irritation his words bring. He would never say that to Charlie and the feminist inside me roars like a lion at his words. However, once again the woman in me betrays my ethics and giggles like a school girl inside.

I've always been the same and present an impression of a hard-edged businesswoman who excels in a man's world. However, I'm also a woman and it's comments like this that reminds me of that. So, I just smile and take my seat opposite him and wait for the inevitable.

He sits and smiles mysteriously. "You must be wondering why I've called this meeting, Victoria."

I shake my head and try to remain cool and composed. "I have an idea but would never dare comment until I know the facts."

He laughs. "There she is. The Rottweiler lawyer I know and love. I wouldn't have expected any other answer from you."

He grins as the door opens and I immediately feel irritable as I hear a cheery, "Donald, sorry I'm late, just something that came up at the last minute that needed dealing with first."

Charlie bowls into the office and flops down beside me with no sense of occasion or respect. He looks across and grins what he believes to be his secret weapon. "Hey, Vicky. Looking hot, gorgeous."

My lips tighten and I see the gleam in his eye as he waits for the explosion that his words were designed to create.

Instead, I nod and say thinly. "Charlie."

Mr Rowanson looks between us and leans back in his chair. Suddenly, there is an awkward silence in the room as he regards us both coolly. I'm not sure why but a sense of unease creeps over me at his expression. Today has started out badly and it may continue that way judging by his expression.

I dig my fingernails into my palm as I wait for him to speak. Even Charlie has grown quiet which is a miracle in itself making me more on edge than ever.

Mr Rowanson taps his pen on his blotter and sighs.

"Thanks for taking time out of your busy day but I'm guessing you know what I'm about to say."

We say nothing but you could cut the atmosphere with a knife as we wait.

He leans back and sighs heavily.

"Ever since my brother died I've struggled. We started this company together and have worked side by side the entire time. Of course, we bickered occasionally, its what brothers do but mostly we got along and put the company first. Now he's gone it's not the same anymore. This no longer interests me as it did before and has made me re-evaluate what's important in life."

He shakes his head and looks at us sadly. "I have a wife I barely see and wouldn't know what to say to when I do. My children never visit because why would they? I never had time for them when they were growing up so why do they owe me their time now? This company was my life, my family were just what was expected of me. The trouble is, I am now realising that I got it wrong all these years. It should have been the other way around. My company should have come second place to my family, and it's taken my brother's death to highlight it."

He reaches for a silver-framed photograph of his brother and their respective families that has always lived on his desk.

"I should have studied this picture and seen the truth that has been staring out at me all these years. I have worked hard and ignored what life is all about. Well, now it's time to put them first and try to salvage some sort of relationship with my family before it's too late. I have grandchildren I want to take to the park and sons who have turned into men I want to know. I want to spend time with the woman I love and rediscover the girl inside her, alongside the young man in me. I want to rise late and go to bed early. I want to go on picnics and waste time watching old movies. I want to travel and discover the world outside this country and I want to laugh again."

I hold my breath as he fixes us with a hard look and says briskly, "But first I need to put someone in place to safeguard this company and protect its future. Someone who will treat it as their own and take it forward to be even bigger and better than it is now. As far as I'm concerned there are only two people who I trust enough to care for our life's work and I'm looking at them."

Just for a moment, there's silence as he watches us absorb his words. I feel a little confused and say, "So are you saying you want us both to take charge?"

He laughs. "Maybe, maybe not. What I'm saying is that I'm thinking of it. The trouble is, you are both good at certain things but not the complete package."

I feel the shock hitting me hard as I absorb his words. What does he mean, of course, I'm the complete package, is he mad?

He sighs heavily. "On the one hand, I have Charlie here. Loved by all his staff and a great favourite with the clients. His work is exemplary and yet there is a disorganisation to his office that can no longer be ignored."

Charlie makes to speak but is silenced by a hard look from the boss who refers to his computer screen. "It appears that there's a lot of sickness in your office that goes unchallenged. Productivity is down and your idea of a staff meeting is a few drinks in the pub after work. You also have a high turnover of mainly young assistants, who leave almost as soon as the ink is dry on their contracts. One in particular, gave her reason for leaving as she could no longer work with you every day knowing that she would never be yours. She couldn't watch you with another every day knowing how much she loves you."

I roll my eyes as I sense the self-satisfied grin on Charlie's face. There is no such grin on Mr Rowanson's face.

"You treat your interviews like a personal dating service. Even Mark Jacobs left after he realised you would never 'come out' and declare your love for him. Then Miss Gray who is old enough to be your mother folded when she overheard a rather explicit conversation you were having with one of the young interns. You may have it all, Charlie but you need to learn a professionalism that has eluded you so far."

He turns to me and frowns. "However, nobody could accuse you of being unprofessional, Victoria."

I smirk but he glares at me. "It's not a compliment. Your staff may be productive and have the lowest sick record of the whole company but they are also the unhappiest. You treat your staff meetings like the boardroom in the Apprentice. You pull them apart and leave them shaking and quivering with a sense of inadequacy. You have no compassion and no understanding of life outside these walls. A certain Samantha Farers left because she asked you to grant her leave to watch her son's Nativity last Christmas. He was going to be Joseph, and she wanted to attend with her husband and support him. You granted her 30 minutes spare time to watch as her husband live streamed it via his iPhone. You may think that was ok but she apparently didn't as she resigned on the spot."

I feel a flash of irritation as I remember it. I thought it was the perfect solution. Her husband was there, so it didn't need them both taking time off.

Mr Rowanson sighs. "The trouble with you both is you are poles apart. One has too much of something the other lacks. These challenges are designed to bring out the best in both of you and separate the person from the professional."

Charlie chips in. "So, what are you saying, Donald?"

He smiles mysteriously. "I'm saying that you have one month to prove to me that you are the man for the job."

He smirks. "Or should I say woman?"

He leans forward and stares at us with a hard expression. "I'll set you both a series of challenges that you must complete. Every day of December there will be the same challenge set to you both and you must show me that you can deal with the task set. On Christmas Day, one of you will get the gift of a lifetime and start the New Year as the Managing Director of this company. So, tell me, do you accept the challenge on offer?"

Just for a moment, there's silence as we absorb his words. I'm not going to lie, I feel as if I already have this one in the bag. I am organised, controlled and efficient. Any task I'm set I will excel at. Charlie, on the other hand, will just try to pass the buck to his staff and take his eye off the ball.

Almost as if he can hear my thoughts, Mr Rowanson looks at us sharply. "The one condition is you do them together with no outside help. You must work together to get the job done and the person who impresses me the most will win the company. Do I make myself clear?"

My heart sinks as I realise what he's saying. Work alongside Charlie for one whole month, day in day out until these challenges are completed. This is bad. However, I want this more than I hate him, so I just nod and look at him with determination. "That's fine by me."

Charlie looks at me and grins. "No problem."

Then we turn to Mr Rowanson and he laughs softly. "So, you must be wondering what the challenges are?"

I lean forward with interest. Whatever they are, I am so ready for this.

He sits back and looks at us with amusement. "As it's Christmas, I thought I'd make it a little more fun. Every morning at 8 am, you'll receive an email. It's designed to resemble an Advent calendar. On day one, you open the door to see what's inside. Then it's up to you how you deal with it. One for every day of December finishing on

Christmas Day. What do you say, are you up for a special kind of Advent?"

I look across at Charlie and see the competitiveness in his gaze. I narrow my eyes and turn to face Mr Rowanson as we both say at once. "Bring it on."

4

I don't have time to dwell on things before the business of the day takes over. Every hour of it is always meticulously planned which is why I am so hard on my staff.

I must admit I feel a little prickly about the way Mr Rowanson spoke to me. How dare he say I'm lacking in anything? Charlie, on the other hand, deserved all he got. He's always been a bit of a playboy and keeps the office in gossip for most of the year. I've lost count how many of his assistants he's dated and yet he's always forgiven. He's your stereotypical playboy who charms his way through life and always gets what he wants. Well, not this time. This is too important for me to let slip through my fingers. He may think he has this but I know better.

I make my way to the meeting room set up for the Mackenzie's and ignore the malevolent stare from Annie as she waits. I can see her son sitting in a chair through the glass partition looking a little frail in the oversized chair with his head on the table. I feel a little pang as I see that he is indeed suffering and yet push the feeling aside. I have no time for compassion. Time is money and the Mackenzie's are paying us a great deal of it to sort out their divorce.

He is a successful surgeon who has risen high in his profession. His wife stayed at home and supported him through it all and has inevitably grown tired of his huge workload and found fulfilment with her fitness instructor. They have been arguing a settlement for close on a year and a half and we are in the final negotiations. We are representing the wife and I fully intend on getting her everything she deserves.

My thoughts return to Mr Rowanson and I wonder if his wife ever strayed from the marital bed. Maybe it's what happens when you pursue your dreams. Success is a lonely path to tread and only the fully committed reach the end of it. Not many understand the sacrifices needed to see it through which is why I've never tried. I've had dates, but that's all. Usually, two minutes in I'm bored and ready to leave. I need mental stimulation as well as the physical kind and it's hard to find someone who has both.

Occasionally I allow myself to indulge in the physical side of things but the subsequent mess is distracting. Dodging their phone calls and text messages becomes tedious as I try to focus on the most challenging area of my life - my work.

So, I gather my professional self together and set about bringing this deadlock to an end. Mr and Mrs Mackenzie won't know what's hit them when we finish today. I have devised the perfect solution to their problems, and its why Mr Rowanson would be mad not to award the position to me. Charlie wouldn't even dream of doing what I am intending to do which is why he will trail in my shadow.

Mr and Mrs Mackenzie are sitting like frozen statues on either side of their respective counsel. Annie is representing Mrs Mackenzie and our rival Sullivan and Ames are representing her husband. The air in the room is cold and thick with acrimony and I fix them all with my razor-sharp stare.

Annie looks miserable and I feel a flash of anger that she has brought her personal grievance into the meeting. I stare at her pointedly and she has the grace to look down and seemingly collect herself.

Clearing my throat, I sit at the head of the table facing my counterpart who sits beside his assistant and the surgeon.

"Good morning. This meeting has been a long time coming and I think we are all looking for a solution."

Everybody nods and I glance at the papers before me.

"Mr Mackenzie. You are resisting signing the settlement because you feel as if you have brought more to the marriage in the financial sense than your wife and feel it wrong that she gets half of your fortune."

He slams his fist on the desk and roars. "Half you say. I don't think the house, the cars, the villa in

Portugal and the pension set up for our retirement adds up to half. More like it all in my book."

His lawyers nod and I shrug dismissively.

"Mrs Mackenzie you say that you deserve it because you gave up a career as a teacher to support your husband through shift work and 18-hour days. In the early years you supported both of you and without your financial contribution he would have no chance to study and reach the top of his profession."

She nods as he narrows his eyes and rages. "Give me a break, we both contributed to the finances and her role was of her choosing. She wanted to be the stay at home wife who lunched with her friends and spent my money on designer clothes. When I did want some attention, she was too busy with her art classes and fitness regime. Now I know it's because she was focusing her attention on that man all the time."

I shake my head as the other lawyers look as if they've lost the will to live.

I stand up and walk around the room as if thinking about something. Then I turn to them both and say with steel in my voice.

"Mr Mackenzie. You have the ability to earn good money for the rest of your life if you wish to. Far from being left with nothing you have the knowledge you have learned and the skills to achieve great things. I happen to know that you are currently in talks to move to America and work for an extremely lucrative private health organisation. The money you are set to earn far excels any you have earned before. Therefore, the pot of gold you have amassed in the past is nothing to the one in your future."

Mrs Mackenzie looks shocked and makes to speak but I silence her with a raised hand.

"Mrs Mackenzie. You have been married for fifteen years and have spent most of it at leisure. I am not saying that is wrong, I am just stating the obvious. It was an agreement made between the two of you and so must stand as such. I believe that you should take the offer on the table which will enable you to continue living in the manner you have become accustomed to. What you do in the future is yours to decide as is your husbands. You want half of his future earnings but I have worked out that the fifteen years you have been together is payment enough. You have the opportunity to make a new life for yourself, as does he. I recommend you call it quits and sign the contract now. If you insist on pressing for half of his future earnings by way of a pension, then you will have to prove to the courts that you deserve such a settlement."

She looks at her husband angrily.

"I will go to the bitter end."

I shake my head. "Then it's up to me as your advisor to point out that details of your extramarital affairs will become public knowledge. There is also the matter of the business you have on the side to take into consideration."

I relish the sight of the blood draining from her face as she realises what I know. Her husband's team lean forward and he looks confused. "What business on the side?"

I reach for my folder provided by the usual detective I appoint for the more annoying cases that linger on my workload.

"It appears that your wife has not been idle during your working day. She has set up a company entitled Vulcan productions where she performs for selective customers via the Internet."

There is silence in the room as they all look at me with astonishment. Mrs Mackenzie hisses. "You bitch. You're supposed to be on my side."

I shrug and ignore the daggers Annie is throwing in my direction.

"I'm on the side of the law, Mrs Mackenzie and you have wasted far too much time already. I have the reports of your PayPal account set up in your stage name which shows you have amassed a considerable fortune independent of your husband. You have kept all the money for your own gain while living off the money he earns. Therefore, if you want to take this to court, you will no doubt have this all taken into consideration amid an extremely lengthy process. Therefore, as your lawyer, I can only advise you to settle and gather up any dignity you have left and move on with your life."

I sit down and look at the stunned faces around me. I don't care that I've spilt her secret. She's a vicious woman who has used her husband shamelessly all these years. He saves lives and carries out admirable work while she uses him to fund her lavish lifestyle and affairs. All the time she indulges in dubious activities while coming across as the injured party. No, my sympathies are with her husband on this and the sooner she ceases to be a client of ours couldn't come soon enough for me. We have fought and battled for 18 months to get her an honest settlement but it was never enough. We tried every trick in the book to get her to settle and she stood strong and determined. Sometimes enough is enough and getting her what she thinks she deserves ceases to matter. I feel sorry for her husband and when I found out about her hidden assets, it made me sick.

She glares at me and says icily. "Fine. I'll settle. But just for the record, you're a cold-hearted bitch who shouldn't be allowed to be called a lawyer. I'm your client, not him and I will seriously look into having you dismissed."

I shrug. "As you wish, Mrs Mackenzie."

Her husband looks bewildered. "What's going on? What business?"

His lawyer looks interested. "Yes, this has brought a new light to the case. Maybe we need to reconsider our position and look into this deeper before signing anything."

I shrug. "If you insist but this way everyone wins. They get their divorce and are free to move on. If you draw this out, it will sit tied up in red tape for years. Is this really what any of you want? My advice is to sign and move on before everybody loses."

Mr Mackenzie looks defeated. He slumps back and says sadly. "I'll agree to the terms but want to walk away. I want to keep my future earnings and the house in America. She can have the rest, I don't want to be reminded of her, anyway."

He turns to his wife and says sadly. "I never thought it would come to this. I loved you and thought you loved me. Maybe I should have recognised it was failing years ago. Maybe I'm as much to blame for this as you, maybe more. But I can see now that you aren't the woman I thought you were. I want to move on with my life without you in it."

He stands up and looks across at me gratefully. "This sounds strange when you've taken me for everything I've ever worked for but, thank you. You have given me a way out and a new start without the tainted past to slow me down. You've done the right thing and ended this. There are no winners here but lessons have been learned."

He looks at his lawyers and shakes his head.

"Do what you have to. I have a life to move on with."

Then he leaves without a backward glance and his lawyers stand to follow.

My counterpart grins and holds out his hand.

"Congratulations, Ms Matthews. I think we have a settlement agreement in place. We will draw up the necessary contracts and end this for good."

They nod to Mrs Mackenzie and leave her fuming in their wake.

Annie looks bewildered and I fix our client with a hard look.

"You may think I acted against you, Mrs Mackenzie but sometimes what's right takes precedence. I don't have to like my clients, it's not a pre-requisition of our contract. For the record, women like you put the rest of us to shame. My advice is to take what you've earned and try to do something right for once. Move on and leave your husband in peace."

She storms out closely followed by Annie and I watch them go with relief. Finally, we can close this case and move on. I don't care that I betrayed her secret, she deserved it. Now another case is closed and we can reap the rewards of it. Charlie would have had this one running for years.

I'm not averse to bending the rules to get what I want. That is why I will win this company and win it well.

5

December 1ˢᵗ

24 Days to Go

The next day starts off much the same. The builders are no longer showing their appreciation but at least my coffee was served to my liking. My seat was once again restored to me and I have a feeling that everything is now back on track and going my way.

Today is the 1st December and signifies the start of the Advent calendar. I wonder what it will be? I know that I can definitely win this if I apply myself properly.

As usual, I'm the first one in and feel strangely on edge as I fire up my computer. I wonder what it will be?

I almost can't concentrate on my usual routine but push my curiosity aside and channel my mind onto the list before me.

It must be a few minutes after eight that I look up and check my Inbox. I feel a shiver of excitement as I see the notification and the email waiting innocently for my attention.

Advent calendar.

With shaking fingers, I click on it and watch in disbelief as the screen fills with a little window. The pictures of a snowy scene with a deer looking cute in the snow. I click on the number 1 and think I hold my breath as the screen changes and the door opens with the caption *24 days to go*.

Then a message flashes up and as I read it I feel confused. This can't be right, there must be some mistake.

Write a holiday greeting to someone in the armed forces.

Is this a joke?

I read the message again, but it's still the same. I shake my head as my phone rings.

"Yes."

There's a small laugh on the other end and then I hear Charlie's teasing voice.

"Have you seen it?

"Yes."

"What do you think?"

"I think it's a joke."

He laughs softly. "I thought you'd think that. I like it though. What about you?"

I suppress my inner eye roll. Of course, he likes it. It's easy.

I say dismissively. "Well, I can't say I'm impressed but will find this one easy. So, what's your plan?

I can almost imagine him grinning as he says, "Well, we have to do this together so I'm guessing we should agree on it. How about we choose the same regiment and select a name at random? We send them a card by way of thanking them for all their hard work on defending our freedom and tick this one off the list."

Sighing, I realise he's right. This is almost too easy and is getting in the way of actual work. I say tightly. "Fine. Do you have a regiment in mind?"

A slight pause and he says, "You draw up your shortlist and I'll do mine. We can meet in my office in 30minutes and nail this."

I retort. "Fifteen and in *my* office."

He laughs. "Have it your way, I know it's important to you. But just so you know, I play to win and I always do."

I just hang up. Whatever!

Feeling irritated, I research the names of various regiments and look at the work they do. I find it quite fascinating really and never realised how much goes into defending our country.

My own personal preference would be a naval ship. They are away at sea for months on end with little contact with civilisation. It can't be easy so I google the names of a few ships and the address for corresponding with the armed forces.

Fifteen minutes pass quickly and I'm surprised when the door opens and Charlie races into the room. I shake my head. "Don't you believe in knocking?"

He grins and jumps into the seat in front of me and leans on the desk facing me. "I think you were expecting me so thought there was no need. Anyway, that would take away a couple of minutes of precious time in your day that would be best spent winning some case or another to tick off your productivity list."

He leans back and smirks. "So, what have you got?"

Sighing, I say, "I have decided on HMS Daring, a destroyer currently deployed in the Gulf. They have been away for six months and are not expected home this side of Christmas. I have the contact details of the Ministry of Defence and was about to call them to explain what we want and ask them to email over a list of possible recipients."

Charlie grins. "Good start but I'm one step ahead of you. I went to Eton with a guy who ended up in the armed forces. He's an officer currently deployed in manoeuvres in the Baltic sea. A quick catch up on Facebook gave me the answers I need. He's messaging me some names of possible recipients within the next thirty minutes. Luckily, I caught him when he was at a loose end so we should have our list by the start of business today. That way it shouldn't interfere with any meetings we have set up."

The sight of him grinning sets me on edge. He thinks he has this - it's all there in his cocky grin. However, even I know this is the best option. We will carry out the task and have time to carry on with our day. Grudgingly, I nod.

"Ok have it your way, I don't have time to argue. Let me know when you have the list and I'll sort us out a couple of cards."

Charlie grins triumphantly and leaves me to it and I sigh.

This is not what I was thinking at all. I thought it would be a test of our business skills which I would win hands down. This is just time wasting as far as I'm concerned. Maybe Mr Rowanson should step back a little as he is obviously not in his right frame of mind.

Luckily, I remembered we still had some cards left from last year. The ones we send our clients printed with the company greeting. I'm sure they will do, with just a handwritten message inside as requested.

The phone rings about half an hour later and Charlie says annoyingly, "Are you ready to nail the 1st of December, honey?"

I grit my teeth and say shortly. "I'll be right in."

I head to Charlie's office and push down the irritation his words always bring. He knows I hate the way he litters his speech with endearments and patronising nicknames, yet he still does it probably hoping to get a rise out of me. Well, I am one step ahead of him and just march right into his office as he did mine.

He looks up and smirks. "So, the list is in. Do you want the first choice, or should I?"

I shrug. "You choose, it's not as if it matters, anyway."

Charlie smirks and looks at the list. "Hm, well obviously I choose a woman. It would feel a little creepy writing to a guy and isn't really my style."

Now it's my turn to smirk. "Are you sure about that, *Chaz*? I mean, why did your last assistant leave really?"

I savour the flash of annoyance on his face as he says shortly. "We all know why he left, and it was nothing to do with me. No, I'm choosing Sandra. She works in the Sonar department and according to my friend is a great girl who's up for anything."

I snort. "She'd have to be to put up with you."

He grins and pushes the list towards me. "Your turn."

I speed read the list and see it's made up of about twelve names, their job title is listed beside them and I immediately zero in on someone called Nathan Miller, Jet Pilot.

I thrust the list back to Charlie and say, "There, he'll do."

Charlie snorts. "I never had you down as the predictable type, Vicky."

Handing him one of the cards, I roll my eyes. "I don't care what type you had me down as. Now fill this in and let's get on with our day."

Charlie laughs out loud. "Are you kidding me?"

I look surprised. "What?"

He shakes his head. "Who wants to receive a stuffy corporate card from last year imprinted with the greeting, *S & D Rowanson Ltd values your business and wishes you a happier New Year.*"

I look surprised. "Why, what's wrong with it? I was going to write a personal message underneath."

He laughs which instantly gets my back up.

"Well, you can send some stuffy boring card if you like. I'm getting a rude one off the Internet and emailing it to her. I'm guessing she would much prefer that."

I shrug. "Whatever. Anyway, hand me that pen over there and I'll get on with it while you continue to demonstrate that your mind has never really left the playground."

We work in silence and I think about what I'm about to write. This man is a stranger to me so it can't be that familiar. He must be starved of conversation and would probably appreciate a few motivational words to keep his head in the game. I chew the end of the pen as I always do when I am thinking hard and lean back and cross my legs. Charlie is tapping away on his computer and I can only dread what sort of card he is inflicting on that poor woman.

Then I start to write.

Dear Mr Miller.

You don't know me but I just wanted to put pen to paper and say how much we, the British public, appreciate your work on our behalf. Do not think that we aren't thinking of all you brave soldiers out in the field defending our freedom. I would like to offer you a resounding pat on the back and assure you that we are thinking of you in the festive season when you are unable to return home to your loved ones. I will raise a glass or two to you and your brave comrades on Christmas Day in salute to your sacrifice.

Yours sincerely,

Ms Victoria Matthews. LLP

There that will do nicely.

Taking the envelope, I attempt to seal the card in it as Charlie looks up and reaches for it. "Let's see."

I pull it back and glower at him. "It's private."

He smirks. "I need to verify that you did what was asked. So, what do you say, Vicky? I'll show you mine if you show me yours."

I push the card towards him and say in a tight voice. "Ok, have it your way."

I watch as he reads the card and then laughs fit to burst. "This is priceless."

I snarl. "Shut up, what's wrong with it?"

His shoulders shake as he struggles to speak. "God, if I received a card like that I'd shoot myself. Not very jolly is it?"

"Ok then Shakespeare, what have you written?"

He swings the monitor around and I see the card he has designed for Sandra.

CHRISTMAS IS LIKE SEX

IT HAPPENS ONCE A YEAR

ITS OVER FAR TOO FAST

AND YOU NEVER REALLY

GET WHAT YOU WANT!

I gasp. "You can't send that, it's pornography."

He winks. "I'm betting she'll be happier to receive this than old Nate will his."

I stare at him and snarl. "Listen, I'm sure he will be more than happy to receive a genuine greeting rather than the filth you'll send. Not that it matters anyway. As far as I'm concerned, I've completed the challenge and maintained the dignity of the company while doing so, which is more than can be said for you."

Just for a moment, our eyes lock and the challenge is there mirrored right back at me. For all his laughter and joking around, I can see that Charlie is taking this as seriously as I am. At this moment we are locked in a battle of wills and shared purpose. This may look like a game but it's far from that. It's a war.

6

Now that the first challenge is complete, I breathe a sigh of relief. That wasn't so bad. I mean, I can put up with Charlie for thirty minutes every day if it means gaining the upper hand in the end.

I'm still fuming with his reaction to my card though. It wasn't that bad. I'm sure Nathan will be only too happy to receive it. He must be an educated man to rise to the rank of a jet pilot. I'm not sure why I picture him as Tom Cruise in Top Gun but I like to think of him that way.

Just for a second, I imagine him receiving the card. His hands will touch where mine were last. He will smile and be intrigued by the woman who sent it. I am sure he will write back and then will begin an amazing correspondence between us. We will become pen pals and share many a witty exchange. Then one day he'll surprise me and blast his way into my office in full dress uniform and sweep me off my feet with a rendition of '*You've lost that loving feeling.*'

He will sweep me in his arms and kiss me passionately in front of the whole office and rub Charlie's face firmly in the fact that I was right all along.

Feeling happier, I head back to my office and the Robertson file. A fraud case where he cheated his company out of millions. This is a difficult one and will take all of my concentration.

Luckily, I'm kept busy for most of the day and push the Advent Calendar to the back of my mind.

As I head home for the evening, I pass many brightly lit shop windows on the way and note the Christmas displays behind the glass. They are designed to excite and tempt the observer inside. Little room sets with fireplaces spilling many presents from them and Christmas trees twinkling with lights and gifts.

It all looks exciting and promising and heralds the approach of the happiest day of the year.

The wind blows and I pull my coat even tighter around me. There is a chill in the air that promises snow and I shiver as I walk briskly along.

A homeless man sets up for the night in one of the doorways and I wonder how he can possibly survive on a night like this. I think about my warm apartment waiting for me and a fridge stocked with more food than I can eat and feel a flash of empathy for the man down on his luck.

I wonder about his life. What has driven him to such desperate times? Why is nobody looking out for him and where is his family at his time of crisis?

I see the doorway of a local coffee chain and completely out of character I step inside with one aim in mind. Scanning the menu, I select a flat white and place my order, throwing in a panini at the last minute.

Then I head outside and approach the doorway. The man is slumped in the corner with a sleeping bag that has seen better days wrapped around him.

Feeling slightly nervous, I approach him and my heart constricts at the weary defeated eyes that stare back at me. Thrusting the coffee and sandwich towards him I say softly, "I hope it's ok, I thought you could use these."

He blinks and looks at the cup and sandwich and then raises his eyes to mine.

All around people scurry past not giving us a second look. Two women walk past talking about their night ahead and a bus screeches past drowning out their words. It's as if time stands still as he reaches to take the offering from my hand and smiles wearily. "Thanks, darlin'."

I smile. "You're welcome, sir."

I turn away and feel cold no longer. It wasn't much for me to do and completely out of character but I'm happy I did. It's not much but maybe will help him just a little. It wasn't charity it was compassion, something I don't have a lot of.

However, as I head home, it's that exchange that makes my day worthwhile. It's that meeting that means the most and that man that stays in my thoughts as I turn in for the night. For the first time in a very long time, I feel happy.

7

December 2nd

23 Days to Go

December the 2nd arrives and with it the second challenge. This time it's a picture of Santa with a sack of toys. Once again, I feel the little flutter of excitement at the unknown as I open the window.

23 days to go flashes onto the screen and I read with interest what follows.

Donate a toy to the local children's hospital.

Once again, it takes me by surprise. What on Earth has this got to do with running a successful company? This time I reach for the phone and call my nemesis who answers almost immediately.

"Vicky, darling. I've told you to stop calling me, it would never work between us, darling."

I roll my eyes and count to ten, swallowing the retort he is looking for and just say sharply.

"Ok, this one's straightforward. We can get this done in our lunch hour. First Hamleys and then a short tube ride to Great Ormond Street Hospital. Job done and back in time for our afternoon work."

Charlie laughs. "Typical, Vicky. You've got it all worked out, haven't you?"

I sigh with exasperation. "Well, somebody has to. Is that ok? I mean, I know you like your liquid lunches but that will have to be sacrificed in the line of duty."

He laughs again which reinforces the fact that he takes absolutely nothing seriously.

"I can cope with that, although I may need a stiff one after an hour hunting down kids' toys with you."

I hang up before he can throw any more pointless remarks my way.

The morning flashes past and I look up in surprise as once again he barges in my office without so much of a knock.

"Ready, darling."

I grit my teeth. "I'm not your darling, and never will be."

Grabbing my bag and coat, I stomp out of my office without looking at his conceited face.

We travel in silence to the tube station. This feels so awkward. Despite working at the same company for many years we haven't had much to do with each other. He runs his side of things and I mine.

Even though we're a similar age, we are poles apart in every way. He is good looking, charming and has an easy way about him that people appear to love. I, on the other hand, treat everybody in a professional and business-like fashion. I have no room for friends at the office because it would get in the way of our professional relationships. I know most people prefer to work for Charlie. He is easy on them and lets his staff get away with things I would come down hard on mine for. I never like to admit it but a part of me envies him his popularity. He finds it easy to fit in where I never have.

It's always been the same. Throughout school and college, I focused on learning. I wasn't interested in joining clubs that had no bearing on my goals and any friends I made were in my study groups. I never went to parties unless you count the one that ruined all others for me forever.

I try not to think of that night if I can. The one time I let my guard down and suffered the consequences. No, from that day on I never did again. There were no more parties for me and people soon stopped asking me to go. I'm betting there were more parties than study sessions in Charlie's education and yet here he is, still succeeding despite it. He obviously never had to try as hard as I did and maybe that's why I dislike him so much.

We take the journey in silence. I'm not one to speak for the sake of it and Charlie just appears withdrawn and brooding on something. By the time we reach Hamleys, I'm glad to see the brightly coloured interior beckoning us inside.

As we step through the doors, I look around me in awe and stare in wonder at the brightly coloured toys crammed on every surface. It's a child's paradise and there are many of the little people running around and screaming with excitement.

I don't miss that Charlie's eyes light up as he turns to me and says happily, "What do you have in mind?"

I shrug. "I was thinking something educational. They are in hospital so won't be learning much and their education will be suffering. However, they may be ill and so will need something that won't tax them too much. I was thinking maybe a jigsaw puzzle, what do you think?"

He rolls his eyes. "Of course. I should have guessed you'd choose something like that."

I feel annoyed and glare at him, "What's wrong with that?"

He shrugs. "I was thinking something much more exciting. They must be bored out of their tiny minds and looking for fun. I was thinking a magic trick set to keep the nurses on their toes. I bet they will have great fun with that and it would be good for both girls and boys."

I shake my head and sigh wearily. "Whatever. Anyway, we don't have long so you grab yours and I'll grab mine."

Charlie winks. "It would be much more fun to grab each other's."

I shrug. "Maybe that would be best. You go and choose an educational jigsaw and I'll check out the magic sets. Make sure it's suitable for a sick child and not one of your usual immature offerings."

He salutes me and says cheekily. "Whatever you say, ma'am."

I watch him head off and shake my head. I'm not sure if the guy ever grew up and I can't quite believe I am in this challenge with him. Fate is very cruel sometimes.

It doesn't take long and I grab a magic set that looks educational enough while also looking like fun. The shop is busy with mums frantically piling baskets full of toys for their children.

I wonder what it would be like to have a family. My sister has two children who I rarely see. Come to think of it, I rarely visit any of my family anymore. My sister lives a stone's throw from the council estate where we grew up and is on her second marriage already. My brother lives in Scotland where he manages a bar with his girlfriend and my mum still lives in our old maisonette despite me begging her to swap with the local housing association. She's a proud woman though and won't leave her home or friends who are more like family to her than I ever was.

I see Charlie in the distance looking bored as he chooses a puzzle. Just for a second, I study him. He is good looking with short blondish hair that lies slightly spiky on top. He has beautiful blue eyes that would be the envy of many women, with long dark lashes that crinkle at the edges when he smiles. Despite his desk job he looks fit and trim and wears his suits with style and ease.

As I look at him standing there without a smart remark spilling from his lips or a wicked look in my direction, I realise just how attractive he really is.

Shocked, I lower my gaze. Oh no, this is all I need. I can't think of Charlie in any other way than as my adversary. Who cares if he looks hot and available? I have no business thinking of my competition in any other way than I want to decimate them.

Quickly, I move to the checkouts and reach for my credit card. This stops now and any thoughts I have towards Charlie outside of this challenge should be firmly left in the jigsaw section of this store.

We meet by the exit and I look at his brightly wrapped parcel with surprise. "How did you get this gift wrapped? Is there a service I missed?"

He grins. "No, Katie the assistant offered when I told her what it was for. She also threw in a card and an extra-large bow."

I look at him in surprise. "How do you do that?"

He looks surprised. "Do what?"

I sigh. "Get people to do nice things for you. It's a gift that I could use right now."

We start walking and he looks interested. "I don't do anything, just be myself. If you talk to people, they are usually interested in what you say."

I stare ahead gloomily. "That's the problem, Charlie. Nobody ever listens to what I have to say. In fact, they can't get away quickly enough."

We reach the tube station and quickly walk to the platform and I regret my words. I mustn't show any weakness or let him inside my head. He can't see any hint of vulnerability because then he'll use it to his advantage.

The train arrives and we sit next to each other in silence. As the train hurtles through the blackened tunnels, I feel strangely unsettled. He says nothing yet there's an atmosphere building that I can't ignore. I'm conscious of his every move and sit as straight as a statue, afraid of the direction this is taking. Charlie is also quiet which is most unlike him. Occasionally, he shifts in his seat and my heart leaps with every movement he makes. I scream inside. No! This can't be happening. Stop! Think about something else—*immediately!*

The train lurches from side to side and I tense in my seat to avoid any brief moment of contact. Something has changed and I don't like it one bit. I need to nip this firmly in the bud and immediately vow to look up Tinder again when I get home. It's been months since I've had a man's company which is obviously why I am having these disturbing thoughts.

Charlie and me - don't make me laugh.

8

Luckily, the journey is short and we waste no time heading to the reception area of the children's hospital. I leave Charlie to explain to the receptionist and fully intend on leaving as soon as we deposit our gifts. However, once again Charlie's charm prevails, and the receptionist flashes him a grateful smile and beams at him with total adoration.

"Oh, you must give these gifts personally. We have two very deserving recipients who would love to meet you."

I look at Charlie in surprise and shake my head imperceptibly. We don't have time for this. We're already running late and will be much longer than an hour if we deviate from the plan.

To my annoyance, Charlie just grins and says sweetly, "Oh we would be honoured to meet them, wouldn't we, Vicky?"

The woman smiles at me as I stutter. "Of course. Thank you, we would love to meet them."

I shoot daggers in Charlie's back as we follow her to the lift. She beams at us and says brightly, "Squirrel ward. Tell the nurse I sent you and she will direct you to the right rooms."

As soon as we step foot inside the lift, I turn on Charlie.

"We don't have time for this. I have a two-o'clock that's urgent and it won't look good if I'm late."

He shrugs. "Come now, Vicky, we're on company business after all. This is more important than any old stuffy meeting you've got planned. I'm sure these kids would love to be able to walk away and carry on with their day. Unfortunately for them, they can't, so it's the least we can do."

I throw him an angry look. "Don't you dare make out I'm unfeeling! I feel as sorry for these kids as you do and wish with all my heart they were safe and healthy at home and looking forward to a Christmas with their families. You don't get to take the moral high ground in this."

The doors open and I stomp outside and head towards the nurse's station. She looks up and smiles. "Oh, you must be the lovely couple who have come with gifts for Maddie and Ben. They will be so excited to see you."

She stands and beckons us to follow her, chatting all the way. I leave Charlie to answer her because I'm feeling stressed already. Not only will I be late for my meeting this afternoon, which is enough to send me delirious but I also have to deal with these feelings that have come out of nowhere towards the extremely annoying man in front of me. This is a disaster. I've always prided myself on keeping it cool with the opposite sex. In fact, I keep it cool with just about everyone I meet, even my own family. I have my reasons for this and I've managed to keep that part of me locked away for many years now. The trouble is, it's still there in the background of my life. I have tried to shut it away inside a little box marked *danger*. It won't go away though and today has shown me how close it always is despite how hard I try to shut it out.

We reach a door and the nurse walks inside and says brightly, "Hey, Ben it looks like Christmas has come early, these nice people have a gift for you."

As I follow Charlie into the room, I do a double take and my heart shatters into a million pieces. Lying in the bed, hooked up to all manner of machines, lies a frail little boy. His eyes could melt butter and he smiles sweetly but with so much pain behind it that I feel as if I'm about to fold right here and now. My heart breaks at the sight of this poor little boy. His hair is gone and his skin white and translucent. He looks frail and weak and I stifle a sob that works its way from deep inside me.

Charlie moves towards the bed offering him the carrier bag. He sits next to him and smiles gently. "Hey, little guy. We thought you may like something to annoy the nurses. Maybe next time they make you do something you don't want to you can make them disappear."

Ben reaches for the gift and his little eyes light up with awe as the box appears almost too big for him. He says in a small, voice. "Is this really for me?"

Charlie nods and looks at me and smiles. My breath hitches as I see the same feelings inside me reflected back in his eyes. For all his joking around, Charlie is as affected by Ben as I am.

He smiles and says, "You can thank Vicky for choosing this one. She's an expert present chooser that I drafted in especially for you."

Ben's eyes turn to me and I approach him, smiling softly. "Hey, Ben. You'll have your work cut out with this box of tricks. Do you think you're up to it?"

He nods vigorously. "I promise, Vicky. Whatever it is, I won't let you down."

We laugh as we realise he hasn't even opened it yet. Charlie grins at me as I say jokingly. "Well, open it then. You don't have to wait until Christmas Day for this one you know."

Ben giggles and pulls the bag apart at the top. My heart sinks as I see how weak he is and even the act of removing the gift is hard for him.

Charlie reaches over and helps him, saying jokingly, "I'm sorry, Ben. I see a present and have to rip the paper off even if it's not mine. You don't mind a helping hand, do you?"

Ben smiles at him gratefully and a little piece of my soul melts as I watch his eyes light up as the big box of magic reveals itself. The nurse laughs. "Oh my. There's trouble ahead for us here. We won't be safe from this little wizard, will we?"

Ben laughs and his face transforms with a wicked smile that reveals the cheeky boy he has hidden inside the sick one. "Can I practice now?"

The nurse nods. "You can play with this as long as you like. As soon as I've shown Charlie and Vicky to Maddie's room, I'll be back to help you set it up."

He looks at us both and I am hit by a gut-wrenching blow to my heart at his expression. "Thank you, Charlie and Vicky. I promise to play with it forever."

I see Charlie swallow hard and I smile at Ben and wink. "I'm counting on it, Ben. Make sure you get full use of it though and when you're ready, we'll be back for the show."

He smiles. "I promise."

We leave him to it and follow the nurse from the room and Charlie asks her the question that I was afraid to ask. "What's wrong with him?"

She sighs. "Rare form of cancer. He's a fighter though. He's weak at the moment because he just had another chemo session but I'm sure he will bounce back from it. The prognosis is good but cancer has a way of making its own rules. That gift is just what he needed. Something to focus on away from his illness."

I interrupt. "What about his family, they must be devastated?"

She nods. "They are. His mum and dad live in Yorkshire and have two other children. It's hard on them all and the only reason he's alone today is because his sister is in a sport final and the parents have gone to support her. Life goes on despite how much it pains them to leave him. Usually one of them is here but sometimes it's impossible so he's left to his own devices. His grandparents help out when they can but they're on holiday at the moment so couldn't cover."

I fall silent. I wonder if I would help out if my niece or nephew needed it. I'd like to think I would but I know me and I've always put work first. They hardly know me at all except via the sterile Christmas and birthday cards I send them with money inside. No thoughtful gifts wrapped in bright paper that would bring excitement to their eyes like Ben's. I actually feel ashamed of myself and vow to visit them as soon as possible.

We follow the nurse to another door and I'm not sure if my heart can take any more. This time the little girl that is waiting looks at us shyly from her hospital bed. She can't be any older than seven and yet looks so frail I wonder how on earth the nurses can face such heart-breaking sights every day? She isn't strapped to any machines but sits upright in bed with her legs under a huge frame that keeps the sheets from touching her. She looks at us curiously and the nurse says cheerfully. "Hey, Maddie, these lovely people have a surprise for you."

She looks surprised and I see a flicker of excitement light up her eyes and I swallow hard.

Charlie seems strangely quiet beside me, so I venture forward holding the gift-wrapped package out to the shy little girl, all the time thanking Charlie for getting it wrapped. It's just a little thing but means more to these children than just retrieving a package from a carrier bag. I am fast learning the importance of the wrapping and realise that it's as much a part of gifting than the actual present itself.

I sit gingerly next to her and say softly, "I hope you like this, Maddie. If not please say and I'll change it for something you would really like."

I see Charlie stand the other side of her and just for a second our eyes meet. I almost think I see a tiny bit of respect before he looks away towards the little girl smiling shyly beside us. Unlike Ben, she is more than capable of unwrapping the package herself and I'm feeling strangely anxious at what she'll think of the contents. Maybe Charlie was right and she will hate it on sight. However, her eyes fill with tears as she pulls the jigsaw from the wrapping and looks at the picture of a zoo filled with animals. She smiles which totally lights up her face and looks towards the nurse. "Look, Betty, a jigsaw. I've never had a grown-up one like this before. Can I start it now? Please?"

Betty smiles. "Of course, you can, darling. You've even got a little table set up in front of you so it was the perfect choice for you."

She smiles at us. "You must have known."

She turns towards the door. "Wait for a second though, I have one of those jigsaw mats somewhere. Then it won't be spoiled when we take you for your physio."

The little girl nods excitedly and looks at us and says shyly. "Thank you for my present."

Charlie smiles sweetly at her. "It's our pleasure, sweetheart. That should keep you busy for a while."

She nods and turns her attention back to the picture and we leave her to it. We meet the nurse on her way back and I say sadly, "What's the matter with her, Betty?"

She shakes her head sadly. "Car accident. Lost one of her legs and her father at the same time. Her mother survived but is bad in intensive care at another hospital. Her grandparents do all they can and despite it all, she's a positive little soul."

Then she looks up and says gratefully. "Thank you for taking the time to light up their day. It matters more than you could ever know. The world carries on for most of us but is a different kind of world they now live in. It's easy to forget that there is pain and suffering existing not a stone's throw from the bright lights of the streets outside. Not many people give it a second thought as they pass these doors every day."

She smiles and heads towards the room holding her board and I say shakily, "This was nothing, Betty. What you do is worth far more than the two small gifts we have brought. You deserve all the thanks, not us."

Betty just smiles and shakes her head. "I do it because I love it. Don't feel too sad guys. Despite it all, these kids have a lot of love thrown their way and we will make sure they have an amazing Christmas."

She heads off and as I watch her go I feel ashamed of myself. Charlie moves beside me and says gently. "Stop it, Vicky."

I look at him in surprise. "Stop what?"

He smiles softly. "Stop beating yourself up. You weren't to know any of this and I'm guessing that if you knew you would have bought half of Hamleys and brought it here. Sometimes something happens that knocks our life back into perspective. Ours seems pretty ridiculous now, doesn't it?"

I nod slowly. "You're right. Everything seems irrelevant when you see the struggle these poor children have to deal with. Meetings are no longer as important and I would miss them in a heartbeat if I thought I could help just one of these poor little souls have a better day."

To my surprise, Charlie smiles and my heart stops beating for just a second as my breath hitches. Gone is the cheeky, cocky nemesis who I hate. In its place is a man who looks kind of sad and lost and it throws me completely. Then he smiles ruefully and holds out his hand. "I don't know about you but I need a drink."

I raise my eyes and he laughs. "I mean, a coffee. Come on, I'll treat you on the way back to reality. That is if you don't mind being back a little later than planned."

Thoughts of my urgent meeting are pushed firmly away and I smile. "Ok, but if Mr Rowanson asks, I'm blaming you for leading me astray."

He rolls his eyes and grins. "If you wanted me to, honey, I could lead you astray in a much more wicked way than a coffee."

I roll my eyes and spin on my heels, hiding the grin that threatens to betray my indignant façade. Thank goodness for that. Charlie has broken the mood and set us back firmly on the path we were on before. I need to remember he's my opponent and not start thinking of him any other way because I've come too far to lose it all now at the last hurdle. Today was a one-off. Nothing that Advent calendar can throw at us can be worse than the feelings this challenge brought out in me.

However, as we walk outside the hospital, I feel like a different person than the one who walked in.

9

As I head to the office, I'm dreading today's challenge. Yesterday took a lot out of me and I know it affected Charlie too.

We did grab that coffee and made small talk until we reached the office. Like me, Charlie appeared anxious to get things back on track and neither one of us mentioned what happened at the hospital. Once I got back, I threw myself into my work to drive away the feelings the day had awakened in me.

Charlie had been uncharacteristically quiet, and it made me wonder about him. I'm sure he's led a very sheltered life and never seen pain and suffering like that. I never have and my upbringing was hardly the stuff of storybooks. It made me realise just how lucky I am never to have faced such pain. Maybe I should visit my family this weekend. I've not been the most attentive of daughters or sisters not to mention my niece and nephew who probably wouldn't even recognise me if I walked past them in the street.

I have a pretty full day planned and hope the challenge is an easy one that doesn't mean I have to leave the office. I pride myself on leading by example and our extended lunch did not go unnoticed yesterday. I'm pretty sure the office gossip is rife with tales of me and Charlie as, of course, nobody knows about this little challenge we have going on. All they will see is us spending an unhealthy amount of time together and I feel irritated that I can't set the record straight.

I don't have long to wait before today's mission flicks up on my screen.

The picture is of a post-box with a robin sitting on it and as I click on it I look incredulously at the words on the screen.

Send a letter to Santa.

Really? Is he having a laugh? I grin and lift the receiver to call Charlie. At least this one doesn't involve me spending any time with him, so I breathe a sigh of relief as he answers on the second ring.

"Yo, Vicky. Have you got your wish list prepared?"

I feel myself bristling at his constant insistence of shortening my name but say curtly.

"This one's a piece of cake. I'll have mine typed out and in an envelope inside the next ten minutes. I appreciate this one may tax you a little as you will have to actually use a little imagination but when you're done, bring it to me and I'll send it to the post room."

Charlie laughs. "Oh, I'm sure that would look good in front of the staff. It would be all around the office by morning break that its executives are writing to Santa. This isn't like you, babe, not thinking of the bigger picture."

I grit my teeth as I realise he's right and say shortly, "Fine, have it your way, *babe*! When you're done, bring it to me and I'll post it in the post-box on the corner, then we can get on with the important matters of the day."

He laughs and says annoyingly, "Later, babe."

I slam the phone down and actually feel myself grinding my teeth. Why on earth did God give me such an annoying child to work with? Where are the professional men with no sense of humour and a solid gold work ethic? I actually feel as if this whole company is riding on my success. If Charlie wins this, God help our futures.

Once again, I chew the end of my pencil as I figure out what to write. It's obvious I won't get away with a few lines. We have to read each other's to verify the challenge and I can't face Charlie's derision if I write something without any thought involved. Mind you, I couldn't if I tried. Like everything in my life, I take this challenge seriously and intend on giving every last one my best attempt.

If Mr Rowanson wants a letter to Santa, then it will be the best letter Santa has ever received.

Feeling inspired, I start writing.

Dear Santa, aka, Father Christmas, aka Mr Claus

It has been a while since I last wrote which I apologise for. The years have passed since I last asked for the Barbie dream castle but I would like to thank you for delivering it to me.

However, I am no longer that little girl who innocently asked for the latest toy. I have grown up and my tastes have somewhat changed.

Although I have everything I wanted, a good job and a nice home and lifestyle, I want something that may be out of your comfort zone.

I have listed the requirements below in order of preference and if you can but grant one of my requests, please let it be the first one?

That the children in hospital get the happiest Christmas they have ever had and the gift of health. Please pay special attention to Ben and Maddie. They are kind of special.

Please find a home for the homeless at Christmas. There's a particular man in the doorway of Selfridges that I am particularly worried about. If you can't find him a home, a new sleeping bag might be most welcome.

Please deliver everything on the lists of my niece Sophie and Thomas Anderson. They are good kids who don't deserve the Aunt that fate threw at them. Please keep them safe and healthy and allow them to grow up happy.

I am also feeling a little bad for Annie's son, Edward, who I dragged into the office when he was feeling ill. Please deliver him the biggest smile on his face on Christmas Day with the gift he wanted the most.

While we're at it, please can you deliver Charlie a sense of professionalism and the inability to shorten people's names? In particular, the pet names that irritate the life out of the people who strive for excellence in their day. Maybe a good dose of adulthood to stifle the child inside him may make for a much more orderly life.

Finally, something for me. Please, can you give me peace of mind? It's something I've wanted for a very long time and is proving quite elusive. I am sure you know what I'm referring to and had hoped that the memories would have faded by now. Any help on that front would be greatly appreciated.

Thank you for your time and for all the hard work you do in making children's Christmas dreams come true.

Yours sincerely

Victoria Marshall LLP

Ps. Please can you make Charlie less annoying? I know it's a big ask but vital to my sanity. If not, please just put him on the 'Naughty list.' It's nothing he doesn't deserve!

I lean back and feel somewhat proud of my first attempt. I have thought of others before myself and not provided an endless list of trivialities.

It must be half an hour later that Charlie bursts into my office waving his letter.

I snap. "Come in, Charlie. I'm sorry, I must have missed hearing you knock."

He grins and comes over and sits on the edge of my desk, slapping his letter down in front of me.

"Here you go, Vick. One letter to Santa signed and delivered."

I make to pick it up and he slaps his hand firmly down on mine.

"Not so fast. I need to see yours, remember?"

I withdraw my hand from under his as if it burned and glower at him as I thrust my letter towards him.

"There. Laugh if you must and then you can leave me to carry on with the important business of the day."

He winks and takes the letter around the other side of the desk and sits in the chair facing away from me.

I feel curious as to what he thinks and sigh inside as I reach for his. This is all so pointless.

Yo Santa!

It's been a while, dude but I'll never forget the time I saw you around the side of the house putting it on my mother Christmas Eve 1980. She seemed to appreciate the happy Christmas you gave her so thanks for that. Just one complaint. I asked for an Action Man, not the Ken doll you delivered instead. Sorry to be picky but I was kind of scarred by the experience. Just saying, be a little more attentive to the details in future, a kid's childhood counts on it.

Well, you must be wondering why I'm back in touch. I could sure use your help in spreading a little Christmas cheer around here. There's this chick you see. She could certainly use some and I'm sure it's not her fault but you see she's lost sight of the fun side to life. Maybe if you could deliver it life would be a lot more interesting around here.

If you can't do that, I mean, it would be a miracle if you could, let me win this challenge and I'll order her to have fun as her boss. I would make every Friday fun day and make everyone wear Hawaiian shirts and drink rum. Work would be a lot more fun and I'm betting the sickness record for Fridays would be halved, so as you see, it's a win-win situation.

Well, sorry to disturb you but there's a drink in it if you come calling.

Your best friend forever.

Charlie

I roll my eyes. Typical Charlie. However, I feel a tad annoyed at his reference to me. So what if I'm a professional and keep any frivolity firmly away from my working day? What sort of message would that send to my clients, not to mention my staff?

Charlie spins around and just for a minute stares at me. He looks thoughtful and then looks down at the letter while I squirm with embarrassment. Why did I write that last bit? I might have known he would judge me for it. Feeling unsettled, I do what I always do when I feel cornered, I attack.

I snarl. "Typical. You couldn't resist using this as an opportunity to beg for this company, could you? It was such an obvious thing to ask for and I'm disappointed in your lack of creativity. Friday fun day, don't make me laugh. And don't think I didn't notice it's me you were referring to. Feeling threatened, are we? Well, you should be. I fully intend on winning this challenge for everyone's sanity. As far as I'm concerned this whole charade is just bringing me one step closer to what I want every day this farce continues."

I fold the letter and stuff it angrily in an envelope and reach out for my own one. Charlie, however, just holds it tightly and his eyes soften and he stares at me with a soft expression which completely unnerves me.

"Do you want to talk about this final paragraph? You know I'm a good listener."

I feel the mortification setting in and growl. "What, the one about making you less annoying? I don't even think Santa can deliver that."

I feel my cheeks turning red as he hands me the letter and says softly. "You know the offer still stands. If ever you need anyone to talk to my door is always open. Hell, we could even really go town and grab a drink after work one night. Just say the word and I'll arrange it."

I stare at him in total astonishment and look for the wicked grin and mocking eyes. Instead, all I see is the concerned look of an extremely hot guy sitting across the desk from me and I shrivel up inside with embarrassment. Way to go, Victoria. Expose the one thing in your life nobody must ever discover and to your sworn enemy at that. However, there is a part of me that craves folding into his offer. The eyes that are looking at me are filled with concern and something else I can't quite place. It catches me off guard and for a moment it would be the easiest thing in the world to give in and pour my heart out. Then my guard slips back into place and I harden my heart once again, saying briskly. "Thanks for the offer but no thanks. If I do ever need to offload anything you can rest assured it won't be to you. Now, if you don't mind, I have business to attend to."

Just for a moment, he stares at me and I think I see a flicker of disappointment in his eyes. I hold my breath as he shrugs and stands, saying quietly. "Fine. Have a good day, Victoria."

Then he is gone leaving me feeling like a first-class bitch. He was only being kind and once again, I used his kindness and threw it back in his face. I can't deal with it and it's my first defence to go on the attack. I wonder if I'll ever be able to lower my defences and let anyone in? God knows I want it more than air sometimes. It's very lonely being me but one thing I've learned is the only person you can truly count on in life, is yourself.

I try to push my feelings aside but they stay with me for most of the day. Even Sarah notices when she arrives to discuss the afternoon's appointments.

I feel her studying me as we go through the list and by the end of it I've had enough. Fixing her with a cold stare, I say roughly, "Is there something you want to say, Sarah?"

She looks surprised and clears her throat, saying softly, "It's nothing, Ms Marshall. It's just you seem preoccupied, and it's not like you."

I fix her with a blank stare and say coldly. "I can assure you there is nothing wrong and the only thing on my mind is the upcoming trial we are discussing. We can't all be sweetness and light all the time you know, some of us have a hefty workload that is getting increasingly longer all the time I have pointless activities to attend to. Forgive me if I seem a little off but I'm working on a secret project with Mr Monroe which is proving extremely testing."

She looks interested and I don't miss that her eyes light up at the mention of Charlie. She grins. "That explains it all then."

I stare at her in surprise. "Explains what exactly?"

She laughs. "Word is, you're having a relationship with Charlie and are keeping it secret. I must say, it's all anyone is talking about."

She doesn't notice the horror on my face and actually winks at me. "I wish it were true, you would make a perfect couple. You look good together and have shared interests. Not to mention your personalities balance one another perfectly. God, I wish it was true. Just think of the gorgeous babies you would have."

I can't believe what I'm hearing and say angrily. "Enough. For the record, there is nothing going on with me and Mr Monroe. As if that would ever happen. We are poles apart and I have zero interest in him outside of the work we do. Do me a favour and spread that bit of gossip around the office. If I were looking for an emotional partner, he would be the last man on earth I'd ever choose. In fact, even if he was the last man on earth, I'd choose to be alone. Do you really think I would stoop so low to date him? A man who spends more time in the pub than his own home. A man who thinks allowing his staff to bring in bottles of wine on a Friday afternoon is good business practice. A man who enjoys offering incentives such as karaoke Thursday and lucky dip Tuesday. That man has never transitioned into adulthood and has absolutely no place in my life whatsoever. Do I make myself clear?"

Sarah nods miserably. "Yes, Ms Matthews."

I exhale sharply and gather myself together. "Right then, good. That's that then. Anyway, maybe we should get back to work now that matter has been settled. You may go."

As I watch her walk from the room, I feel bad. I totally overreacted and feel a bit silly now. I glance around the office and my eyes fall to the book facing out from my bookcase. The biography of Karren Brady. Super businesswoman and personal role model to me. If I could get away with it, I would have her picture framed on my desk as a constant inspiration. Many times, I ask the question, "What would Karren do?"

As I look at her successful face staring out at me I ask the same question. She looks back at me with her stern authoritative gaze and I know what she would say.

"You can have it all, Victoria. You're a strong independent woman who doesn't need a man to define her. Then again, you are a woman with needs and definitely need a man to take care of them. What's wrong with lowering your defences once in a while for the greater good?"

Yes, Karren would say that I just know it. She married a footballer after all. Not what I would have expected but understandable. I mean, she is a woman and a hot footballer kicking his balls your way would be hard to ignore. Maybe it wouldn't be so bad to lower my defences just a little and test the waters. It may be fun.

10

For some reason, I'm looking forward to the challenge today. Yesterday's was easy and made me think about the letters I sent to Santa over the years. I used to enjoy writing to him and mailing the special note in the post-box at school. I was always so excited on Christmas Eve and marvelled at how the presents appeared at the end of my bed by morning. I tried to stay awake several times but never managed it. There was always the excitement of picturing him speeding through the night on his sleigh with his trusty reindeers delivering gifts to the children of the world. I never questioned it, why would I? It was true after all. Santa delivers the spirit of Christmas to each and every child in the world and it's only when they stop believing that the magic fades. Well, I always believed in the spirit of Christmas and feel sorry that it's been missing from my adult life. Maybe when I have children of my own it will return. I hope so because Christmas without it is a bleak place to be.

I meet Charlie in the lift and look at him in surprise. "You're early today. I didn't have you down as an early riser."

He grins as the doors close. "Maybe I'm turning over a new leaf for my future responsibilities. I have discovered you can get a lot done before the staff check in."

I narrow my eyes and don't miss the fact he's wearing identical clothes to yesterday. He also looks unshaven and his hair is all over the place. I raise my eyes and look at him pointedly. "If I were guessing, I'd say you haven't been home. Am I right, did you burn the midnight oil and forget to blow out the flame?"

He laughs and winks cheekily. "Nothing gets past you does it, Vicky? What do they say, oh yes, 'busted'. So, what are you going to do about it, phone my parents and tell on me?"

I shrug and look disinterested. "As if I'd be that bothered. No, what you do with your private time is your own business. I'm sure it won't affect your work, even if you did stay out all night."

The lift doors open and he throws me a wicked look as he heads towards his office. "Who says I stayed out all night? Maybe, I just stayed at a different house to mine."

The door closes behind him and I stare at it feeling strange. As I turn and walk to my own office, I feel an alien feeling of jealousy rearing its ugly head inside me. The thought of Charlie staying with someone else has floored me. Why do I care?

The trouble is, it's becoming increasingly obvious that I care very much indeed.

As usual, I throw myself into my work as soon as I set foot in the office. Nothing else matters but doing what I love. Even though I may be found lacking emotionally, I understand that particular flaw in my character, I make up for it by striving for excellence in my working life.

The trouble is, no matter how hard I try, I can't get Charlie out of my mind. Despite my irritation and obvious hatred of him, I am fast looking forward to seeing him every day. I suppose a part of me loves the thrill of opening that little window and seeing what's behind it. Part of me craves the intrigue and excitement and as much as I protest publicly, the private part of me is more than happy I am taking this adventure with him.

8 am arrives and with it the anticipated email.

This time the picture is of an angel looking sweet and serene.

I look with excitement at the message that says simply

Watch a Christmas movie

Well, this is more difficult than I thought. How on earth are we going to manage that? As I sit pondering the challenge another email flashes up on my screen from Charlie.

Hey, V

Christmas movie night at mine tonight. I'll pick you up after work. Dress to impress, babe!

Despite myself, I grin. Maybe I'm spending too much time with him because I'm kind of getting used to his cheeky ways and don't even mind as much when he shortens my name. Maybe because it feels as if someone actually likes me for a change. God only knows why he tries? I would have given up ages ago if it had been me. Then I remind myself of what's at stake. Maybe he's just playing the game, and this is part of his tactics. Get me to drop my guard and take the coveted prize.

Sarah comes in and interrupts my thoughts.

"Excuse me, Ms Marshall. Your 9-o'clock's here and waiting in the boardroom."

I nod and turn my thoughts to the business at hand.

I don't see or hear from Charlie for the rest of the day. I do however hear *of* him while using the ladies. I am happily going about my business when I hear two voices outside.

"Charlie's looking hot today as always."

"You're not wrong there. You know that new temp in his office, you know the one with the huge assets?"

Laughter follows and I think I hold my breath as I wait for the conversation to continue.

"Well, I heard she saw him the other night in that bar by the river. You know, the one the MPs go to by Westminster."

"Typical. I bet she spends all her spare time looking for the best hangouts where she can find the sugar daddy she so obviously wants."

More laughter.

"Anyway, she saw him there and was going to approach him when he got a call. Apparently, he looked angry and started shouting at whoever was on the other end."

A gasp and then she says urgently.

"Wow, that's not like him. I can't imagine Charlie shouting at anyone. Did she hear what he said?"

"No, the noise was too loud, but she said he stormed out and left his drink on the side. She did say that she watched him go and saw him getting into a flash car outside. Some woman was driving it and they looked to be arguing as she drove off."

Another gasp and then I hear a terse,

"Oh my god, I'm two minutes late! The dragon will have my guts for garters if I don't get back to my desk, pronto!"

Laughter, followed by the door slamming and then I'm alone with my thoughts.

I think about what I heard. I wonder who this woman is and why Charlie feels the need to go drinking after work, anyway? It sounds as if he was on his own in that bar which is a little sad when you come to think of it. I'm not going to lie though, I did feel a prickle of jealousy as I heard about him leaving with a woman. Why should I care? He irritates me most of the time and any time spent with him is annoying to say the least. But I do care very much and I'm even more annoyed at their reference to me as they left. I'm not stupid, I know what people think of me but hearing it is another thing.

Sighing to myself, I head out of my solitary confinement and head back to the office, pushing any thoughts of Charlie firmly to the back of my mind. After all, what he does in his spare time is no concern of mine, anyway.

6 o'clock comes and I feel a little nervous if I'm honest. I know it's not really a date, but I'm used to finishing up here and then heading home to a microwaved meal for one. Just for a moment, I

think about my life. Am I happy? I always thought I was. For longer than I care to remember this has always been my dream. Other girls discussed their wedding and where they would go on their honeymoon. I researched business opportunities while they watched, 'Say Yes To The Dress.'

I never thought of myself as being strange. In my spare time I devoured biographies of strong women. Karren Brady—of course, and Hillary Clinton to name just two of them. While everyone was reading Harry Potter, I was reading about JK Rowling and how she made it to the top. In fact, I didn't stop at women either. Richard Branson, Barack Obama and Alan Sugar also found their way onto my bookshelf. I was on a mission and never questioned it. Why would I? I had a goal, a purpose and a plan. I am so close to achieving my goal I can taste it. I can't let myself down on this, it's my lifelong dream.

My thoughts are interrupted by a sharp knock and then Charlie bowls in grinning.

I roll my eyes. "Good of you to knock. Maybe the next step of your training will be to actually wait to be asked in."

He just grins that cheeky grin and I can't help but forgive him everything. He winks. "Are you ready, babe? It's not far."

I let the babe go and just look at him with interest. "Where is home exactly?"

He looks almost embarrassed and sighs heavily.

"Knightsbridge."

I blink and then look at him in shock. "Wow, you're being a tad overpaid if you can afford to live there."

He shrugs. "I didn't say it was mine, did I? Let's just say I still live at home. Well, one of them anyway."

Once again, I feel irritated. Of course, champagne Charlie born with a silver spoon in his mouth. Unlike the rest of us, he is handed life on a silver platter. I push my irritation away and say briskly, "Come on then, let's get this over with."

Charlie nods and heads outside and I follow him closely behind.

11

We take the Tube to Knightsbridge and I can't help but envy him his short commute to work. Gosh, if I lived so close, I could manage an extra two hours' work every day. That's impressive and I feel quite jealous of him.

We don't talk much as he seems preoccupied which is fine by me. I'm not sure I can be trusted not to snap at him, anyway. I don't know why but he completely rubs me up the wrong way.

It's only a short walk from the station before he stops in front of a beautiful white Georgian house in a very smart road. I wonder which floor his apartment is on? These houses are beautiful inside, I've seen them on TV and I wonder what his will be like?

He heads up a few steps and puts his key in the lock.

As we step inside, he flicks on the light and I see a beautiful hallway in front of me. Marble flooring stretches endlessly in front of us and huge mirrors dominate the walls. The lighting is modern and illuminates the space beautifully, creating a cosy entrance that beckons you inside.

Charlie throws his keys onto a table in the hall then turns and smiles somewhat guiltily.

"I'm sorry about this, Vick. I would have asked to go to yours but really had to head home tonight. I need a shower and a change of clothes more than food at the moment."

I raise my eyes. "Well, if you will stop out all night, that's the downside of it and what makes you think I'd want you to come to my home anyway? You would certainly be returning home afterwards if you did."

He laughs softly. "Listen, I wasn't presuming anything. Well, now you're here you may as well make yourself at home. I'm heading off to shower and change, so I'll show you to the kitchen and you can make yourself a coffee or something. If you prefer you can wait and I'll make it, I know how stubborn you can be."

I open my mouth to retaliate and he holds up his hand. "It's ok, I didn't mean anything by it. Anyway, come on, I'll show you downstairs and leave you to settle in while I change."

As he leads me down a flight of stairs, it dawns on me that there are no apartments here. This is Charlie's house - all of it and that annoys me even more than I was already. This house must be worth millions. Why the hell does Charlie want to work when he obviously has more money than sense?

I almost groan with longing when I see the kitchen. It fills the whole of the basement and is state of the art, with sleek lines and hidden lighting illuminating different areas. Bifold doors run the length of one wall at the end and if it wasn't dark outside, I'm guessing there's a garden outside.

Charlie smiles somewhat apologetically. "Help yourself to a drink, Vick, I won't be long."

I watch him head off and shake my head in utter surprise. This place is everyone's dream. If it were mine, I would never leave.

I walk around just running my hand over the sleek, cool, marble tops and resist the urge to open every drawer and cupboard. I see one of those built-in coffee makers and marvel at the complexity of it. The whole place is gleaming and I doubt there is even a speck of dust in the room. How is this possible? I've always thought of Charlie as a bit of a slob and yet this home is screaming OCD.

As I explore, I wonder about Charlie's family. They obviously have a lot of money. I know he went to Eton and Oxford but other than that I know very little about him. He is well spoken, despite the phrases he uses and I'm sure his childhood involved many foreign holidays and an extravagant lifestyle. This is worlds away from my own childhood on the rough council estate I grew up on. It's what I've dreamed of having all these years and here it is, handed to Charlie on a plate.

I resist the urge to take selfies of myself in this luxurious kitchen. Ok, maybe I did take one or two but only to remind me of how angry all this makes me feel. I will work for everything I get in life and won't take any handouts, unlike Charlie. Seeing this has just strengthened my resolve to win.

As promised, it doesn't take him long and I don't miss the butterflies that flutter inside me when I see him enter the room, freshly showered and wearing track bottoms and a tight t-shirt. His feet are bare which can only mean one thing - underfloor heating.

In fact, this whole place is so cosy and warm despite the chill outside. I almost can't look at him as he runs his fingers through his wet freshly washed hair and grins that cheeky grin that does things to my lady parts.

"So, you decided to wait for me to get the coffee."

I feel a little embarrassed and say quietly, "I'm sorry, Charlie, I didn't want to break your coffee maker. I don't know the first thing about how it works."

He smiles softly as he reaches inside a cupboard for two mugs. "Don't worry V, I had an hour's lesson on how it works when it was installed. You can't be expected to know just by looking at it."

I watch as he makes the drinks and say with interest. "Your home's amazing, Charlie. Have you lived here long?"

His smile fades a little as he says edgily, "Too long, babe. As I said, it's not mine, it's my family's.

My father has a few houses around the place and this is one of them. It's convenient for the office and free, so I'd be stupid not to use it."

Suddenly, he looks across and says almost desperately. "Don't let it change your opinion of me. This house—it isn't me. It's my family. It may be super impressive but my father has a strong work ethic. I only get to live here if I can prove I'm making my way in life independent of him. He may have money but he wants his kids to make their own way. There are no handouts here except the free bed and board. If I'm caught slacking, I'm out on my ear."

He hands me the coffee and I look at him more closely. There's a weariness to him that I've never noticed before. He looks unhappy when he should be the happiest man in the world living in a place like this. The atmosphere has changed, and he smiles sadly. "Don't judge me, Vick. I'm still the same man you know and hate. Now, haven't we got a challenge to complete?"

I smile and follow him from the room, carrying my mug with me. As we walk, I can't stop staring at this magnificent home as he says brightly, "I've ordered us some pizza. I hope that's ok. What do they say, movie night is also pizza night? Well, we should do it properly."

He heads inside another room and I gasp out loud. "Oh my god, Charlie, you even have your own cinema."

He laughs as I look around the small room filled with large seats set before a huge screen. He jumps into one and places his mug on the table beside it.

"Come on, Vick, make yourself at home and I'll start the movie."

I look at him in surprise. "Don't I get a say in what we watch?"

He shrugs. "If you like, what do you fancy?"

Gingerly, I sit on a nearby seat and think. "What about Scrooge? You know, a classic that delivers the Christmas message."

Charlie laughs hard. "You crack me up, babe. I was thinking of watching Elf. Nothing says Christmas as much as that film."

I roll my eyes and he grins. "Ok, have it your way. A Christmas Carol is on its way."

I nod and feel happy that I've got my own way for once.

Charlie flicks a remote control and zips through a selection of films. Then he grins and says loudly. "Here we go, make yourself comfy, this is one of my favourites."

As the credits roll, I shake my head. A Muppets Christmas Carol takes over the screen and I laugh to myself. Typical Charlie.

Despite myself and god knows I try to keep up the ice queen routine, I start to soften. The film is actually hilarious and I can't help but be drawn into it. Charlie is a complete kid who laughs all the way through it and his laughter is infectious. About halfway through, the doorbell rings and he pauses the film and grins. "If I'm not mistaken dinner is served."

Once he has retrieved the boxes of food, I follow him to the amazing kitchen and watch as he grabs some plates and serviettes from a nearby cupboard. Then he opens what looks like a fancy wine store and says, "Red or white?"

I should just stick to soft drinks but I don't want to come across as churlish, so just smile. "Red if that's ok with you?"

He nods, grabbing a bottle and the corkscrew and shouts over his shoulder. "Grab the boxes and we'll eat in front of the movie."

I follow him out and watch as he leads the way. Seeing him here at home, relaxed and in his own environment, he seems different. I've always known he was good-looking, but the relaxed, casual, Charlie is a knockout. Me, on the other hand, I must look a complete mess. I'm still wearing the trousers and jacket from my day at the office and my hair is pulled tightly back. We are like chalk and cheese and I envy him his ability to switch from professional to casual effortlessly.

Once we settle down again, I throw caution to the wind and remove my shoes and jacket and untie my hair. Maybe it's because Charlie is so laid back that I feel comfortable with him. Despite everything, I am enjoying the film. I haven't watched such a frivolous one in years and find myself enjoying it more than I thought. Charlie obviously loves it and just laughs his way through it. Occasionally, we share a look and a smile and I find myself wanting to know more about my hospitable partner.

One empty pizza box and a bottle of wine later we watch the credits roll and he switches off the set. Suddenly, there is silence where once there was laughter. He looks at me with interest and says softly, "You know, Vick, I was kind of dreading tonight but you've surprised me."

I look at him and raise my eyes, "In what way?"

He shrugs. "You don't need me to tell you, you're quite a hard nut to crack. I mean, you are ultra-professional and I can't fault that but I've never discovered the human side of you."

My face must say it all because he immediately looks guilty. "Listen, that came out wrong. What I mean is, I've never taken the time to actually get to know you. These last few days have shown me more of you than all the years we've worked together."

Normally I would feel quite hurt and defensive at his words but even I know he's right.

I shake my head sadly. "I know how I come across and I've told myself on numerous occasions it doesn't matter. I am hard on my staff and clients and believe me when I say this, I am hardest on myself."

He looks interested but then I catch sight of the time and say in horror.

"Oh my god, look at the time, I should get going. The last train leaves in an hour and I can't risk missing it."

Quickly, I scrabble around for my things and then look up in surprise as Charlie's hand grasps my arm and he looks at me with concern.

"Listen, Vicky. No strings or anything but you can stay here if it's easier. We have seven bedrooms and only one is currently occupied by me. Stay here and then you'll be closer to work tomorrow. I promise not to bother you and you can treat this house as your own."

He looks so worried that just for a second my resolve almost gives way but instead, I smile gratefully and say gently. "Thanks for the offer but I'll pass this time. I need to head home because I'll need a change of clothes and there's a file I need for a meeting tomorrow. Thanks for the offer though, I appreciate it."

He smiles and follows me to the door. As we pass through the magnificent hall I say with interest, "What does your father do, Charlie?"

He pulls a face. "He owns a building company. He started it from scratch and it grew bigger than he thought it ever would. He went into partnership with a rival company and they never looked back."

"Do I know of it?"

He smirks. "It's Wilson-Monroe."

The penny drops and I see a shadow pass across his face as he sees my expression.

"What, the Wilson-Monroe, global corporation responsible for buildings all around the world?"

He nods and I see a pulse start beating in his cheek as he anticipates the barrage of questions that are sure to follow. But I can see he doesn't need to answer them now. Whatever his problem here, it's not for delving into tonight.

There's a story here that runs deep. Maybe I'll discover what it is the more time I spend with him.

Instead, I smile and say brightly. "Thanks for a great evening. Despite everything, I enjoyed it."

I look at him in surprise as he grabs his coat and follows me out. "Here, let me walk you to the station as it's dark. It's the least I can do."

I go to speak but he holds up his hand. "Non-negotiable. I don't care if you are a strong independent woman who probably does karate on her days off after mountain biking and god only knows what else. I've been brought up to never let a lady walk on her own at night and you can argue all you want but I'm still coming."

Swallowing my usual tart comment, I just smile and say softly, "Thanks, Charlie, I appreciate it."

As we walk through the streets of Knightsbridge, he says cheerily. "What do you think it will be tomorrow?"

I grin. "Who knows? This whole experience is completely unpredictable and well out of my comfort zone. It wouldn't surprise me if it was to train Eskimos to make crackers."

Charlie laughs. "It's taken me by surprise too but I'm enjoying the whole experience, are you?"

Looking into his gorgeous eyes that twinkle in the darkness, I admit to myself as much as to him. "Yes, Charlie. I am enjoying it way more than I ever thought I would."

It's a thought that keeps me warm on my journey home. For the first time in what seems forever, life is more interesting than it has been in a very long time.

12

December 5th

20 Days to Go

Thank God it's Friday. This has been the strangest week of my life and that's a fact. However, it's with an alien smile on my face and a spring in my step that I head to the office.

Still no whistles from the builders which surprises me but has ceased to be important. Everything else is exactly as it should be and I'm even looking forward to today's challenge.

By the time the next one appears in my Inbox I am desperate to find out what it is.

A picture of a mug of hot cocoa and a pair of woolly mittens flashes onto the screen and I open it with excitement.

Make a playlist of your favourite holiday tunes.

My heart sinks. I am so out of my comfort zone with this one. I wouldn't know what a playlist was if it sat in front of me with a sign around its neck saying 'playlist.' This one is my fail.

I reach for the phone but there is no answer today. That's odd. Charlie usually answers it immediately or at least barges into my office. I head outside and say to Sarah. "Is Mr Monroe in yet?"

She shakes her head. "No, he has a meeting across town today. He told us not to expect him in and clear any meetings."

I nod and return to my office. Bother. This isn't good. My traitorous heart has run away with itself and is reading far more into Charlie's attention than it has any right to. Why should I care if he isn't in today? I don't usually keep tabs on him and it shouldn't concern me in the slightest. However, it does. I want to hear his teasing voice or see his cheeky grin. I want him to annoy me and to throw a sharp retort his way. I sit at my desk and sigh heavily as a text flashes up on my phone.

Yo, V. Meet you at mine after work, unless you want to do this at yours. I'm sure we'll nail this one in no time. Let me know if you've got plans but we need to do this today as per the terms of our challenge.

Charlie X

Grinning, I type my response.

To Charlie

No problem. I am fully aware of the terms of our challenge and will meet you at 7 pm at your house. Hopefully, it shouldn't take long this time. If you need me to pick anything up on my way, please let me know.

Victoria Marshall. LLP

I wait for a second and he replies with an emoji of a laughing face and I shake my head. Typical response. The guy is the most unprofessional man I have ever met, yet the most brilliant at what he does. I'm in no doubt he could run this company with no problem but it would be the most chaotic place to work in the world.

No, Mr Rowanson needs me to steer this ship into the future. Not Charlie, who can't take anything seriously. The trouble is, I need to learn how to make a playlist and fast.

I have a short window of opportunity before my staff meeting to Google making a playlist. It appears that I just need an iPhone, iTunes and a computer. Well, I have all of those but have never bothered with the music side of things. In fact, I only ever listen to motivational, self-help audiobooks when I take the daily commute to work. A much better use of my time and yet another way to reach my goals.

I have trained my mind religiously over the years to treat every minute of the day as another step towards my goals. Charlie may have been joking about my weekend pursuits but fitness does play a part. I train my body as well as my mind to be in tip-top condition. I research power foods and prepare recipes that will feed my mind as well as my body and I train in the ancient arts of jujitsu and karate. However, I'm beginning to see that I'm creating a monster and I'm fast realising that there's one area of my life that I've severely neglected - my personality.

It doesn't take long and I soon learn how to compile a playlist. It looks pretty easy and I shake my head. Of course, it's easy. Just because I haven't made one before it doesn't mean I couldn't learn in a heartbeat. Once again, I wonder at Mr Rowanson's sanity. Why on earth does he think these challenges will show him who is the best person for the job? I mean, he must be seriously losing it.

Now that's done I concentrate on my staff meeting. We have one every Friday morning and Monday afternoon. I like to end the week with a roundup of what was required and then we have the afternoon to get up to speed. Nobody can leave for the weekend until we are on track. Monday afternoons are spent making sure the week is planned methodically, which enables us to reach our goals.

I gather my files and head to the boardroom where my staff are waiting. There are six of us who work in my department. Me, Sarah my PA and four other junior lawyers. all detailed with various cases that I oversee. I know I'm hard on them but I am for a reason. I want us to be the best. Any sign of weakness and we would lose the case. This wouldn't do either our company or clients any favours so I am ruthless out of necessity.

All eyes turn to me as I walk in and the way the conversation stops short tells me that the subject of the conversation was me. I shrug it off. I know they hate me, I would in their shoes but I'm not here to be their friend. I am here to do a job and if that makes me unpopular then so be it.

Annie nods as I sit and turn to face her. "Any news on the Mackenzie contract? Have they sent over the drafts?"

She nods and pushes a file towards me. "It's all here ready for your green light."

I say in a hard voice, "Have you checked it over?"

She looks nervous as she nods and says, "With a fine-tooth comb. It all looks to be in order."

I hand the file to Sarah, "Add this to my list. I'll check it over this afternoon and sign it off if agreeable."

I turn my attention to Mark, one of my longest serving juniors. "Anything to report on the contract for Starline?"

He nods and pushes another file my way. "It all checks out and we're about to draft the contracts this afternoon."

I fix him with a hard look. "And it hasn't been done already because…?"

He actually squirms in his seat as he looks at me guiltily. "We only heard back from the searches this week. I was running late on the Goodman case and so it was held up."

The silence in the room is palpable. Everyone holds their breath and looks anywhere but at me. They know this is an excuse that I find unacceptable.

I say grimly, "Why were you running late?"

He has the grace to blush and says in a small voice. "Because I had to take time out to sort out a personal matter."

I hold my breath and count to ten. I know he's scared of my reaction. They all are. They are waiting for me to explode like an atom bomb and wreak devastation to the room. Maybe I would have done last week but for some reason, which shocks me more than them, I don't. Instead, I exhale sharply and turn to the next victim. "Louise, what about the land deal with Hardy and Asquith?"

She speaks in a firm, controlled, voice and tells me everything I would have expected to hear and I sigh with relief. Of all my staff she is the most switched on and I rely on her more than anyone.

The meeting carries on but today, for some reason, I notice things that I never have before. I notice the animosity in their eyes as they look at me. I see the grim set of their mouths and the unhappiness on their faces and Mr Rowanson's words come back to haunt me. '*You treat your staff meetings like the boardroom of the Apprentice. You pull them apart and leave them shaking and quivering with a sense of inadequacy.*'

Now I know he was right. I do. Guilty as charged. I am a monster with no feeling or humanity and it may have got me up the ladder quicker than most but was it worth this atmosphere? Was it worth the hatred these people feel for me? It's not the respect I always thought it was, it's fear. Suddenly, I feel weary. I feel ashamed and dislike the person I've become. For once in my life, I am struggling inside and they don't even know it.

Just for a moment, I sit in silence as Louise finishes and just stare around the room. Then I do something so out of character it takes them by surprise. I smile and look around at my staff and say brightly. "I think we'll leave it there for today. Make sure you're all up to speed by Monday's meeting but before you go, there's something I need from each of you."

The looks on their faces almost make me laugh. They look worried, surprised and wary. They suspect a trap and I can't blame them. I smile again and look around the room. "Can you all write your favourite Christmas song on this piece of paper before you go?"

They look at me with shock and I sit back in my seat. I don't say anything more and just enjoy the confusion in their expressions. Sarah gingerly takes the paper and starts writing before handing it to Annie. One by one, they write their favourite and then leave the room. When the last one leaves, I glance down at the list. Good, it's a start and it will prove to Charlie that I know what I'm doing. So what if Christmas songs leave me cold? This is war and I am going to win. That much I'm sure of.

13

I arrive at Charlie's door just before seven armed with my newfound knowledge of playlists and song choices. He answers the door and a little piece of my soul melts. He has changed already into jeans and a t-shirt and once again is barefoot. His hair is messy, and he flashes me that cheeky grin that seems to reach parts of me that I never knew were there.

"Vick, babe. Looking amazing as always."

I glower at him and he laughs, holding the door open for me to enter.

My heels click on the marble tiles as I follow him into an impressive study. I look around in awe as I take in the wood panelling and plush carpeting. A huge oak desk dominates the room and there are many framed certificates on the walls and bookcases stuffed with impressive looking hard backed books.

Charlie heads over to the desk and grabs another chair, setting it beside the large padded one in front of the largest computer I have ever seen.

"Here, rest your legs while I grab us a drink. What do you fancy? We'll make it the hard stuff as it's the weekend."

I watch as he heads across to a drinks cabinet and grabs what looks like a bottle of whisky.

I raise my eyes. "What if I don't drink spirits, Charlie? Have you got any soft drinks over there?"

He smirks as he splashes two measures of whisky into a glass and then repeats it with another one.

"Come on, darling, don't make me drink alone. This will warm you up inside and give you the courage to tackle our latest challenge."

Rolling my eyes, I take the glass from his outstretched hands.

"Only one then. I have to get home earlier than last night as I have things to do."

He doesn't say anything just winks as he takes a large gulp of the drink in his hand.

I on the other hand merely wet my lips with the demon drink. I'm not a spirit's girl, never have been and I'm not about to start now.

Charlie starts fiddling with the computer and then looks at me and raises his eyes. "Do you have some songs you want to include?"

Pushing the list towards him, I smirk. "Here you go, all done and dusted."

He looks through my list and dare I say it, looks impressed. "You've surprised me, babe. I never had you down as a Slade fan."

I look at him smugly. "There's a lot you don't know about me, Charlie."

He looks at me with an expression I can't quite place and then the loud sound of 'Merry Christmas Everybody,' comes blaring out from hidden speakers making me jump.

Charlie smirks as I can't help it and cringe at the loud music that blares from the speakers. Then I remember it's one of my choices so I pretend to love it and tap my foot in time with the music and plaster a look of joy on my face.

Charlie laughs and turns to the computer and appears to start downloading the song and I try to look as if I'm enjoying it. Then, one by one he downloads all my choices and to my surprise there are a couple I recognise. 'Last Christmas' was always a particular favourite and I have no problem humming away to that one. I even forget I don't drink whiskey and quite enjoy the burn as it works its way through my body.

Charlie sings along loudly and grins as I try to join in. By the end of it, we are giggling like school kids, which I'm sure is helped along by the Christmas spirit in the glasses.

Soon my choices are downloaded and we start on Charlie's. I'm surprised to find his taste is not what I expected. Old classics such as Nat King Cole and Bing Crosby fill the room. Then he adds a modern twist with Michael Bublé. I actually prefer his choice to mine and find myself swaying to the songs and smiling happily as the beautiful tunes fill the room.

Charlie appears to be caught up in the moment and mouths the words to me as he sings along to the lyrics. He moves around the room and makes me giggle at his stupid ways before he pulls me from my seat and twirls me around to the seductive sound of, 'Baby Please Come Home.'

Maybe it's the whisky, or maybe it's the company but I feel more relaxed than I have in ages. If somebody had told me I'd be dancing with Charlie to Christmas songs in his father's study last week, I'd have thought they were stark raving mad.

By the time the playlist has been compiled, I've had the best evening with Charlie. I pushed aside our challenge and obvious differences and just relaxed and let my guard down.

Once Charlie switches off the computer he grins ruefully. "Job done. Another tick on the list and another day closer to the prize."

I nod and look around for my things. "Thanks again, Charlie. I'd better be going and let you continue with your weekend."

As I turn to leave, his hand reaches out and pulls me back. I see a lost look in his eyes as he says softly, "Stay a while."

I look at him in surprise and he smiles softly.

"Listen, Vick. I don't know about you but it gets pretty lonely living on your own. I don't know the first thing about your life outside of the company but I'm guessing you don't have a lot to rush back to. This job we do, it takes over a bit, doesn't it?"

I nod in agreement. "You're right for once."

I wink as I say it and he grins. I smile softly and say, "How about we head out and grab a bite to eat. I don't know about you but I'm hungry. Also, I probably need something to soak up this Christmas spirit."

He laughs and says happily, "Just give me five minutes to make myself presentable. I know a great little restaurant around the corner. It's not far and we don't need a reservation."

He hurries out of the room and I sit in the chair and wait. He has surprised me again. I always thought of him as the party king with a string of women waiting for his call. From what I've seen though, he is actually quite lonely. A lot like me really and I never thought that his job affects him the way it does me. Maybe I've misjudged the wrapping with Charlie. I think I'll delve a little deeper tonight and see if I can discover more about the man behind that cheeky grin and the smart mouth.

Charlie takes me to an intimate looking Italian restaurant on the Brompton Road. We walk past Harrods and I gasp at the amazing windows that shine out in the dark sky. They are very impressive and we stand and look at a recreation of a warm and cosy scene in front of a fireplace. Stockings hang either side and are bursting with designer gifts and sparkling jewellery. There's a Christmas tree that holds more gifts and sparkling gems, with expensive fragrances littering the foot of it and expensive watches hanging from the branches. As we look at the display, Charlie says in a tight voice. "I hate that scene."

I look at him in surprise and see the tightness of his jaw and the anger in his eyes. I look back at the scene and say softly, "Why, what's wrong with it?"

He shrugs. "It's vulgar and demonstrates everything I hate about Christmas."

I stay silent and he carries on. "Look at the gifts hanging from the tree and stockings. They cost a small fortune and pander to the materialistic in our society. It's all about buying the most expensive present and looking as if you're the most generous. It's almost as if the more you spend the better the gift. People drown in debt to buy gifts that will be tossed away quicker than the debt is paid. I hate this side of Christmas, it's devastating."

He pulls me with him and walks away from the decadent scene angrily. I almost struggle to keep up, wishing like crazy I had worn flat shoes. He must calm down a little because he slows down and looks at me apologetically. Reaching for my hand, he says gently, "Sorry, Vick. I forgot I walk quickly. Here, let me help you along."

I should pull away, I know I should but I don't. Charlie's hand in mind feels good - so good it's as if it belongs there. I like the contact with him and the warning bells ring loudly in my head.

'No! Move away from the hot guy who is running off with your heart. Step aside and save yourself before it's too late. This man's a player and is playing you now. Protect yourself at all costs. Mayday! Mayday! Save yourself before it's too late.'

Well, it is too late. I'm not sure how but Charlie has worked his way through the iron exterior and softened the defences that have taken years to build.

Charlie Monroe has done the unthinkable. He has worked his way inside my heart and I don't know how to get him out.

The restaurant's impressive as I knew it would be. The atmosphere's seductive and peaceful and there is soft music playing. Dim lighting is aided by candles burning on intimate tables and I can tell this isn't going to be cheap. The waiter greets Charlie like a long-lost friend and shows us to an intimate table in the corner.

This is bad - very bad because someone had better tell my heart that this is all pretend because just for a moment, it thinks something may actually happen with this gorgeous man.

We make our selections and Charlie orders us a bottle of red wine. I protest but he shakes his head and holds my eyes with his. "Come on, Vick. It's Friday night and we deserve to unwind. You can crash at mine tonight and then we'll both be in place for the next challenge."

I shake my head but he isn't having it. "Come on, darling, what have you really got to go home to? An empty flat with a meal for one if I'm guessing right. Knowing you it would involve working to the small hours and then waking up to some sort of punishing regime you set yourself in your spare time. Tell me I'm wrong and I'll pay for a cab for you myself."

I look down and the realisation hits hard. He's right. There is nothing but work in my life. I'm a sad lonely woman with no friends.

He reaches across and lifts my face to his and I see the concern in his eyes. "Don't feel bad. If it's any consolation your life mirrors mine. It's some sacrifice we make to succeed isn't it?"

I look at him in surprise. "But you must have a bunch of friends to keep you busy. You're so full of fun and I imagine you have a great life. I mean, look at your amazing home right in the centre of everything. I don't believe you for one minute, Charlie Monroe. You're just trying to make me feel better."

He shakes his head sadly. "I know it seems that way but I don't. My life isn't all champagne and wild parties you know. I don't even date much because I can't deal with the inevitable. Girls want commitment and it gets messy. I've never met a girl I want to see more than a few times, which makes me even more of an idiot than you thought I was."

I lean forward with interest. "Why not?"

He shrugs. "The sort of girls I meet are either gold diggers or career women. The girls that run around with the crowd I grew up with are society girls with no common sense or knowledge of real life. I don't want to be saddled with a trophy wife so I stay away."

"But what about your friends? Surely you enjoy spending time with them?"

He shrugs. "Occasionally. Most of them are from wealthy families and I never really fitted in with their world."

I snort and he raises his eyes as I blush deeply. "Sorry, I don't know where that came from."

He grins as I say incredulously. "But look at you, Charlie. You live in a house that costs millions, and you went to Eton and Oxford. You *are* one of them whether you like it or not."

He almost looks angry. "You'd think so, wouldn't you? The thing is, I was always a bit of a joke. Champagne Charlie with the common family from humble beginnings who was never really accepted. You see, my family doesn't speak like them and are more at home with normal people doing normal jobs than the people who think they are above everyone else. Having money was a double-edged sword growing up. I was sent to the best schools and yet never really accepted. My parents were from rough beginnings and didn't have the connections or past to ever truly fit in. Not that they cared, my family have rules of their own they abide by. Family is everything and you have to work hard to look my father in the eye. He made his fortune with no handouts and no leg up in life and wants the same from his children."

I am fascinated by Charlie's life. If anything, it sounds better than I thought it was. I wonder about his family and say with interest. "Do you have any brothers or sisters?"

For some reason, he looks angry and nods. "One sister, Emily. She's younger than me and a bit of a handful."

"In what way?"

He shakes his head. "She's a wild one. Where I have to work for everything, she gets to live in the fast lane. It appears that the usual rules don't apply in her case and she gets away with everything."

I'm intrigued and press for more. "What does she do?"

He laughs, but it's without humour. "What doesn't she do more like? She's running around with a wild crowd and has got herself in deep with some politician. She works as an intern at the Houses of Parliament, an unfortunate introduction by one of her society friends. The trouble is, she has declared herself in love with the man she works for and he's encouraging her."

I look at him in horror and say in a whisper, "What's so bad about him?"

Charlie sneers. "The fact he's married has a lot to do with it. He's also old enough to be her father and the sleaziest guy I've ever met."

He looks so worried I want to reassure him and reach out and grab his hand. He looks at me in surprise and I smile softly. "She's young and easily impressed. Maybe it's not that bad. It may not be anything at all and I'm sure it will fizzle out. I mean, you yourself are no stranger to office infatuation. You have to deal with it on a daily basis and you're ok. There are no scandalous stories associated with you or I would have heard about them."

He smiles and I hold my breath as his eyes power into mine. "You mean well, Vick but this time you're wrong. The trouble is, I can't bring myself to open that can of worms tonight. What do you say to a nice dessert here and then a coffee back at mine? You must be done in and we have another challenge to face tomorrow, remember?"

I can see he wants to wrap this conversation up and respect his wishes. However, I'm not a Rottweiler lawyer for nothing and vow to get to the bottom of this for Charlie's sake. There's more to this than he's telling me and for god only knows what reasons I have, I want to help him.

14

Waking up at Charlie's is an experience I never thought I'd have. We returned home after a fabulous meal and drank coffee until the early hours. Most of our conversation was centred on the office and we laughed and shared stories of our staff and clients and generally put the world to rights. Then he lent me one of his t-shirts to sleep in and rustled up some spare toiletries that they obviously keep for guests.

He showed me to an amazing guest room and then left me to it. To say I'm happy is an understatement. I think this advent calendar challenge is just what the doctor ordered. I am having the time of my life and discovering things about myself that I never knew existed. Far from questioning Mr Rowanson's sanity, I now think he's a genius.

It must be about 10am before I venture downstairs. I can't believe I've slept so late. It's so out of character and definitely not something I've done for several years. It must be the alcohol I consumed and the fact we didn't get to bed until the early hours.

Charlie is sitting at the breakfast bar when I venture into the kitchen and smiles looking so hot I feel uncharacteristically shy.

"Morning, Vick. Sleep well?"

I nod as he pushes a coffee towards me. "Here, you may need this when I tell you what the challenge is today. Check your phone, you'll be surprised."

I reach for my phone and check my emails. This time the pictures of a snowy scene and as I read the message, my heart sinks.

Go ice skating.

I look up and see Charlie grinning at me. "Have you ever been ice skating before?"

I shake my head feeling suddenly nervous. What if I injure myself? I mean, you hear all sorts of stories about people falling on the ice and getting a body part sliced off by an out of control skater. What if I break something and end up in plaster for the festive season? What if I make a complete fool of myself and never live it down? This is so far out of my comfort zone it's not funny. This is the worst one yet.

Charlie laughs happily. "This is great. I love ice skating. I warn you, I'm quite a dab hand at it."

Great, just great. He just cotton picking would be, wouldn't he? Well, I'm certainly no Jayne Torvill to his Christopher Dean. This will be a disaster.

My head spins with every excuse under the sun as to why I can't do this. My voice actually shakes as I say "I can't go ice skating. I'm totally wearing the wrong clothes."

Charlie looks at me hard and I see a twinkle in his eye as he says in a teasing voice. "What's the matter, Vick, are you not up for the challenge?"

I start to speak really quickly. "Of course not. If you must know, I could have been a professional. I fact, I was asked to try out for Team GB but couldn't be bothered."

He folds his arms as I babble on. "In fact, I was asked to train this year's athletes but had to pass because of work commitments. Actually, the reason I stopped was because I broke my ankle. In fact, I broke the ankles of several other people near me as I ploughed into them and I was in therapy for months dealing with the pain of causing such human suffering. I've only just got over it and I'm sure I'll have a relapse if I hit the ice."

Charlie laughs and takes my hands in his and says softly, "Breathe, Vicky. It's ok, I've got this. We'll head back to your place and you can change. You don't live that far from Hampton Court and we can do it there."

He must see the panic in my eyes because he says gently, "I won't let you back out. You can do this, babe. You're the strongest woman I've ever met and I won't let your fear stop you from overcoming it. Even if I have to hold you up all the way around the ice I promise I won't let you go. You're safe with me and nothing will hurt you when I'm around."

Oh. My. God. Charlie is officially my superhero. This man was fashioned out of dreams and made for me by God. Can he really get any better than he is and can I get any worse? I'm ashamed of myself. I've just exposed a major weakness of mine to my opponent and far from throwing it back at me like I would probably do, he is actually being nice about it.

Just for a second, I look into those gentle eyes and melt inside. He is looking at me with a warmth and determination that makes my soul sing. So, I smile weakly and just nod. "Ok, but once around the circle thing and then it's done."

He grins cheekily and I can't help but smile. "Good for you, V. Let's go and you can show me how it's done."

Charlie drives us to my home. He has changed into jeans a jumper and a huge padded jacket. He grabbed a woolly hat and gloves and looks just like a Christmas card himself. I look strange sitting next to him in my business suit and yet it feels like the most natural thing in the world to be here.

He is so easy to talk to and we play our Christmas playlist on the way, singing along to the songs as if we don't have a care in the world. By the time we reach my apartment, I've forgotten the hell that is about to be unleashed on me.

He parks in a visitor's bay and follows me up to my first-floor apartment just outside London.

For a moment, just before I put the key in the lock, I feel unsure what he'll think of me. This place is nothing like he's used to. In fact, it would fit inside his kitchen and I think back to my childhood home. We lived in a maisonette that wasn't anything like this. It was in a rough neighbourhood and I always vowed to move on and make something of my life. This is the best I could do, and I was always proud of how far I've come. However, as I'm about to let Charlie inside the most private part of my world, I feel as if I have failed a little.

He leans against the wall watching me and god only knows how he does it, says gently, "Stop it, Vick."

I look across and he smiles sweetly. "Stop comparing your place to mine. At least this is all yours. Mine isn't. I live with my parents, so if anyone has cause to feel embarrassed it's me."

I shake my head and say softly, "How do you do that, Charlie?"

He looks confused. "Do what?"

I laugh. "Read my mind as you do."

He shrugs. "It's easy. For a lawyer your face is an open book, to me anyway. I see all your emotions pass across it and watch them unfold in your eyes. You may be a closed book in your professional life but take you away from your comfort zone and I see a scared woman afraid that she doesn't measure up."

He reaches across and tilts my face to his. "What you don't realise is that you measure up way more than you think. You're an amazing woman, Vicky. I've always known it and spending this last week with you has confirmed it. You just need to lighten up and let go for once. It's all there inside you trying to stay hidden. Maybe Mr Rowanson saw what I see. Maybe he saw something in both of us that we couldn't see ourselves. Who knows, by the end of this challenge we may just walk away better people because of it."

I raise my eyes and smile. "You know, Charlie, you're not so bad yourself."

I let us into my home and as he follows me in I feel a warm feeling inside. It's good to have a friend at last.

As I walk back inside my personal space, I breathe a deep sigh of relief. Home at last. I may have only been away for one night but now I'm back in my own domain my world rights itself.

I look around at the place I call home and relish the sight that everything is firmly in its place where it should be. This is how I like to live. In an orderly fashion where things are supposed to be. Nothing is out of place and I run my home as I do the rest of my life - like a military operation. The décor is neutral and practical. There are no frivolous furnishings, just tasteful pieces that serve a purpose. Charlie follows me and laughs softly. I turn to look at him and frown as he smirks. "Just what I expected. Your home is exactly as I pictured it."

I frown. "What's that supposed to mean?"

He shakes his head. "It's you, babe. Miss practical and efficiency. I bet you never go to bed without clearing up first. I'm guessing if I looked in your cupboards everything would be in its proper place facing the right way. I'll bet there isn't anything here that isn't useful and I'm guessing there's not a pillow out of place or a speck of dust on the mirrors. I've got to hand it to you, you're one impressive woman."

I scowl at him and he winks making me even more infuriated than I was before.

"For your information, Charlie I like things like this. Why live in chaos when it doesn't take long to have everything in place? It's the slippery slope you know. Once you let one part of your life go, the rest soon follows. If you don't like it maybe you should take a look at your own place. If I remember rightly that was much the same."

He shrugs. "Not my doing, we have a maid."

Words fail me. In fact, for the first time since I can remember, I'm speechless. Actually, I'm disgusted. A maid. For one man. Incredible.

He looks amused. "What's got in your knickers?"

Ok, this man is now seriously annoying me despite his mega hotness and the fact I thought he could possibly be my soulmate two minutes ago. Now that ship has firmly sailed. I mean, what an utter asshole. In fact, he is the King of assholes. The Prince of stupidity and the Duke of men to be avoided at all costs. This man is as far from being my soulmate as that homeless man in Selfridges.

Gritting my teeth, I say curtly, "Now you've finished analysing my life I'd better get changed for the task we've been set. Don't worry, I won't keep you long, *babe*! The sooner you get on your way the happier I'll be."

He looks surprised. "What's rattled your cage?"

I don't even answer him and head off to my room to change, leaving him to entertain himself with his stupid childish ways without me.

As I slam the door behind me I rant inwardly. Stupid idiot. A maid for Christ's sake. What sort of man thinks a maid is acceptable in this century? Can't he do his own cleaning like the rest of society? He sits in his multimillion-pound luxury home pretending he's just like the rest of us. Turning his nose up at the luxurious gifts in Harrods like he has a social conscience, when all along he probably has an account there and orders his groceries from the food hall. What an idiot, judging me for making something of herself while he thinks he's suffered because he still lives at home.

I pull on my jeans and sweater and reach for my boots. Stupid idiot and I'm not talking about him now. I'm thinking of how close I came to actually thinking he could be the man for me. Well, when I meet the man of my dreams, he won't be the judgmental asshole through that door.

I sit on my bed and suddenly an image of Tom Cruise in Top Gun springs to mind. Of course. Nathan Miller fighter pilot and all-around hero. Yes, he's my future. I expect he's dreaming of it now. Maybe fate has had a hand in delivering me my dream man in a roundabout way. I wonder when I'll get the reply I so badly need right now to rub in Charlie's face. If he thinks he has me figured out, then he's in for quite a shock. Victoria Marshall is better than the picture he paints. I'm going to show him just how wrong he is about me.

My resolve firmly set in place, I stride into my living room and fix him with my most disinterested look. "Come on then, let's get this over with."

He looks a little sheepish and just follows me back to his car. I give him the cold shoulder and fume inwardly for most of the journey. After about twenty minutes he sighs and says softly, "I'm sorry, Vick. I didn't mean to offend you. Quite the contrary. I admire you more than you know and just wish I was half as organised as you are."

I snap. "It doesn't matter what you think of me. All that matters is the challenge. I fully intend on passing every one of them and proving to Mr Rowanson I'm the best person for the job."

The air grows instantly hostile between us. I have reminded us both of what's at stake and any friendship that may have been forming between us stops now. We are at war and need to remember that. There will be no guard lowering and no alliances. We are both out to win and this has just reminded us both of that.

15

By the time we reach the makeshift ice rink set up in front of Hampton Court Palace, any familiarity between us has been left firmly at my apartment.

However, in my tantrum, I forgot a very important thing. I can't skate and am terrified of the thought of it. As we check in and get issued our skates, I almost hyperventilate with nerves.

Then, as we head outside, I look around me in awe. Sparkling before me in all its winter splendour is an open-air ice rink. One of the Queen's most amazing palaces provides the backdrop to this glorious sight set beside the River Thames. All around us is the laughter and enjoyment of the masses as they skate with abandon across the frozen ice.

We join a line of people waiting for their turn and I shiver. Charlie is quiet and subdued and I know it's because of my behaviour towards him. I don't care. A maid - really?

There is a family in front us kitted out like your typical movie family. Mum, dad and two children, one of each. They are dressed like an advertisement for happy families out on a winter skating expedition. Bright bobble hats and ski suits. The mother and daughter have their hair in braids and look as if they ski in the alps at weekends. The man looks lovingly at his wife as they share a smile at the eager faces of their offspring. They speak in clipped accents and look as if they drive a Range Rover and live in a mansion in Oxshott. These people have it all and I'm betting they can skate like pros. God, I hate everything about them and yet I want to be that woman more than I've ever wanted anything in my life before.

Suddenly, the loneliness hits me. The void in my life that swirls around me like a black hole. I have nobody to smile at me and make me feel like their world. I'm not surprised given the way I treat people. Even my own mother flinches when I show up and my brother and sister look at me with horror whenever we meet. I have no friends and my staff hate me. Suddenly, I feel ashamed of myself. I don't even like me most of the time. In fact, I haven't liked what I've become ever since that night.

The tears burn behind my eyes and I try every avoidance tactic I've learned over the years to push the memory away. No, not now. Please god, not today.

Then a hand takes mine and squeezes it gently. I turn in surprise and see the concern in Charlie's eyes as he smiles apologetically. "It's ok, Vick. I promised you I'd look after you. I won't let you fall."

I look into his eyes and it hits me hard. It's too late. I've fallen already.

As I thought the perfect family take to the ice like a scene from Holiday on Ice. The parents take a child each and they hold hands as they take off across the ice doing little turns every now and again. God, I hate them.

Charlie takes my hand and grips it tightly. "It's ok, Vick. Just concentrate on standing up and I'll propel you along."

I feel so self-conscious as I watch the little children whizz around me like professionals. There are teenagers looking ultra-cool as they zip around with bored faces trying to impress the giggling girls on the side-lines.

As my feet slip and slide on the ice, I curse Mr Rowanson. How could he subject me to this humiliation? I would like to see him travelling around this death trap without a care in the world.

All I can do is cling onto the edge with one hand and hold Charlie's hand tightly with the other. As we start to move I stumble and my heart skips a beat every time I think I'm about to fall. Charlie is holding me up like I'm some sort of drunkard and yet I'm grateful for that.

We inch our way along the side of the rink, trying hard not to focus on the rest of the people who appear to understand what to do to keep upright. Occasionally someone stumbles and falls and I swallow the shriek that threatens to explode every time it happens. In my mind, my life will end on this ice rink. Somebody will misjudge a leap or turn and the blades of their skates will embed themselves in my head. The rink will turn red with my blood and I will haunt the Hampton Court ice rink for eternity. The ghost of Victoria Marshall will become the stuff of legends. They will sell t-shirts with the image of me lamenting my death with a skate stuck out of the side of my head. Yes, this is very much a possibility as I struggle to complete this near-death experience.

We haven't even got a third of the way around before Charlie stops and spins around to face me. He looks at me kindly and leans his face to within inches of mine. Grabbing my shoulders, he says in a calm, comforting, voice. "Breathe, Vicky. You've got this. If you can walk, you can skate. If you can run, you can skate. Look at these children. They can skate because they have no fear. Relax and let the ice guide you. You've got this and if I know you at all, it's that you're a fighter. Don't let your fear bring you down."

His eyes twinkle and I swallow hard. Wow, Charlie is gorgeous. I've been such a bitch to him and yet here he is trying to help me complete this challenge. He could let me fail and report back to Mr Rowanson that I failed. But he doesn't and I feel so grateful for his kindness I almost do something alien to me - cry. So, I swallow hard and smile bravely. "You're right, Charlie, I'm being a baby.

Come on, let's nail this challenge and I'll treat you to a hot chocolate to say thanks."

He smiles and says softly. "That's my girl."

As he takes my hand again, I very much wish I was.

The impossible has happened and I can now officially skate! Ok, not in the professional sense of the word but I managed to do one circuit of the rink without falling, with only Charlie's superhuman efforts at holding me up to guide me. However, I did it. I'm not going to say it's now my most favourite pastime but even so, I feel a sense of accomplishment as I reach the exit and look back on a fear challenged.

Charlie grins as he sees the triumph in my eyes. "Well done, Vick. A few more lessons and you'll be spinning with the best of them."

Shaking my head, I stumble off the rink and look at him with horror. "I won't be rushing back that's for sure. Thanks for your help but quite honestly that was terrifying."

We grab our boots and head towards the exit. As we leave the challenge behind, I smile at Charlie with a little touch of warmth thrown in. "Come on, I'll buy you that hot chocolate as payment for your services."

He laughs. "Well, I normally charge a lot more per hour than the price of a hot drink but as it's you, babe."

Despite myself, I just grin and we head towards a coffee shop opposite.

Two hot chocolates with whipped cream and sprinkles later, we sit in the window of the warm and cosy coffee shop and look out at the people bustling along the pavement outside. As we watch, it strikes me that I don't usually do this. In fact, I would be at my Jujitsu class right now and be thinking of my fat-free lunch for one.

As I take another sip of the carb-infested drink and look over at my companion, I get a warm feeling inside. This feels so normal and I haven't had any normal in my life for many years now. I decide to find out a little more about my companion who appears as emotionally redundant as me. "So, Charlie, tell me about your family. Do you see them much?"

He shrugs. "Not much. Mum and dad like to live abroad most of the time. They have a house in Florida they prefer because of the weather. They don't like the British winter so mainly stay away. My sister, as you know, lives here but I hardly see her because she prefers to stay with her friend Sammy and tear up the town."

He looks a little angry and I remember what he said. "So, you don't approve then."

He looks at me moodily. "Neither would you if your younger sister was making the biggest mistake of her life and you were supposed to be looking after her. She's meant to be living with me where I can keep an eye on her. If my parents knew half of what she gets up to, I'd have a lot of explaining to do."

He looks so worried I say softly. "What's so bad about being a little wild in your youth?"

He looks angry. "Because what she's doing is devastating for everyone involved."

He looks around and lowers his voice. "She's 20 years old and involved with a married man. He has two children and a famous wife and if the newspapers got wind of it, you can imagine the scandal. He's a politician and the scandal would blow everyone's world apart. I'm trying my best to make her see sense but she's welded on those rose-coloured spectacles and is having none of it."

He takes a sip of his drink and looks moodily out of the window. I think back to the conversation I heard in the toilets and remember that he was waiting in a bar one night by the Houses of Parliament. I look at him thoughtfully.

"So, have you spoken to this man?"

He shakes his head. "I've tried several times, but he's managed to evade me. I've tried calling him but nothing. Short of shadowing her there's not much else I can do and actually, she has every right to do what she's doing. She's old enough to take responsibility for her own life but I can't just sit back and watch her destroy it along with the rest of us."

I'm not sure why I should care but I do. Charlie looks so upset and for some reason that makes me upset. Leaning forward, I reach out and take his hand which I can tell takes him completely by surprise. "I'll help you, Charlie."

He looks shocked and yet I see the gratitude in his eyes. Then he shakes his head and smiles ruefully.

"It's ok, babe. You don't have to get involved. It's not your mess to worry about."

I grin and lean back in my seat. "You forget I'm rather good at bringing complete assholes down. This is what I do best and as it's you, I'll even waive my usual fee. It will give me something to get my teeth into and I kind of like the idea of messing with a politician. That's a new one, even for me."

Charlie is spared from answering as his phone rings and he looks at the screen and sighs. "Sorry, V. I should take this it's Emily."

I watch as he takes the call with resignation in his eyes. "Ems, what's happening?"

There's a short pause and I see his mouth tighten and his eyes fill with anger. "Slow down and speak clearly."

I can hear someone speaking quickly on the other end but no words come through.

Charlie catches my eye and I see the pain, panic and disbelief in his as I hold my breath.

He says curtly. "Stay where you are. I'll be as quick as I can."

As he ends the call, he says sadly. "That was my sister Emily. It would appear the guy's wife found out and has gone crazy. I should go and sort this out."

We stand to leave and as we hurry from the coffee shop, I say with determination. "I'll come with you."

Charlie looks at me in surprise. "Why would you want to? This is going to get nasty, you should keep well away for your own sake."

I shrug. "You can say I'm your lawyer, Charlie. Two heads are better than one and I may be able to help."

He looks at me so gratefully that I can see he's been shouldering a huge burden. The look he shoots me is one of gratitude and relief and my resolve hardens. Charlie helped me today and now it's time to repay the favour doing what I do best. The bitch in me is rubbing her hands with glee because this time it's personal.

16

Charlie drives us back to his home and fills me in on the way.

"Emily was introduced to Marcus Adams the MP for Cirencester last year at a party and they got on well. So well, in fact, he offered her a position on his team as an intern."

He laughs hollowly. "It appears it was her other skills he was interested in and they soon became much closer. She knew he was married, but he did the usual job of convincing her that his marriage was a sham. She told me she fell in love with him and his wife was some sort of ogre that had trapped him in a loveless marriage. You know the sort, Vick, one hundred percent bastard."

I nod. "Yes, I know the type. All too well as it happens."

Charlie doesn't know this, but I jumped at the chance to help him for more than just the kindness of my heart.

It doesn't take long and we are soon back at Charlie's amazing home. I notice a red sports car parked outside and think back to the comments I heard. It must have been his sister who picked him up from the bar that night. For some reason, I feel happy about that and my heart sinks. Way to go

Victoria. Fall for the pretty boy with the cheeky grin. When will you ever learn?

I feel slightly nervous as we head inside. What if Emily's angry that I'm here? Turning to Charlie, I whisper, "Is this such a good idea? She may not like a stranger listening in on her private business."

Charlie nods. "Why don't you make yourself a drink while I find her and suss it all out?"

Nodding, I follow him into the beautiful kitchen and try to make myself at home as he heads off in search of his sister.

As I wait, I think about her predicament. Rather than make myself at home, I do what I always do - work.

I take out my phone and search for the MP for Cirencester. Immediately, his picture flashes up and I look curiously at the man who smiles pompously out at me. He must be in his early forties and is slightly greying at the temples. He looks like a man who has it all even in this photograph. He has that supercilious pompous air that men of power radiate and I hate him on sight. I carry on and click on his family and look with interest at his wife, Sally Adams.

I recognise her immediately. She's a news reader on one of the major channels and it surprises me that she would have married someone like him. She always seemed so sure of herself, so cool and collected and I always thought we could have been friends if we ever met. In fact, she always seemed like a girl after my own heart. However, now I question her sanity. I mean, she must be out of her mind to have married such an idiot and just like that my illusions have been shattered in a heartbeat.

I delve a little deeper into their world and find that they present an image of the perfect family. They have two children who attend public school and there is not a whiff of scandal to their name. But I know these types and if there is any, I know just the man to ask.

Quickly, I dash off a quick message to my usual spy and brief him on what I want. If anything, he's quick so I fully expect to receive an update within hours.

Almost immediately, I hear voices and look with interest at the young woman following Charlie into the kitchen. She's a pretty girl, but that doesn't surprise me, she is Charlie's sister after all.

She has amazing long blonde hair and the most beautiful blue eyes I've ever seen. I thought Charlie's were something else but hers are captivating. However, I can see that they are currently clouded with pain and as she looks at me, I see the questions enter them. I smile as she remembers her manners and looks at me curiously. "Hi, you must be Victoria."

Finally! Somebody related to Charlie can use my full name. I nod. "Pleased to meet you, Emily isn't it?"

She smiles shakily. "I'm sorry to ruin your date."

Charlie grins as I shake my head so hard it may fall off any minute.

"No, you've got that so wrong. Charlie and I are just work colleagues who are working on a secret project."

I think I'm almost hyperventilating as I deny any thought of intimacy with my annoying nemesis.

He rolls his eyes. "Deny it all you like, babe. We know the truth."

Emily's eyes widen and she looks between us in confusion. I glower at him and he laughs.

"It's ok, Vick, I've got this. Vicky's right, Em. We are just work colleagues, nothing more. You interrupted an important part of our work which is why I brought her back with me. Tell her everything because nobody deals with problems quite like Victoria Marshall."

Emily sits next to me at the breakfast bar and proceeds to fill me in on what she has obviously told Charlie.

"You must think I'm an idiot, Vicky. Typical clueless girl falling for a married man who has fed her the usual line."

I don't say anything just smile with encouragement.

She sighs. "I thought Marcus was different. He told me that his wife was just in name only and they were together for the sake of appearances and their children. I never saw her and he was always with me so I never doubted him for a second. I suppose I had the blinkers on because it's obvious now. I mean, we always used to meet in secret away from prying eyes and possible discovery. He never invited me to his apartment, and we only met on business trips where I accompanied him as his assistant. The trouble is, his wife found out. I suppose she's not a reporter for nothing and confronted him."

As she tells her sorry tale, I wonder what can be so bad that makes them both look worried. Surely, it's over now and a lesson learned.

Charlie looks at me with a hard expression as Emily puts her head in her hands.

"Sally, his wife, is threatening to expose our affair. It appears this is just one of many and she's had enough. She wants revenge and half his fortune, not to mention custody of their children. I wouldn't mind but Marcus has denied everything. He dismissed me as a stupid infatuated child and terminated my employment on the spot. I now have no job, no boyfriend and no chance of getting one when this hits the fan. He will come out of this unscathed because he's already got his clean-up crew onto it."

She starts to cry softly. "This will hit the media if she's got anything to do with it and our family will be dragged into it. My parents will find out and it's their disappointment that hurts me the most. Charlie will also get in trouble for not looking out for me and it will be all my fault."

I glance over at Charlie and he looks destroyed. I can tell he feels responsible and the look on his face shows me that he can't deal with this. It's too personal.

I fix them both with a blank look, one that I've perfected over the years and switch on my inner bitch. They may not be up to this but I certainly am.

The rest of the evening was spent going over everything she knows. I set up a temporary office in their kitchen and started my planning. Charlie ordered takeout, and we set about sorting out the mess Emily has found herself in.

For the second night in a row, I stayed at Charlie's. This time, however, it was with my business head on.

17

I'd almost forgotten about the Advent calendar until my phone buzzes waking me up at 8 am. Just for a moment, I wonder where on earth I am and think I must still be dreaming? Then it all comes flooding back and I think back to last night. Despite her situation Emily was lovely. She was so similar to Charlie it was lovely to watch. Despite the fact they have so much they are as down to earth as they come. We watched a film and Emily made popcorn. By the end of the night, we had almost forgotten about the events that brought us all together.

Reaching over, I grab my phone and scroll to the messages. There it is bang on time. A picture of a family laughing around a tree.

I feel the usual excitement as I click on it and read the message.

Skype a family member.

My heart sinks. Great, just great. This is going to look great. All of my family hate me and now Charlie will see that with his very own eyes. However, there is a little part of me that's curious to see his family. If they're anything like his sister, he'll be laughing at this one.

There's a tentative knock at the door and it sends me into a major panic. Surely that can't be Charlie? He wouldn't come knocking on my bedroom door, would he? I mean, nobody and I mean nobody, sees this girl pre-makeup routine. There are reasons why I live alone and this is just one of them. Maybe I should pretend I'm still asleep, surely, he'll go away then.

I watch in horror as the door handle turns ominously and my heart beats rapidly. This can't be happening and images of the horror movies I've seen in the past come back to haunt me. This could be some sort of ploy to get me alone and defenceless. Charlie may be an axe murderer in his spare time and his sister his accomplice. I've been lured here on a pretend mission to get me out of the picture and leave the way clear for Charlie to seize control of the company and now I will pay with my miserable life.

I shrink back against the pillows and prepare to scream like a banshee if what I suspect is true. All of my self-defence lessons have deserted me during this vital time.

As if in slow motion the door handle turns and the door edges open a little. A small hand reaches inside and my heart beats so loudly I think I'm about to have a heart attack.

I watch as the door opens and Emily looks over at me and smiles apologetically.

"I'm sorry, Vicky. I hope I haven't disturbed you but I wanted a word before Charlie gets up."

I smile and pat the bed beside me. "Of course. Come in and tell me what's on your mind."

Yes, just like that my fears dissipate at the promise of some alien girly chatter.

She scoots over and jumps in beside me and images of high school slumber party like films spring to my mind. Not that I was ever one for that. Nobody asked me anyway, but I always wondered what it must feel like.

Emily looks upset and I smile reassuringly. "It's ok, you can talk to me. I won't tell anyone. Client confidentiality and all that."

She smiles thinly and looks at me gratefully. "It's about Charlie, actually."

She laughs as she senses my surprise.

"He always works so hard and what with keeping an eye on me all the time he hasn't had much of a break lately. Last night was the first time I saw him actually smile in a long time."

I shake my head in astonishment. "But he's always smiling. Well, whenever I see him anyway."

She smiles a secret smile. "I'm glad. The thing is, Vicky, Charlie hasn't had a lot to smile about lately. Our father is a force to be reckoned with and puts a lot of pressure on Charlie to succeed. He doesn't want him turning out like some sort of rich and spoiled playboy and as a result is on his case rather a lot. He's also been on at him to settle down for ages and take on some responsibility. You're actually the first girl he's brought home, and I was kind of hoping there was more than just that colleagues' story you've cooked up between you."

I think all words have failed me. If I can remember how to speak the skill has deserted me in an instant. Me and Charlie. Charlie and me. 'Oh, hi, have you met my other half, Charlie Monroe? Hi guys, this is Charlie, my boyfriend.'

Images of us walking through the snow chasing two padded to within an inch of their life children. Twins probably with Charlie's blue eyes and irresistible smile. I see us skating like that family and attending parties together as an item. In fact, my whole life with Charlie flashes before my eyes in an instant before reality crashes brutally in and I gasp, "You must be kidding me."

She looks disappointed. "What, have I got it wrong?"

I nod vehemently. "So wrong. In fact, nothing can be further from the truth."

I laugh like a mad woman on speed. "How on earth could you think that? That's so funny, I mean, Charlie and me, oh that's priceless. As if that would ever happen. Funny one, you got me there."

I'm almost hyperventilating as she slides off the bed and looks at me with a strange expression. The one usually reserved for those looking at the clinically insane. She shrugs with a disappointment that's obvious and says sadly, "Oh, I see. I just hoped that… oh well, never mind."

She heads to the door and looks back and smiles. "Sorry to bother you. I'll let you get ready and then I'll treat you both to breakfast."

As she closes the door her words stay with me. Charlie and me? Whatever next.

By the time I finally make myself look presentable, it must be half an hour later. I feel a little worried as I head into their amazing kitchen because the trouble is, I appear to have forgotten that I'm still wearing Charlie's t-shirt.

I wonder what today will bring? Not my usual Zumba class that's for sure. In fact, I'm so behind on my regime I'm feeling totally out of sorts and my usual confidence has deserted me. I am used to everything being rigidly planned and meticulously executed. This week/ weekend has completely thrown me.

I almost blush when I see Charlie sitting at the breakfast bar watching Emily cook bacon and eggs. The smell is out of this world and my stomach growls hungrily. Charlie grins and pats the stool beside him.

"Here you go, babe. Park yourself here. Ems won't hear of us helping."

I feel as if I'm as red as the tomato ketchup that I'm hoping will accompany this feast as I see Emily grin at us knowingly. I want to shout out loudly and firmly that she's got it wrong but instead resign myself to sitting next to Charlie in a dignified manner.

He pushes an orange juice towards me and smiles. "So, who are you going to call?"

I'm not sure where it even comes from but I retort. "Ghostbusters."

Charlie laughs and Emily giggles. I think I'm more in shock than they are. I don't make flippant remarks or attempt to joke around. I wonder where on earth I've gone because I don't recognise the girl who has taken over my body.

Charlie laughs. "Good one, Vick. No really, which one of your interesting family members are going to get the pleasure of your call today?"

Sipping the orange juice, I think hard. There are only three possibilities and all of them bad ones. My mother would be the best bet but the most embarrassing. Then there's my sister, but she has an annoying habit of trying to make me feel bad at every opportunity. Then there's my brother. He is the most annoying of them all but may make the shortest call.

I shrug. "I'm not sure, maybe my brother. What about you?"

Charlie looks at Emily and I see a flash of sympathy in her eyes. He shakes his head. "I owe my mum a call. Let's just hope dads out and we can survive what could turn out to be twenty questions."

He reaches for his iPad and sighs. "I'm getting mine over with now. He could be playing golf or still in bed. Unless he's teeing off at 9 am he'll still be in bed reading the papers."

I watch with interest as he makes the call and I don't miss the worry in his sister's eyes. This could go badly wrong and I think I hold my breath as we wait for the inevitable.

Suddenly, I hear a loud, "Oh. My. God! Is that really my baby boy calling up his old mum?"

I look with interest at the screen and see a beaming lady looking so happy that my heart leaps. She looks like an older version of Emily and nothing at all like I imagined. She's wearing a full face of makeup and yet is dressed in some sort of satin robe; her hair is immaculate, and she looks tanned and healthy. Just for a moment, Charlie looks confused. "Mum, where are you? It can't be Florida unless you never went to bed."

She squeals with excitement. "Then why did you call you stupid boy? Not that I'm complaining. I mean, it's not too much to ask is it? The odd call from her favourite son once in a blue moon."

I laugh at Charlie's expression. He looks ashamed and embarrassed and yet I can see the softening around his eyes and the twitch to his lips. He's happy to see her, it's obvious.

Suddenly, she looks across and her eyes widen and a hand flies to her mouth. She says loudly, "What the… is that a girl? Charlie is that your girlfriend?"

Before he can answer she starts waving madly. "Cooee. Oh my god, let me look at you."

She shouts over her shoulder. "Harry, look Charlie's got a girlfriend. She's gorgeous, a real looker. Come and see."

Charlie groans and I watch Emily back out of the room. Then I see a man appear beside his mother peering into the screen like we are exhibits at the zoo. "What? Yes, I can see her. Wow, darlin', you're a sight for sore eyes."

He looks across at Charlie and gives him that look that men pass between themselves when they're impressed. "Punching above your weight a bit there, son. Is she mad? I mean, she has got all her marbles, hasn't she?"

His mum elbows him and shrieks loudly. "Oh, Harry you crack me up. Leave the lovebirds alone."

I feel slightly awkward as they continue to stare at me in amazement and I just smile. "Um… hello, I'm Victoria, Charlie's colleague from…."

They look at each other and burst out laughing. His dad roars with laughter. "Is that what they're calling it now?"

He leans closer to the screen and whispers loudly. "It's ok, darlin', we don't judge. After all, Linda and I weren't that innocent in our youth."

She grins and pokes him hard. "Still aren't, babe."

Charlie looks positively ill, and that makes me happier than I thought it would. I laugh softly as he shakes his head. "Both of you stop it. Vicky is my colleague. We are working on something huge."

His parents look at each other and burst out laughing. His dad says loudly. "I bet you are son."

He winks at me. "It's ok, babe, we won't embarrass you anymore."

His mum looks at me with excitement. "This is such good timing. We were going to surprise you, babe but you've blown it wide open. We are home for Christmas and you and Vick are invited to Oxford for a good old family Christmas. What do you think about that?"

Silence. Stone cold, cotton picking silence. In fact, if there was tumbleweed in Knightsbridge, it would be blowing around this kitchen now. Words have obviously failed Charlie as he looks to be in complete shock. Emily is nowhere to be seen so I do the only thing I can think of. I smile and snuggle up next to Charlie and say sweetly, "That sounds amazing, doesn't it, babe?"

Charlie looks at me in shock as I put my hand over my mouth and say quickly, "Oh no. I completely forgot. I've already told my mum I'll go there."

I look apologetically into the camera and smile softly. "I'm so sorry, you'll have to count me out. Thanks for the offer though, maybe next year."

I watch as a look passes between his parents and Charlie remains stiff and disbelieving beside me. I don't know why I just did what I did, but all I knew was I had to nip this in the bud. Charlie can pretend we split up when he next sees his parents and all the attention will be diverted from asking awkward questions about him and Emily. Perfect.

Then his mum shouts excitedly, "That's ok, darling, bring your family with you. We would love to meet them, wouldn't we Harry?"

Charlie groans and I look at him in horror. Quickly, I shake my head. "Um...I'm sorry but we can't do that. Mum never leaves the house. I mean..." I lower my voice. "She has an um, illness, so we go there. I would invite you but there wouldn't be any room and she would worry. Maybe next year."

His mum looks at me sympathetically. "Oh, your poor mum. How awful. You know, I knew someone like that once. It took a while, but we soon snapped her out of it."

She turns to her husband. "You remember Harry, don't you?"

He looks a little lost and then says with a resounding, "Of course, I do. We flew her out to Florida, and she met Chuck. I don't think she ever looked back. Nice couple. He could do with manning up a bit in the boardroom but he's a good chap."

His wife leans forward and whispers, although god only knows why she is whispering because we can all still hear her. "Listen, babe. Don't worry about it. Come to us on Christmas Eve and then head home on Christmas Day. It's what happens when you fall in love. You have to split your time between families. Maybe next year she'll feel more like herself and manage to take a trip out to Oxford. Don't worry, we hear you."

Charlie coughs and looks towards the door. "Sorry, mum, dad, I think I hear someone at the door. Nice to chat and all but we've got to go."

His dad grins and his mum rolls her eyes. "If you say so, babe. Don't worry, we know what it's like when you're in the first flush of love. Just make the most of it while it lasts."

His dad winks and then lowers his voice. "Seriously though son, it's good to see you growing up at last. Vick's a great girl and you'd be wise not to let her go. Come up next weekend and bring her with you. Grab hold of Emily while you're at it and we'll make a weekend of it."

Then his expression hardens, and he says, "I insist on it."

Charlie smiles weakly and ends the call. The door opens and Emily pokes her head around it looking worried.

"Have they gone?"

Charlie nods and looks over to me. "I'm sorry, Vick, but why on earth did you say that?"

Emily looks at me with the same curious look and I shrug. "I was trying to divert the attention away from any awkward questions. It's fine. You just have to say we broke up, no Biggy."

Charlie groans. "I'm sorry, Vick but that won't cut it with them. If I tell them that I'll be in even more trouble than if I said I was single. You've just given them the best Christmas present they could have asked for and Emily is about to give them their worst. If you feel anything for us at all, you'll keep up the pretence until we get Ems off the hook."

As I look at their defeated expressions my heart sinks. Me and my big mouth. I've just made things a lot worse and now I'm caught up in something I can't walk away from.

Emily finishes cooking us breakfast and then heads to the gym. It's the wrong way around in my opinion but I'm keeping my mouth shut for the rest of the day - if not forever.

As we wash up, Charlie looks at me and smiles. "Thanks, Vick. I know why you said what you did, and it's not your fault it all went wrong. Don't worry, I'll think of something to get you off the hook."

He folds up the tea towel he's been drying the dishes with and grins.

"Anyway, your turn now. Who are you really gonna call?"

My heart sinks under the pressure of the inevitable. "Ok. If you thought that call was bad, you haven't met my sister."

I'm not going to lie, the butterflies flutter around my stomach like they're on a mass exodus for the winter - if that is even what butterflies do. I chose my sister because she is unlikely to ask me embarrassing questions like my mum would and her house is much tidier than my mums. I know I'm a terrible snob but the sight of mum's living room is one I could do without Charlie witnessing first hand.

The call is duly made and I bite my fingernails as I wait for the inevitable.

It doesn't take long and then I see her incredulous expression. "Good god, Vicky. What's the matter, do you need a kidney or something?"

I hear Charlie snort beside me and I plaster the usual stern expression on my face that shrieks duty call.

"Good morning, Lisa. Long-time no see."

She shakes her head and peers into the screen, much the same as Charlie's parents.

"Where are you? That doesn't look like your flat."

I groan inwardly. "I live in an apartment, Lisa, as well you know. No, I'm staying with friends and thought it would be nice to call my sister and see how she's doing."

Lisa shakes her head and I don't miss the sound of screaming coming from another room. She shouts, "Bradley, go and sort Thomas out. He's trying to batter Sophie again and I can't think straight."

I daren't look at Charlie and just try to wrap this up quickly before it can get any worse.

"Anyway, I just thought I'd say hi and maybe ask what the children would like for Christmas."

Lisa leans back and folds her arms, fixing me with that disapproving look she's perfected over the years. "Maybe a visit from their aunt once in a while. I mean, they hardly know you, Vick and it's not right. You never babysit and god only knows I could use the help. It's not as if you have much in your life except for work and you get the luxury of wallowing in self-indulgence at the weekend. Mum hasn't seen you in months and it's not normal. Now you ring up out of the blue and just say 'hi.' Now tell me, what's really going on?"

I desperately try to think of an excuse to end the call but fail miserably. Then Charlie lays his arm around my shoulder and leans toward the screen. Lisa's eyes widen as she sees I'm not alone and gasps, "Who's that?"

Charlie kisses me on the cheek and says, "Hi, I'm Vicky's boyfriend, Charlie. Hasn't she mentioned me?"

He looks at me and ruffles my hair playfully. "You're priceless, babe. But I love you."

I swear my face turns bright red and I feel a strange sort of buzzing in my head. Lisa looks in shock as I push Charlie away and say hurriedly, "Oh don't mind him, he's just joking."

Lisa eyes narrow. "Then why are you obviously wearing his t-shirt in a strange kitchen on Sunday morning? I know you Vicky and that's not like you. Come on, fess up and tell me what's really going on. Are you pregnant, is that it?"

Oh god, can this get any worse? I fix on my blankest stare and say haughtily, "For your information, I am not pregnant. Charlie is not my boyfriend and if you must know, I'm helping him with a project for work. Anyway, I just thought it would be nice to see how my family is, that's all. No big secret and no big deal. Anyway, it's been nice to chat but I must go."

Before I can, a little face appears and looks into the screen. "Who are you talking, to mummy? Is that Aunty Vicky? She looks scary."

Charlie laughs as I try to plaster on my best Nanny McPhee expression. "Hello, angel, this is your Aunt Victoria. I just wanted to see what you would like for Christmas."

Her face lights up and she shouts excitedly. "I'd like an iPhone please, Aunty Vicky. Mummy says I'm too young but Emma Jones has one and she's one month younger than me. She has some really great Apps and a cool Facebook profile."

I look at her in horror. "Are you sure? Don't you want a Barbie or something?"

She pouts petulantly. "That's for babies. I'm seven now and past all that."

Lisa looks angry and shouts, "I've told you, no! Now go and do something grown up if you want to be treated like one and tidy your room."

Sophie goes off grumbling as Lisa looks after her angrily. When she's gone, she looks at me and shakes her head. "It's another world, Vicky. You don't know what it's like dealing with the little people. They aren't content with a Barbie and Ken and it's all 'I' this and 'I' that these days. Nothing costs less than £100 and it has to have a label on it. They all want to grow up quickly and it scares me. I don't know what to do about it because everyone else gives in for a quiet life. Mum's no help either. She spends all her spare time at bingo and gossiping with Marjorie Watson. Bradley spends all his time fixing his motorbike and won't go out and get a decent job. I tell you I'm drowning here and my sister is missing in action. If you could get us anything this Christmas please make it a one-way ticket to somewhere exotic for me with Justin Timberlake. I can't remember the last time I did something selfish and I'm on the edge."

She leans forward and whispers and I shake my head. They're all nuts, what's with this whispering epidemic?

"You know, I start with the wine at frigging 3.30 these days. 3.30 when the kids come home from school. We exist on burgers and frozen peas and the only escape I get is in my imagination. If you think anything of me at all please come and take the lot of them away and GIVE ME A BREAK!"

I hear screaming coming from the kitchen and she sighs heavily. "Got to go, good to talk, sis, don't be a stranger."

Then she is gone leaving me one hot, guilty, sister abandoning, worthless aunt and daughter mess.

18

December 8th

17 Days to Go

When I wake the following morning, I pray the weekend was just a horrible nightmare. My eyes flicker open and focus on the familiar. Thankfully, I'm in my apartment – alone and can pretend for a few minutes that none of it ever happened.

However, as soon as I swing my legs from the bed and stand, it all comes rushing back like a bad dose of acne. I groan inwardly as I think about what a mess I made of things.

After skype-gate, there wasn't much to say except to think of every excuse under the sun for a hasty retreat. Then I spent the whole evening worrying about the mess I'd created with a few badly chosen words. More than anything I surprised myself by being so impetuous. I never speak without carefully considering the implications of my words and now I can see I was right to do so. This is a disaster.

Sighing heavily, I get ready for work and start the arduous journey to the office and I only hope back to my well-ordered professional life where everything is exactly as it should be.

It's a cold frosty morning and I shiver as I pound the pavements on the way to the station. The chill in the air matches my mood perfectly and I pull my scarf tighter around my neck. Today there is no regard for fashion and I am wearing a thick padded coat and snow boots. I have a woolly hat pulled down low on my head and thick gloves to keep the ice from my fingers.

As I walk towards the building site, I notice the usual group of builders huddled by the gate. It looks as if they are waiting to be let in and I look at them with curiosity. They've become familiar to me over the last few months and I notice the recognition in their faces. Instead of the usual cat calls and wolf whistles they just smile and look down to the floor. Despite myself, my curiosity wins out and I stop and head over to them.

As I draw near, they look at me in surprise as I hop from foot to foot and say breathlessly, "Good morning."

They murmur their greeting politely and I fix them with my usual autocratic stare.

"Excuse me but I have a question. For months you used to call out to me as I walked past. You did it every day like clockwork and then one day it all stopped. Not that I mind of course. I mean, not every woman likes to be objectified and a victim of sexual harassment but I would like to know why you stopped?"

The men look at me as if I'm from Mars and then at each other with mischievous grins. One of them

smiles and winks. "If you must know, darlin',
we've been ordered not to address the members of
the public. If we're caught shouting or calling to
any woman who walks past, we'll get a warning and
could lose our job."

One of the others chips in. "Yeah, the men in
suits think it's degrading to women and will make
them sue our company. So, you see, darlin', it's not
worth the trouble it would bring."

I shake my head and say in an annoyed voice,
"Well, for your information I used to like it. Maybe
you could relay that back to your bosses and tell
them it's a public service bringing a little sunshine
to somebody's day. I agree that not all women
would appreciate it but when it's the only attention
you get it's worth more than you know."

They laugh and I flash them a wicked grin.
"Well, at least that's been cleared up. For a moment
there, I thought I was losing my touch."

The men laugh and one says, "You can touch me
anytime…"

I raise my hand, silencing him with a hard look.
"Quit while you're ahead, *darlin'*."

Then I wink and head off towards the station.

I am soon at the office and as I make my way to
my desk I look at the ones I pass. Today, for some
reason, I am noticing things that I never have

before. Alongside the usual computers and 'In trays,' I see the personal effects of my staff. Framed photographs of their nearest and dearest beam out at them from their silver homes and little ornaments and personal touches litter their space. I notice that Annie has a pink fluffy pencil standing proudly from the pen pot. Louise has a box of chocolates lying open on her desk and I see a small pot plant on Mark's.

They are just little personal touches that bring some humanity to a sterile space and as I head inside my office, I see no such things. Everything here is purely business and serves a purpose. The only personal items are my inspirational biographies. Where are the photographs of my loved ones? There are no plants or little quirky stationery items on my desk and as I sit on my chair and look around me, all I can see is loneliness.

The week passes much like the last one. The only bit of excitement I get every day is the little window that pops up at 8 am every morning. Secretly I crave that moment. It's the unknown and the fact that I get to spend some time with Charlie.

After the weekend we have reverted back to being just polite colleagues. I am still working on helping Emily but haven't had a lot of time to gather my evidence. My contact is taking longer to help than usual which is extremely frustrating.

However, it's the little challenges that brighten my day and warm my heart.

On Monday we cut out paper snowflakes and had a competition as to who did the best one.

Tuesday, we went window shopping and judged the best Christmas window in Oxford Street.

On Wednesday it was to visit the local animal shelter with treats for the poor animals with no homes. It was a near miss on that one because Charlie fell in love with a Labrador called Brigadier who wouldn't leave him alone.

Then Thursday came.

19

December 11th

14 Days to Go

The picture is of a table laden with treats and my heart starts beating rapidly as I click on the image. For whatever reason known only to Santa, I am starting to absolutely love these little challenges.

As I read the words, they reach out and grab hold of my heart.

Serve a meal at a local homeless shelter.

Sitting back in my seat, I smile. This one means something to me. Ever since that evening when I bought the homeless man a drink, I have wondered about him. I think about him when I head home to my warm apartment and wonder what makes a person live that way. I'm not sure why I've become so obsessed with it but the image of his grateful eyes has stayed with me and I'm more than happy to help out where I can.

I make my way to Charlie's office with a spring in my step and knock loudly, then head inside without waiting for an answer.

The look on his face stops me in my tracks and I feel the anxiety grip me as I see the worry in his eyes.

He says quietly, "Close the door, Vicky, you're not going to like this."

Now I feel super anxious and head towards him and say quickly, "Is it, Emily?"

He shakes his head and sighs. "No, it's my father. He's reminded me we're due to visit them this weekend. I tried to tell them you couldn't make it but he insisted. He accused me of trying to keep my life separate from the family and my mother was worried about me. He threw the guilt trip on me and told me she's talked of nothing else all week and has gone to a lot of trouble preparing things for your visit. He also told me that something was up with Emily because she wasn't returning their calls. He wants answers from all of us and if we don't go there, he will come and find us and drag the answers out of us whether we like it or not."

He groans and looks at me apologetically.

"I'm so sorry. You must be wishing you had never agreed to help us last weekend and then this wouldn't be happening."

I shrug. "Listen, it won't be so bad. After all, we could use the time to complete our challenges and work on Emily's case. I haven't got much at home that requires my attention so it will be fine."

Charlie looks at me with such gratitude it takes my breath away. For somebody so cocky, self-assured and downright annoying he has this softer side to him that demonstrates a complex person hiding behind a very attractive shell. We all have our secrets and it appears that Charlie is no different. Perhaps the more time I spend with him will enable me to peel away those layers and who knows, maybe help him.

We decide to use our lunch hour to complete the challenge. I could do without another late night and Charlie told me he had plans this evening. When he told me, I feigned disinterest, but I was burning up inside. That feeling has shocked me the most. Why do I care what he does in his spare time? The trouble is, it's obvious I care very much, which is why I need to move this on and then run screaming for the hills. I need to protect my heart at all costs and I tell myself that the only thing that matters is winning the company. However, the reason I'm doing this is slipping further from my mind the more time I spend with Charlie. What I look forward to the most is spending time with him every day. I am now officially—as the American's say—Screwed!

The homeless shelter actually turns out to be quite nice. I had visions of a scruffy makeshift sort of shelter with burning fires and sleeping bags on the floor. However, this one appears to be like a

YMCA and is clean, tidy and welcoming. It's still pretty basic but a million times better than sleeping on the streets.

We are met by a man called Steven who shows us around. He explains how it all works as we follow him with interest. "The homeless come here and get showers, clean clothes and a meal. Some get to stay in a proper bed and there are volunteers on hand to give free haircuts and doctors to check them out."

I look around with surprise. I never knew that people were so kind and once again, I feel guilty at my own self-absorbed life.

As we follow Steven to the kitchen, Charlie says in awe, "Wow, Steven, this place is impressive. You're doing a great job here; do you get many um… customers?"

Steven nods. "Too many. We must operate a strict policy to give everyone the opportunity. It's a shame there aren't more of these places because there are more homeless people than spaces. We do what we can but could do with so much more. Like everything in life, goodwill and charity are in short supply as people's lives take over. We all want to help but very few people actually do."

I feel embarrassed as he speaks. I've never thought about volunteering for anything in my life. I was too busy, too tired and too disinterested. I never gave it a second thought and walked past anyone collecting money as if they were invisible. I would cross the road to avoid being accosted in the street to sign up for something I convinced myself was a scam. The one act of charity I have ever done was to take the homeless man some food and I must say it felt good to do so.

I say with a warmth that shocks even me. "You're an amazing man, Steven. All of you are and I never knew so much went into helping others. It puts my own life into perspective and I don't like what I see."

Charlie looks at me with an understanding in his eyes and nods. "Yes, our lives seem rather shallow when you come to think of it. The clients we deal with and their problems are not real life like this. They are all chasing the material side of life where these people are running in the opposite direction. Their problems are superficial in comparison and yet their problems follow them every day. They breathe them, sleep with them and become them. There's no escape and a hard journey to leave them behind. I'm sure that behind every unkempt exterior is a story waiting to be told."

The tears burn behind my wide eyes. Charlie's right. The challenge these people face is far greater than any case we deal with. Serving them a hot meal seems trivial in comparison to what they really need.

We head into the kitchen and are provided with aprons and made to wash our hands. Charlie is stationed behind the counter serving up the food and I am on hand to clear the tables and keep the area clean.

As I work, I look out for a familiar face. It was just a short meeting but I can remember every detail of it. However, it's obvious he isn't here and once again I worry about what happened to him.

Mainly the people we serve are content to sit silently and eat. It must feel good to eat a hot meal in a safe environment and I recognise the need for some to have private time. There are also those who chat and smile and appear to be enjoying the experience. It seems strange to see some people who have showered, changed and had their hair cut. They look just like any other person walking to work and yet their walk involves survival.

It also shocks me how many women are here, which shouldn't but it does. I wonder if they have families who are worried about them and as usual turns my thoughts to my own. Would they search for me if I was missing? I see them so infrequently it would take some time for them to realise I wasn't around.

My heart sinks as once again I feel the loneliness inside.

Then I hear a soft, "Cheer up missy. It's not that bad."

Looking across, I see an older man watching me with a smile on his face.

Smiling, I laugh self-consciously. "Sorry, my thoughts run away with me sometimes and I forget what I'm doing."

He stares at me and then points to the seat in front of him. "Sit and spare me a few minutes."

I do as he says because something in his expression compels me to do so. There's an authority to this man and a kindness that is evident in his twinkling eyes.

He smiles, revealing a perfect set of teeth which makes me think he can't have been long on the street.

"So, what's making a young lady look so lost this fine afternoon."

I shrug self-consciously. "I don't know, maybe it's because this place has awakened emotions in me that I've tried to keep buried."

He nods. "Yes, we look at life differently when we are surrounded by the unfamiliar. Things become clearer when there's nothing for them to hide behind."

I smile and hold out my hand. "Victoria Marshall. I'm pleased to meet you, Mr...?"

He grins. "James Sullivan at your service."

He grips my hand in a firm handshake and looks at me thoughtfully.

"So, Victoria Marshall. Forgive me if I speak out of turn but if I didn't know better, I would say you were the one lost and drifting, not me."

I nod sadly. "You are very astute, Mr Sullivan. Nothing gets past you, does it?"

I smile as he shakes his head. "Call me James and you are correct, it doesn't. When you have time on your hands you focus on the things that count. When you have nothing, it's a cleansing experience and you see the world very differently."

As I look into his eyes, something strikes me. He looks strangely happy which shocks me. Leaning forward, I say softly, "Why are you here, James? If I may say so, you don't look like the type of person who would be."

He raises his eyes. "There are many people like me, Victoria. People from all walks of life who have fallen on hard times. Not many of us choose to be in this position but life has its own agenda and so here I am."

I say with interest, "Why are you here, James?"

He looks at me sadly. "The usual route in. Alcohol. I used to have a wife, family and a good job with the fabulous home that goes with it. It all became too much, what with the daily grind and the responsibility of providing for my family. My wife was amazing but had her own problems with post-natal depression. For a while, our lives entered a dark place and the only light I could see was at the end of a bottle. I drank more and more to forget when I should have taken charge. I didn't understand her illness, and it angered me."

He shakes his head. "For a while I blamed her. Can you believe that? I was working hard, and she was at home. I thought she had the easy part but as it turns out I thought wrong. She was in a private hell and I was the Devil. I was unsupportive and wrapped up in my own problems. The family was falling apart, and I blamed her."

Trying not to let the shock show on my face, I nod. "That sounds hard. Did your families not help, or friends maybe?"

"Yes, of course, they did to a point. Like most people, we dressed our problems up to resemble normality. We sheltered from the approaching storm and pushed away our fears. We stopped communicating out of fear at what would be revealed. We soldiered on until it all came crashing down."

I am absolutely riveted by his story. Nothing else matters but hearing what happened. He looks rueful. "I was a mess. Drinking heavily and no longer just in the evenings. My wife was at her wits ends and I stayed away—a lot. I couldn't face my responsibilities in a home that felt increasingly more like a prison. The children were unhappy and my wife depressed. Instead of seeking professional help, I blamed her. Can you believe that? I was so far gone I actually blamed my wife for her illness. It all came to a head when I was dismissed from my job. The drinking was obvious, and I made mistakes. I was unbearable to be around and my work suffered. For two days I drank on the street rather than go home and admit to my wife what had happened. My life closed around me like a pressurised cabin and I couldn't cope. So, I took the cowards way out. I waited until she left the house with the kids and snuck inside. I took nothing but a small bag and whatever money I could lay my hands on. Then I wrote her a note and told her I was leaving her for another woman. I wanted her to be angry and hate me because I hated myself more. Then I disappeared. I faded into the shadows and became invisible to real life. I drift with people similar to me and just walk."

I am so shocked and my heart breaks for this man and his family and I say with concern, "Have you contacted your family since? Do they know?"

He shakes his head and looks strangely proud. "No, it's better this way. I am weak, Victoria and they don't need me in their life. They need to find someone better who will do a much better job than I ever can."

Shaking my head, I say harshly, "How can that possibly be true? There is nobody better than you. Those children deserve the right to a father who will stand up and face his problems head-on. They will respect your struggle and learn from your mistakes.

Running away doesn't solve this, it just delays the inevitable."

I fix him with a hard look. "How long has it been since you last saw them?"

He smiles as if he's heard this all before and says abruptly, "Twelve years."

His words hit me hard. Sitting back in my chair, I let them sink in. Twelve years. I thought he would say twelve days, twelve weeks or twelve months. But twelve years is devastating.

He laughs softly. "Shocked you, have I? Well, you shouldn't be. I have chosen this life, and it's best for everyone concerned. My family have moved on and I'm happy for them."

I say in the barest whisper, "How do you know?"

He looks down. "Because I saw them one day. It must have been three years after I left. I felt compelled to check on them and returned to the neighbourhood. They wouldn't have recognised me because I was dressed in the clothes of the homeless. Not many people give us a second look and would walk past their own mother and not see her. I sat in the park opposite the house and watched them come and go for seven days. They looked happy and content and I saw my wife had replaced me with somebody better."

I say earnestly, "Who could be better than the children's father?"

He smiles with a resignation that angers me. "Just because I created them it doesn't mean I'm the best one for the job. Do you have children, Victoria?"

As I shake my head, he nods. "I thought so. It takes a lot to be a parent. Nobody explains what's involved, and it's quite a wake-up call. You have to be strong to cope with the sheer hard work it involves, and it drains every bit of you. The rewards make up for it but some people can't see past the exhaustion to appreciate that. I am that person, Victoria. I only thought of myself and not my family. A stronger man will put their needs first and guide them along the right path. We don't get to audition a family or interview the best person for the job. We hope that love will see us through but sometimes it isn't enough. The love I have for my family is to let them go. To give them someone who they deserve and remove myself so they don't have to pretend to want to be around me."

As I look at him sitting across from me I feel angry. Far from making me sympathetic to his story it just makes me disappointed. I stare at him long and hard and see the resignation in the eyes looking back at me. Then I say harshly, "You're wrong, James."

He sits back and smiles. "Go on."

"Have you ever wondered what those children and your wife think about when they go to bed at night? Do they wonder where you are? Do they

181

wish you had never left? Is there a part of their life missing that has left a hole in their heart that can never be filled? I think you know the answer to that because I'm guessing you have a huge hole in yours. If you had sought help and faced your problems together, your lives would probably be so different now. Maybe you would have split up but at least they would still have a father. You have let them down and yourself because you choose to walk like some sort of ghost on this earth telling yourself that you did it for the best. *You* are the best, James. The best for those children who must be lost without you. They will see their friends with loving fathers who never gave up on them. They never chose this, you did. Tell me one thing, James, do you still drink?"

He shakes his head. "No, I never touched a drop after I left. It was easy to leave all my problems behind and that was my biggest one. Despite the impression you may have of the homeless, Victoria, we are not all alcoholics drinking from a brown paper wrapped bottle slumped on a park bench. Some of us like the freedom of the open road and surviving on what mother nature provides. I've seen amazing places and had the time to appreciate them. I have no ties which equal no worries. Places like this help and I travel the country a free man. I choose this life because it suits me. We are not all cut out for family life and I can admit that to myself and am at peace with it. You just want to label me like everyone else and believe that the way I live is the problem - it's not. This is who I am, and I accepted that years ago. Don't pity me, Victoria because I am one happy man doing what he loves. I could go back, of course, I could. I could get help with finding a job and start over. My family may even visit me once in a while, but newsflash, I don't want to."

He stares at me with a smile on his lips that speaks much more than his words. The man sitting before me isn't lost, he's found. He has found what makes him happy and done the unthinkable. I don't have children but can't imagine ever leaving any I do have. However, in some way he is right. Who am I to judge him? He has chosen this path, and that's his decision. It may not be the one I would choose but I shouldn't judge him for it. That's for him and his family to do.

He leans forward and says softly, "I'm guessing you came here to help, Victoria. You thought you would give something back to the people who need it the most. That's an admirable thing to do and you should be proud of yourself. But not everybody wants to be saved. In fact, many people are here because they have saved themselves. Don't pity us, just take time to understand us and don't place your expectations for life on others. We all choose to live in different ways. Your way is the normal path most people choose to follow; a good job, nice home, marriage, children and everything that goes with that. I have veered off down the rougher path. The one with many pitfalls and hazards in the way. Unchartered and unknown but so indescribably beautiful not many people get to see it. We must all do what makes us happy and happiness is not wrapped up in a particular package. Maybe that's my gift to you this Christmas. Look at the world through different eyes once in a while and don't judge everyone by your own standards. We are all different and see the world in a different way. Just do what makes you happy, Victoria and you will be, no matter what others may think of you."

His words echo around my brain as they sink in slowly. This conversation has been unexpected, unfamiliar and enlightening. Standing up, I reach for his tray and smile warmly. "Thank you, James. I respect your honesty and accept your gift with gratitude. You are right and I am wrong. I can see that now. I shouldn't judge a person by my own standards and beliefs. I'll never forget what you have shown me today and I hope to be a better person because of it."

He reaches out and offers me his hand. Setting down the tray, I take it and grasp it hard. There is a lightness to my heart that wasn't there before as I shake his hand and smile gratefully, whispering. "Happy Christmas, James."

He winks. "Same to you, Victoria. Remember, stay true to yourself *always* because we only get one life and you owe it to yourself to live it well. Don't be afraid to take the path less travelled by and remember that the only person who can never leave you is yourself. Make peace with that person because they are all you've really got."

As I turn away from James Sullivan, I feel as if I'm a very different person than the one that walked towards him. Who knew it would be me who would be saved - not him?

20

December 12th

13 Days to Go

Finally, it's Friday and for some strange reason, I am actually really looking forward to it. Charlie is pre-occupied and worried about the visit to his parents. I've reassured him that I'll be fine and once the challenges are out of the way, I'll make some excuse to leave.

I'm not going to lie, I am so looking forward to meeting his parents. Mr Monroe is a formidable man who has built up his empire from nothing and I can't wait to find out how he did it. People like that fascinate me and it's why I read so many biographies of powerful entrepreneurs. Now I get to meet one first hand and despite what Charlie and Emily say, he must be amazing. His mother seemed nice too and nothing at all like I imagined. I suppose I thought of them as, well to do and full of pomp and circumstance. It didn't look that way to me and I am so ready to meet them.

However, first we have the challenge to meet and it's with the usual butterflies that I open today's email.

The picture is of a shepherd looking very sweet next to his lamb.

However, when I see what's inside, I groan out loud.

Attend a school Nativity
Scott's Primary
Balham Road
SW12 8DR
10 am—They are expecting you.

Great, I can just see his devilish smile from here as he devised this payback for my past mistake. I've got to hand it to him, he's good.

Reaching for the phone, I dial up Charlie who answers immediately.

"Hey, V. This one's easy. I hope you've dressed down today, you don't want to frighten the little ones."

Taking a deep breath, I say irritably.

"Well, you'll fit right in. I mean, you never really left their wavelength in the first place. I must say, this is ridiculous. I've got three meetings back to back and this will set me back hours."

He laughs. "Where's your sense of adventure, babe, this'll be fun? Work can wait, it will still be there when we get back. I'll just work through lunch, it's fine."

Taking a few deep breaths, I try to see past the horror in my mind. I think I'm having palpitations at the thought of rearranging my day for something so frivolous and unimportant.

I hear the laughter in Charlie's voice as he says, "Pick you up at 9, honey. This will be good training for our kid's plays."

I slam the phone down and put my head in my hands. Really? This is all I need.

Scott's Primary—Balham

After a quick Tube ride, we find ourselves joining a stream of parents making their way inside the little infant school on the Balham Road. I look around with interest at the mothers and fathers who pour through the doors. Many are dressed for the office or whatever jobs they do. Some are dressed casually but they all have one thing in common. They are smiling and happy. There are many loud greetings to other parents and excitement in the air. It strikes me that far from standing out, we actually fit right in. Nobody gives us a second look and I immediately worry about the security of this place. Surely, we should have some sort of lanyard with security clearance to get through these doors. At least there should be a burly security guard swabbing our hands and making us pass through some sort of detector booth like at the airport. You hear of all sorts these days and I don't think I would be happy with this lackadaisical approach to my child's welfare.

I lean over and whisper to Charlie.

"You know, we could be anyone. They haven't even checked us off a register or something. I think I'll put in a complaint to the governors before we leave."

Charlie snorts loudly and I look at him furiously. "What!?"

He shakes his head. "You're priceless, Vick. You think of everything don't you?"

Shrugging, I look around me for potential kidnappers and attackers. "Safety first, Charlie, especially where it concerns children. Come to think of it, why am I asking you, anyway? You're still the same mental age and probably have a nerf gun stuffed inside your jacket as we speak."

Laughing, he pushes me playfully and I stumble into the woman in front. She looks around irritably and her eyes narrow as she says curtly, "I'm sorry, I don't think we've met. What class is your child in?"

I can feel myself blushing under her mama bear gaze, ready to rip my throat out if she suspects foul play. I'm not sure how to answer her really. I mean, I can hardly say we just fancied coming along to watch on a whim, she would call the police screaming 'weirdo' before I finished my sentence.

Charlie interrupts and flashes her his million-dollar smile and I'm somewhat annoyed to see her face relax as she smiles seductively at him.

"Hi, my name's Charlie and this is my colleague, Victoria. We are guests here today of the management on important secret business."

Her eyes light up and I look at him in surprise as he taps his nose and winks. "I'm afraid I can't say more than that but if you're curious, have you ever watched the film, Nativity?"

I watch in astonishment as her cheeks tinge with pink and her eyes shine brightly. Suddenly, she looks as if Charlie is Santa or Zac Efron judging by the smouldering look she's flashing his way. She lowers her voice to a whisper, "Don't worry, your secret's safe with me. Why don't I look after you both? You can sit with me and I'll tell you how it all works."

Sticking out her hand, she grabs his and shakes it wildly, forgetting to let it go. I watch in growing frustration and something that is gnawing at my insides and causing my blood to boil. If I had to label the feeling, I would call it, *Jealously.*

The wanton woman continues to hold Charlie's hand prisoner and drags him inside without a glance in my direction. All I can do is follow them inside, muttering death curses under my breath as I prepare for one hour of utter tedium.

We are guided to a row near the front and the woman pushes Charlie in and then sits firmly between us. She leans towards him and I hear her giggle flirtatiously. "My name's Sarah Mulligan. My little boy Tommy's playing King Herod of the Hamburger. I'll point him out, he's so talented."

I look at her in total surprise. Since when were hamburgers involved in the Nativity? They were very much still living and breathing I'm sure at the Saviour's birth, not residing inside a bun with ketchup on. This is nonsense.

As the hall fills up, I try desperately to empty my mind of the thousand things I should be doing right now. My phones on silent but buzzes angrily in my bag the longer we wait. Charlie is deep in conversation with salacious Sarah and I feel totally on edge—literally. In fact, if she shoved me just a little, I would fall off this wooden bench that should never be used as a seat in a production. I'll get piles at this rate and I can already feel my back seizing up.

It doesn't take long before a hush breaks out among the audience and a teacher stands at the front smiling benevolently and serenely at the expectant faces. I look at her with interest. She looks the sort, yes, practical dress and the pasted-on expression of somebody who can deal with absolutely anything. A woman of many talents and far above the rest of us in the respectability ranks. She is impressive, magnificent and a goddess on earth. She is a teacher.

"Good morning ladies, gentlemen and brothers and sisters. Welcome to our Nativity play, Hoedown in the manger."

What? I look across at Charlie who winks and then turns his attention back to the teacher. Yes, he must remember to pay attention at all times. I bet he was easily distracted as a child and got into all sorts of trouble. Unlike me, of course. I was a model student from day one. In fact, on my first day of school, I cried when I had to leave at the end of the day. Yes, that's how badly I wanted to succeed even then.

I watch with interest as the door opens in the corner of the room and the children start filing in two by two. There's laughter from the audience as the little children shout and point to their parents and I stifle the irritation. Haven't they been taught not to interact with the audience? They have a job to do and must take it seriously.

It takes ages to get them through the door and I'm not even sure where they will all go. Teachers and their assistants whisper their instructions in hushed tones, silencing any disobedience with an angry look. I could so see myself as a teacher. I have perfected that look over the years and know exactly where it's coming from. This makes me relax a little as I feel quite at home here in this establishment of routine and discipline.

The children parade before us in interesting costumes, many of which are homemade. A random tea towel and decorated white t-shirt over leggings; little Angels wearing tinsel crowns and giggling adorably. Then, there are the wise men who look positively regal in their shiny robes and painted on beards.

I am particularly interested in the poor children dressed as sheep and other animals. They even manage to melt my heart as I see their wide eyes and vacant expressions as the piano starts up. Then to call what comes next singing, would make Simon Cowell's eyes water.

There are those children who have obviously paid attention and follow the directions of the teacher who is sitting crossed legged on the floor in front of them. Then there are those who would rather be sticking pins in their eyes than be subjected to this farce. There are the adorable little ones who look bewildered and confused and appear to be wondering if they are dreaming. I like them the most and find myself willing them to make a mistake so we can laugh at how sweet they are. In fact, as I hear the tuneless shouting and watch the circus unfold I am totally absorbed in the whole shebang. The songs are catchy and the reading voices sweet. They stumble over their words and I will them on.

I hear Sarah whisper, "There he is, my Tommy. Look at him, Charlie, he would make a fine actor one day. He would be the perfect choice to star in any film made, shall we say, in the not too distant future."

I look across and raise my eyes but Charlie just nods thoughtfully. "You're so right, Sarah. Outstanding acting."

Shaking my head, I look across and see Herod Hamburger trying to stuff his burger down the boy in front's t-shirt. My eyes narrow as I throw him my death stare. A bully if ever I saw one. Maybe I should record the incident for the governor's inquiry.

Somehow the poor little children manage to portray some sort of story and rather than hating every minute of it I am spellbound.

Maybe it's the heat from the room or the glittering decorations. Could it be the proud faces of the mums and dads as they watch their precious darlings doing something so amazing before their eyes? Or could it be the sheer number of germs being bandied about as children sneeze without holding their hands in front of their mouths and cough their way through the script? Could it be the breath from my neighbour as we share the same oxygen or could it be that there is no fresh air in the room and probably hasn't ever been due to the musty stench of the ageing fixtures? However, something is happening to me inside. I am changing and metamorphizing into somebody I don't recognise. I'm actually enjoying myself and by the end of the play, my mind is made up. I want a child—now—in fact, for Christmas. Yes, that's what I want. A husband who adores me and a family of my own. I want to look proudly at my child obviously starring in the play that they probably wrote. I want to be that parent that everyone admires because of their parenting skills. I want to boast that my child has joined Mensa at the age of five and have everyone congratulating me on a job well done. And as I look across at Charlie, it hits me hard. I want that child with him.

21

By the time we return to work, I have almost forgotten about the cancelled meetings and work piling up on my desk. Instead, we chatter about the play and laugh as we remember a particular child or embarrassing incident. Then I think back to last year and feel ashamed that I prevented Samantha from watching her son's play. In my defence, I didn't know what she would have missed. If I had, then, of course, she could have gone. In fact, we could all have gone and made it the office Christmas treat. There - two birds killed with one stone, metaphorically, of course.

Just before we reach the office, Charlie sighs and looks at me through troubled eyes.

"Are you still on for this weekend, Vick?"

Just for a second, I wonder what he's talking about and then it all comes flooding back. Nodding, I smile reassuringly.

"Yes, of course. Don't worry, it'll be fine. I wonder what our challenge will be tomorrow though? Do you think it will be difficult to carry out when we're not at home?"

Charlie shrugs. "Who knows, but we'll give it our best shot. That's all we can do."

He holds the door open for me and I smile as I pass through. I am actually looking forward to the weekend more than I ever thought I would.

Charlie is fast becoming the person I look forward to spending time with the most. It has surprised me to find we have so much in common. The more time I spend with him the more I realise it.

The journey to the Cotswolds passes by in a flash as we chat about our day. He asks me about my family which I manage to dodge skilfully. He, in turn, does the same when we mention his so I don't probe too much. After all, I'm in the same boat as him and respect his privacy.

By the time we reach our destination any nerves I had pushed aside come rushing back with a vengeance as he sighs heavily. "Sorry, Vick. We're here and nothing can prepare you for the reality of a weekend with my parents."

I look in wonder as we pass through an impressive gate that opens as if by magic when we appear. The driveway alone is like a small parkland and I look around with interest as we drive along an amazing approach to what can only be described as a country estate nestling in the distance.

I say in total awe, "Charlie, your home is out of this world, you are so lucky."

He groans. "Appearances can be deceptive. This is impressive, I'll give you that, but it's not what I would consider a home. It's just one of many that my family own and we have been shipped between them all our lives."

I struggle to understand why that is such a bad thing and say softly, "But your childhood must have been amazing, to get to spend time in wonderful places and see things the rest of us only dream of."

There's a short silence and then he replies in a small voice. "Yes, I suppose it was. The trouble is, it got kind of lonely sometimes. My father was always working and my mother preoccupied with her charities and friends. Emily and I were dragged behind them and wheeled out when the occasion required it. The circles they mixed in weren't the sort of people you would feel comfortable around and their kids looked down at us because we didn't speak like them. Emily had it hard at her boarding school and was bullied terribly. I was too but was more able to deal with it than she was. We never really fitted in anywhere and despite the wealth, it didn't buy us the sort of family life I always wanted. I expect your childhood was richer than mine in many more ways."

I don't have a chance to reply before we pull up outside a large impressive portico. We fall silent as we contemplate leaving the safety of the car to face what appears to be a very trying visit.

Charlie grins ruefully. "Come on, let's get this over with."

As we exit the car, the door flies open and I recognise Charlie's mother standing in the doorway. I blink as she appears to be a walking Burberry advert. She squeals loudly, "Oh my God, you're here at last. I've been so excited all day, haven't I, Harry?"

I watch as she is joined by her husband and I swallow the nerves as I face them. There he is. The self-made man and personal inspiration to me. I must make a good impression and learn everything I can from him on succeeding in the face of adversity—otherwise known as your roots.

He laughs loudly. "Charlie, son. Long-time no see. Introduce us to your delightful girlfriend."

Charlie looks at me apologetically and takes my hand. "Meet Victoria. We work together at S & D Rowanson."

His mother rushes forward and envelops me in a hug, overpowering me with her designer perfume. "Vicky, babe, come here. You know I've waited for this day all my life. The woman who has stolen my baby's heart."

His father laughs loudly. "You mean she's been dreading this day. Mothers and their sons - hey."

She rolls her eyes. "I'll remind you of that when Emily brings her intended home. We'll see what you have to say about it then."

Charlie says in horror, "We're not engaged or anything, don't force that on the poor girl."

His mum winks. "If you say so."

She links her arm in mine and drags me inside. "Don't listen to them, honey. Anyway, you can call me Linda and his dad, Harry. We want you to feel like one of the family. Now tell me all about yourself over a nice cup of tea."

As we walk through the house towards the nice cup of tea, I struggle to keep my mouth from dropping to the floor. It appears that the other half live very well indeed and where the house in Knightsbridge is the epitome of chic sophistication and modern convenience, the house in the Cotswolds has everything money can buy. Despite its size the decor is warm and welcoming and yet I don't miss the expensive antique furniture and art on the walls. This place is stuffed full of every kind of desire and I am struggling to take it all in.

I follow Linda to a drawing room and blink as I see a maid standing waiting next to a tray of afternoon tea. Not the maid again! I think I'm about to have an anxiety attack. Linda pulls me down beside her on the couch as Charlie shoots me apologies from his anxious blue eyes. He must be worrying about the outburst that is sure to follow this maid revelation but I hold it in.

Instead, all my principles have appeared to have deserted me as I take a cup of tea gratefully and just enjoy the whole experience.

As it turns out, Charlie's parents are much like him. Warm, hospitable and so funny my face aches from laughing. In fact, they all make me feel so welcome I wonder what Charlie was worried about.

Then the conversation turns to family matters and the warning sirens sound in my mind as his father says angrily, "What's up with Emily?"

Linda nods as Charlie tries to look nonchalant. "Nothing, why?"

His father shakes his head. "She's avoiding us which can only mean she's hiding something. I thought she was settled in that internship at the Houses of Parliament but then I hear she's looking for a job with an associate of mine."

Charlie disguises his expression well and says somewhat irritably, "So what if she's looking for another job? She's not paid to be there so I don't blame her. It's all very well learning a trade but people do need to earn money you know."

Linda raises her eyes. "She doesn't need money, Charlie. You know she has credit that we pay for. She just needs to fill time until she marries someone who can look after her."

Immediately the feminist in me wakes up and bitch slaps the polite girl I am inside. I'm not even sure I can hold in the reply that is battling with my best behaviour to get out. Charlie looks almost desperate as he stands up and pulls me with him. "Sorry guys, do you mind if I show Victoria around? It's been a long day and it would be good to freshen up."

Linda jumps up. "Of course, I forgot you both work."

She looks at me pitying. "Never mind, babe. If things work out with Charlie boy that job of yours can take a hike. I'm sure you'll be only too glad of that, hey darling?"

Before I can answer I am almost manhandled from the room by a desperate Charlie before his mum's parting shot hits me. "Oh, babe, we've put you both in your old room, just in case you were worried you'd have to sneak down the corridor at night."

His father laughs loudly as Charlie slams the door shut with a resounding thud.

He grips my hand tightly and pulls me speedily from the vicinity before I blow up like Vesuvius.

Charlie literally drags me to his room. Not quite what I had in mind when I pictured this very occasion while lying in my bed alone with my fantasies.

He doesn't speak until the bedroom door slams behind us and then says apologetically, "I'm so sorry, Vick. I had to get you out of there before you exploded. I can't apologise enough and I in no way share their outdated beliefs."

He looks so contrite and miserable my anger evaporates instantly into thin air. Smiling softly, I sit down on his bed and say gently, "It's fine. Thanks for the intervention though. It was close back there."

He sits down heavily beside me and I see his tortured expression. "I knew this was a bad idea."

I shrug. "It's fine. We knew it would be tough. The most important thing is Emily this weekend. Do you think she'll show up?"

"I'm not sure." He sighs, shaking his head. "If she values her sanity, she'll steer well clear. The trouble is, it's easier in the long run to show up and brazen it out. If they found out what she's really been getting up to things will get a whole lot crazy around here."

We sit in silence for a moment and I think about what I've discovered. Charlie doesn't know it yet but my contact came through. The file he sent me made for interesting reading and I was going to show it to him this weekend and go through it all with Emily. Hopefully, we will get the chance but there's a much bigger problem weighing on my mind right now as I say shakily, "Do we really have to share this room?"

My heart is beating so fast at the thought of it and perversely I hope he insists. What can I say, I'm a woman with some very crazy needs right now and Charlie is fast becoming the one I need the most? In my fantasies we are together and in love. We love each other passionately and are a team that can never be broken. The trouble is, I think its one-way traffic and in the interests of self-preservation I try not to let it show.

Then he's back. The cheeky Charlie who has plagued me so well over the years. "What's the matter, babe, don't you trust yourself to keep your hands to yourself?"

I pretend to frown. "Don't flatter yourself. If you must know it wouldn't bother me at all. In fact, you could lie on top of me all night and nothing. Yes, you heard me right, nothing. What do you think about that then, huh?"

He just winks. "Keep telling yourself that, Vick but we know the real story."

Laughing, he looks around him. "You know, I never liked this room; too stuffy and old fashioned. Maybe if you're here, it will interest me more."

Suddenly, we hear a tentative knock on the door. "Charlie, are you both decent? I'm not interrupting anything am I?"

I grin as Charlie groans. "Come in, mum."

The door flies open and Linda looks almost disappointed to see us still fully clothed. "Oh, well... um, I just wanted to say dinner won't be long. I expect you want an early night so I had Lila rustle up something quick."

She winks. "Let's just hope that's the only quick thing this evening, hey Vick?"

I stare at her retreating figure in utter bemusement. This place is mad and I'm fast falling down the rabbit hole of crazy here.

22

Dinner is a loud affair as Linda and Harry talk nonstop about the places they've been and the people they've seen. I am fascinated by the whole experience and am content just to listen. Halfway through the meal, Emily makes an appearance and I watch as she is crushed to both her parents as soon as she steps foot inside the room. By the time she escapes she sinks down in a spare seat next to Charlie and smiles wearily.

"Hi, guys, sorry I'm late. The traffic was horrific."

Linda rolls her eyes. "You should have asked for the helicopter, babe. Dad would have sent Bentley."

I think I choke on my wine as Charlie flinches. Helicopter! Who the hell has a helicopter lying around as a taxi service other than Christian Grey?

Emily shakes her head. "It's fine. I needed the time to chill after the week from hell."

Harry leans forward and says in a hard voice. "What's going on, Emily. I heard you're looking for another job. What's the problem with the internship?"

To her credit, Emily keeps a calm expression and shrugs. "I'm bored with it. I've decided I hate politics and want to work in fashion."

Linda nods knowingly. "I told you it wouldn't work, didn't I, Harry?"

She looks over at Harry and laughs. "Girls like nice things like clothes and makeup. Not stuffy offices filled with boring old problems. I knew this would happen."

She looks at Emily with excitement. "You know, we could call in a few favours, babe. Daddy knows Sir Phillip and I'm sure he'll find you a job in his fashion empire. It will be much more interesting."

She says to Harry. "You'd do that for Ems, wouldn't you?"

He smiles benevolently. "Course I would. You're my little girl nothing is too much trouble."

I actually feel ill. Charlie was right. This is all too much. I've only been here for a few short hours but every principle in me has been sorely tested already. Who are these people? They live in a world so far removed from mine I should have brought my passport. I feel a huge ball of something distasteful growing in the pit of my stomach and it's not the cheesy fries that have accompanied every course we've eaten. I almost can't bear sitting here and listening to it. I should stand up and stick up for women's rights and values. I should tell them to stop assuming that every woman just wants an easy ride and actually wants to work for a living. I should be talking about what interests me and discovering how empires are built from scratch but I can't. These people are Charlie's family and even I know he's hating every minute of this probably much more than I am.

By the time we manage to escape to Charlie's room, I think I'm getting a migraine. Far from being able to grill Harry about his success, all I managed to do was listen to Linda talking fashion with Emily while Harry gazed at them benevolently. Every time I tried to raise the subject he would shake his head and say patronisingly, "You don't want to indulge an old fool just to be polite. Don't worry your pretty little head about the intricacies of big business."

Linda would shake her head and try to get me to join their conversation about fashion. One time she whispered, "It's ok, Vick. You don't have to win us over you know. Even I don't ask Harry about his work, I mean, who can be bothered to talk about the boring things in life, anyway."

I think I finally admitted defeat and just knocked back more wine than I have ever drunk in my life. The world certainly looked a lot more interesting by the end of it. Charlie tried but even his good humour found its way to the wine bottle and we just sat like a couple of winos drowning in unspoken words and misery.

Now, however, I am firmly sobered up and contemplating a night in the same bed as my nemesis. This is awkward to say the least.

By the time I've changed into my funky bunny pyjamas and cleaned my teeth, Charlie is already lying in bed with his arms behind his head watching me approach. He laughs as he sees me and I frown. "What's so funny?"

"You. I never had you down as a funky bunny, Vick."

Shrugging, I face him with a blank expression. "There's a lot you don't know about me, *Charl*! For all you know, I could teach limbo dancing on my days off and run a side business as a Disney Princess impersonator."

He just laughs and pats the bed next to him. "Jump in and I'll tell you a bedtime story."

"Why would I want that?"

"Because I tell a mean ghost story and by the end of it, you will want my big strong arms wrapped around you all night and I would have won."

Shaking the delicious thought of being wrapped in Charlie all night, I just roll my eyes.

"Dream on Casanova, I'm not one of your giggling assistants. It actually may be possible that I can resist your dubious charms. Maybe you're not my type, have you ever considered that?"

He looks at me with interest. "What is your type?"

I smirk. "Well, someone a lot like Nathan Miller I would imagine."

He looks confused and I say airily, "You know, the Jet pilot I am corresponding with. A man who is going places - literally. Well educated, not afraid of extremes and a very interesting life to talk endlessly about."

Charlie looks surprised. "I didn't know you kept in touch. I thought it was just me."

What?!

I try to keep my face devoid of any expression and say with interest. "Oh, do you mean that sonar operator—Susan?"

He grins. "It's Sandra and yes I do. We've been emailing all week. She's such fun."

The pressure in my head is threatening to explode as the green goddess of jealously shakes me inside and screams, *I told you not to play it cool*.

Instead, I try to look unaffected. "Cool."

Did I just say cool? Even Charlie looks surprised and I feel the embarrassment hitting me hard. I so need to go to sleep before I make a complete fool of myself. So, once again, I revert back to type and look annoyed.

"Anyway, I need to get to sleep and there will be no ghost stories."

Looking around the room, I grab some cushions from a neighbouring chair and proceed to stuff them down the middle of the bed creating a barrier between us. Charlie laughs loudly. "What are you doing? Building a fortress to keep the wicked Knight from pillaging your virtue."

Throwing one of them at his insufferable head, I say tartly, "Your reputation precedes you and if you think I'm leaving anything to chance, then you're sorely mistaken."

Jumping in, I pointedly turn my back to him and close my eyes. "Night, Charlie."

For a while there is silence and I lie like an ironing board beside him. The thought of him just a touch away is pure torture. Charlie is like an annoying fungus. Unwanted and destructive but growing on you before you know what hit you. He is all I can think of and when I'm not with him I'm wondering what he's doing and who with? I never thought this would happen and I'm not really sure what to do about it now. Suddenly, a small voice comes out of the darkness. "So, tell me about the Jet pilot."

Smiling to myself, I say in a weary voice, "Not now, Charlie. Go to sleep."

Another silence and then he says, "No, really, tell me about the Jet pilot."

Exhaling sharply, I turn to face him and even in the dim light I see a strange vulnerable expression on his face. I want to reach out and erase those worry lines and brush his lips with mine. I want us to be team Charia, together forever against the world. So, I just smile and say softly, "There really is nothing to tell. Goodnight. See you in the morning."

23

December 13th

12 Days to Go

Morning comes and with it the realisation that somehow my limbs have tangled up with Charlie's during the night. It takes a moment to realise that his leg is over mine and his arm pulling me tightly against his broad chest. The cushions are god only where and I daren't move in case I wake the annoying idiot up.

My heart beats louder than any alarm clock and I wince as I think about the situation I'm in. This is a disaster. How did I ever agree to this? Then again, the woman in me is purring like a Cheshire cat. I can't remember the last time I woke up with a man in my bed—ok, it's technically his bed but that's inconsequential. I am in bed with a hot guy with only the funky pyjamas between us because I am fast realising that Charlie doesn't appear to own a pair.

He stirs and I stiffen up, hating the fact that I want to lie like this all day. I am such a lush. I have been driven to drink and with it came lustful thoughts. Maybe it was the other way around but that's my excuse and I'm sticking to it.

He pulls me even tighter against him and I stiffen, my breathing threatening to land me in the emergency room. Can a panic attack kill you because if it can my life is in danger right about now?

Then I hear a sleepy, "Morning, Vick."

I feign sleep for a minute and then he laughs softly and pulls me even closer, if that's at all possible. Quickly, I pull away and look at him in outrage. "What the hell, Charlie. How dare you destroy my defences and infiltrate my side of the bed? I should have known not to trust you."

He just laughs loudly. "You sure about that? I mean, maybe you destroyed the barriers and threw yourself on me during the night. Maybe you couldn't resist the pull of the inevitable and thought you could blame it on me."

"So, the fact I had my back to you and you had your leg pinning me down and your arms pulling me tight doesn't come into it. No Charlie, the perpetrator in this case is *you* and you have been caught red handed and are guilty as charged."

He just winks, "Don't pretend you didn't enjoy it, because I sure did."

I'm just about to let rip when his phone buzzes on the table next to the bed. He reaches across and grabs it and then looks up and grins.

"Ready for our challenge of the day."

I sit down next to him and look at him with the curiosity burning me up inside. "Ok, hit me with it."

"Ok, December 13th - 12 days to go."

He flashes the screen at me and I see a Christmas tree before an open fire. Then he opens the little window and laughs. "Go to a Christmas tree farm and cut down a tree."

Grabbing his phone, I look at the message and shake my head.

"I never knew there was such a place. Why can't we just go to the Garden Centre and get one wrapped and delivered? I'm pretty sure an artificial one would be kinder to the planet. I'm not sure about this, Charlie. It's akin to murder in my eyes."

Charlie laughs loudly and pushes me playfully. "Murder! A Christmas tree! You crack me up, Vick. Where did you think they came from? Garden Centres don't get them made in a factory you know. Anyway, it will be like one of those movies and it may have snowed in the night and the scene will be all romantic and Christmassy."

"You're an idiot, Charlie."

Reaching out, he pushes me down and starts tickling me. I am laughing so hard I almost forget to be angry at his invasion of my personal space.

We are interrupted by a sharp knock on the door and a loud voice.

"Put her down, Charl. Breakfast in ten."

My cheeks flaming, I jump from the bed and head for the bathroom, Charlie's laughter ringing in my ears. What am I doing? This isn't me, frolicking in bed with a highly desirable player. I'm such an idiot. This is Charlie's way of wearing me down and taking the prize. I absolutely must get a grip and see this all through before he runs away with my heart.

Breakfast is like something out of a period drama or the highest-class Bed and Breakfast, I can't quite decide.

Charlie's family are all sitting at the huge table as Lila fusses round them with coffee and tea and distributing various dishes of tasty looking food.

Emily smiles as we come into the room and I don't miss the interest in her expression as she looks between the two of us. She smiles a little too triumphantly for my liking and says softly, "Morning guys, good night?"

Linda looks at us with interest and Harry laughs from behind the huge Daily Telegraph he is reading. "Not at the breakfast table, Ems. Give them a little privacy for god's sake."

I feel my cheeks flame which makes me look guilty as charged and I can feel Charlie's smirk from here as he says flippantly. "Sorry, I hope we weren't too loud."

I look at him in outrage and he pretends not to notice and grabs a croissant.

I sink down beside him and try to focus on getting through this. Linda looks interested. "So, what are your plans today kids?"

Emily looks bored. "I'm meeting Charlotte in Oxford for some Christmas shopping."

Linda looks at us. "And the lovebirds?"

I grind my teeth as Charlie says flippantly, "Vick talked me into taking her to Christmas world. We'll pick up the tree if you like."

Harry laughs. "She's got you trained already son. Under the thumb and ruled by your…"

"Harry! Not at the breakfast table!"

Linda leans forward. "You know Vick, a word of advice. Mucking around the fields on a cold day isn't much fun, I should know. Get Charlie to take you shopping instead and get him to splash the cash on your Christmas present. Then you could go to lunch somewhere nice and make a day of it."

Trying desperately to ignore the growing torrent of abuse she has coming her way, I just grit my teeth and smile stiffly. "Actually, Linda, I hate shopping."

There is silence in the room as my words sink in. I carry on eating my croissant as I watch Linda share an incredulous look with Emily and then gasps, "You poor thing."

Emily nods and I look at them in amazement. "It's no big deal. I just grab what I need off the Internet. I don't have time with my workload."

Linda shakes her head and looks annoyed. "This poor girl. It's not right, your boss should be told. Heaping all the mundane work on a young girl is all wrong. No wonder you're struggling. It's like slave labour if you ask me. Harry, do something for Vicky. Give her a job in one of your offices and make sure she has enough time and money to hit the shops. It's too much and is abuse in the workplace."

Before I let rip Charlie interrupts. "Victoria loves her work. In fact, she runs the office and could give herself time off if she chooses. She just doesn't want to."

Now I feel like a prize exhibit in the zoo as they look at me in utter disbelief. Even Harry lowers the newspaper and looks as if an alien has landed. He shakes his head as Linda mutters, "It's not right, Charl."

She looks at me with sympathy. "It's ok, Vick. I've got your back and you don't have to pretend with us. I've seen it all before. Young women trying to prove they're as good as a man. We all know women are better at most things but really the boardroom is best left to the men."

Before I can reply, Charlie jumps up, pulling me with him.

"Sorry guys, we need to head off. Lots to do and all that."

He pulls me from the room much like he did last night and I run to keep up with him. Once again, he almost pushes me into his bedroom and turns to look at me apologetically.

"I'm sorry about this, Vicky. Please don't react to them. Mum lives in her own little world and doesn't mean anything by it. Nothing you say will register anyway, so please can I ask a huge favour that I have no right asking?"

I say thinly. "Which is?"

"Please, just drop it. Don't react and tell her what you probably very much want to. We just need to get through the next couple of days and then get back to reality."

Shaking my head, I sink down on the bed. "But it isn't right. None of this is right. Your mum means well but she should see that things have changed. Women are running countries now and making decisions that affect everyone. There is no divide and women run companies and are every bit as equal to the men they employ. Why can't she see that?"

He looks miserable. "Maybe she can but she chooses not to let it affect her. She sees the world very differently and if that makes her happy, then fine. Emily doesn't share her outlook and only panders to her for an easy life. We all do really."

I look at him in surprise. "Why do you pander to her? She will never change if you don't educate her."

Sitting down, Charlie looks at me with a soft expression and I feel those damned butterflies again. "Listen, Vick. Not everyone's the same. You have your values and beliefs and not everyone shares them. It doesn't make them any less of a person because of it. It just makes the world more interesting. My mother doesn't understand this new world we live in. If she does, she chooses to ignore it. All her life she's been the same. Despite everything, she is kind, funny and loyal. So what if she believes something we don't? I have never known her to say any harsh words or speak about anyone unkindly. She is actually an amazing person who often gets underestimated. All of my life my friends have wished they had a mother like mine. Like I said before, we never really fitted in and she has always been a source of amusement to the circles we mix in. They both have really but because of their wealth they have been grudgingly accepted."

I look at him in surprise. "But you said you hated your childhood, Charlie. You told me that your parents didn't have time for you and that you and Emily only had each other."

He smiles softly, "It's true, I did. The trouble was, mum was so busy trying to fit in with the rest of them she forgot about our emotional needs.

Instead she gave us everything money could buy and more. She thought that was the key to acceptance and in their case, it was. She was on every committee going and gave most of her time to charity. She always threw the biggest parties, and it used to make me cringe when I saw the raised eyebrows and smirks of their friends. That is what I despise, Vicky. I despise those people who judge others by their own standards. I despise people who look down on somebody else because they weren't born to the right family. And most of all I despise myself for allowing it to matter. If I were any sort of son, I would be proud of my parents and what they've achieved. However, I am always running from them because I can't bear to see them judged for trying to belong. That makes me no better than the rest of them. All of this with Emily is not because we care what people think—believe it or not, we don't. We do care what our parents think and this would make them even more of a laughingstock than they are already. My mum would be embarrassed in front of her friends, if you could call them that and there would be a lot of, 'I told you so.' So, please, Vick, keep your remarks to yourself for the weekend and please don't judge them."

I feel ashamed of myself. Suddenly, James Sullivan springs to mind and I remember his words.

"Look at the world through different eyes once in a while and don't judge everyone by your own

standards. We are all different and see the world in a different way. Just do what makes you happy, Victoria and you will be, no matter what others may think of you."

Charlie smiles warmly. "Sorry, Vick. I hope you don't mind my lecture. I am actually really protective of my family, despite everything."

I walk across and sit next to him and smile. "No, I'm sorry, Charlie. You're right. I am the most judgmental person I have ever met. Most of the time I hate myself let alone everyone who comes in contact with me. Don't worry, I'll behave myself this weekend. That's one worry off your mind at least."

Just for a minute, we stare at each other. There is total silence around us and the only sound I can hear is my heart beating. Charlie looks at me with such tenderness and something else I can't recognise.

Then he reaches up and touches my cheek gently and his eyes twinkle as he says softly, "I don't hate you, Victoria. Quite the opposite, in fact I'll let you in on a little secret. For quite some time now I've wanted to get to know the girl hiding behind the professional exterior. I've watched you and wondered what makes such a beautiful girl tick. You fascinate me for a whole lot of reasons and I was happy when Donald devised this challenge because I got to spend time with you. I know we're half way through but I have enjoyed myself far more in these two weeks than I have in a very long time. Even if I lose this challenge, it won't matter because I'm hoping I've discovered something far more valuable. You."

As he speaks the tears well up in my eyes. Now I know he's won. He's broken down every defence I've set in place over the years and reached the part of me I have protected for more years than I care to remember.

I say softly, "Thank you, Charlie. I feel the same. Despite the fact you are the most annoying man I have ever come across, you are also the kindest, funniest and craziest one I have ever had the fortune to spend time with. I'm glad I get to do this challenge with you and am not looking forward to when it ends because I don't want to go back to being that girl I was just a short time ago."

Charlie smiles and somehow, we shift just a little closer. I think I hold my breath as I gaze at his handsome face inches from mine. Time stands still as everything falls into place. This moment, this room and what will happen next is inevitable. Charlie and I are inevitable. I can see it as clearly as everything I have ever wanted in life. Charlie and I were always meant to reach this point and as he lowers his lips to mine, I rise to meet his and fate does a merry dance around us. Finally, I am home.

24

Christmas World

Charlie and I are a couple. I can't believe it but we are. One kiss turned to many, and it feels like the most natural thing in the world. We managed to slip out without anyone seeing us and have driven the short distance to Christmas world.

Charlie grasps my hand and we walk towards a shed at the end of a muddy drive. We are dressed in huge padded coats and bobble hats courtesy of the cupboard that Linda has stocked for every season it would seem. I am even wearing wellington boots and have never felt happier.

Charlie and I are now that perfect couple from ice skating. We are connected, and it's not just because I'm holding his ski-gloved hand in mine.

Everything feels new and exciting and I feel as if I can look forward to a bright future whether I win the challenge or not. If he does, I'll be disappointed for myself but happy for him. In fact, dare I say it, I hope he does win because seeing him happy would make me happy. It's that thought that shocks me more than anything. I am actually putting someone else first for once in my life and it feels good.

As we walk, he pushes me in as many puddles as he can and we laugh like schoolkids. By the time we reach the shop we are rosy-cheeked and full of Christmas spirit.

We follow a man outside who shows us the forest of trees all growing happily in their rows and he explains how it all works.

"You choose your tree and we cut it down and wrap it for you. If you need it delivered, we can schedule you in."

As I look at the trees, I feel a little bad. Charlie laughs as he sees my expression and whispers, "Think about it as giving them a home. They were grown for this reason and they deserve to be the most splendid Christmas tree in the world."

Grinning, I snuggle in closer. "Ok, which one then?"

He looks around and says lightly. "Well, my parents don't do things by halves so maybe a 7Ft one. It will look good in the hallway when people come to visit."

We walk along the rows and I look at the trees critically. "Hm. Well, obviously, we want the non-drop variety. I don't expect your mother will want pine needles dropping all over her parquet flooring."

Charlie nods. "It needs to be bushy. We need lots of branches evenly spaced to hold the decorations."

"Yes, that's a must. We need it evenly distributed and not sparse at the top like some I've seen."

Charlie frowns. "You're quite right, Vick. Even light distribution is a must for any self-respecting Christmas tree. Maybe a little sparser at the bottom to reduce wastage when we try to secure it to the stand."

I look around thoughtfully. "Hm, yes, it's a tricky one. I never realised how important a choice this would be."

The man accompanying us looks as if he has lost the will to live by the time we walk through the rows, not once, not twice but three times, pondering the attributes of the trees that are very much the same. By the time we decide on one, I'm a little worried that his axe will slip and he'll use it on us due to the look he is throwing us.

Feeling worried at the thought, I say loudly, "Excuse me, sir but we can chop the tree?"

Charlie looks surprised and I whisper, "It's the challenge. It said chop down a Christmas tree. Maybe it meant us to do it personally."

Charlie nods. "You're right, you always are when it comes to the fine print. Ok, shall I go first?"

Nodding, I watch as he takes the weapon from the disgruntled man's hands which makes me breathe a sigh of relief. Then we watch at a safe distance as Charlie attempts to chop down the tree.

Who knew it would be so hard? I start to laugh as he takes swings at the trunk and only manages to chip a little bark off each time. The man is looking even more irritable and laughing I shout over, "Step away from the tree, Charlie. It's my turn now."

Charlie stands up and his cheeks are flushed and his breathing heavy as the steam from the cold air surrounds him. He grins. "Ok Grizzly Adams, show me how it's done."

I must say I feel a little worried about how this will pan out. Visions of the axe ricocheting off the trunk of the tree like a boomerang and embedding itself in my head come to mind. Images of an ice skate on one side of my head and an axe on the other swim into view as I imagine the horror movie created in my honour. Maybe this wasn't such a good idea. Country life is definitely not for the faint-hearted.

Once again, they stand well back as I take a swing. It actually hurts my hands but I don't let it show. I only manage two goes at it before every part of me hurts with the effort. Now I know I'm more cut out for the boardroom than the great outdoors, so just lay the axe on the ground and face the guys matter-of-factly. "There, the hard work is done. Maybe we should let the professional finish the job and we can get back to civilisation."

Charlie smirks and I grin. The man looks as if God has answered his prayers and makes short work of felling the tree as I snuggle next to Charlie as we watch. As the tree falls so does every last remaining defence I have ever set in place. Charlie kisses my gloved encased hand and smiles. "Challenge completed, Victoria."

I kiss his hand in a similar manner and smile back. "Now the challenge is getting it home."

Somehow, the man manages to strap the tree to the roof of Charlie's car and we gingerly set off for home. Once again, we play the Christmas playlist and sing at the tops of our voices. In fact, all that's missing from this festive jaunt is the snow falling. As Bing Crosby croons White Christmas, I very much wish it was.

As soon as we get home, we set about installing the tree in their huge hallway. Everyone else appears to be out and Lila locates the decorations for us and keeps us supplied with hot chocolate as we work.

Once again, we play Christmas music and look as if we've stepped out of an advert for the perfect Christmas. We are wearing brightly coloured jumpers and jeans and I think I have more decorations on me than on the tree. Charlie has wrapped himself up in some lights and we giggle our way through what is proving to be one of the best days of my life.

Then we stand back ready for the lighting ceremony.

Charlie calls Lila and Graham the gardener in and we make room for Rufus and Billy Bob the two black Labradors that live with Graham. Lila rustles up some mulled wine and we stand waiting for Charlie's tree lighting speech.

He says seriously, "I would like to thank you all for coming to witness the annual Monroe tree lighting ceremony. I would like to thank the tree for making the ultimate sacrifice and being so amazing at what it does. I would like to thank Lila for all her help, not just today but every day of the year and Graham for helping me prune this monster and somehow get it to stand as proudly as it does. Finally, I would like to thank my partner in crime, Victoria, for sharing this journey with me and undoing nearly everything I tried to do because I hadn't done it right."

The others laugh and I grin. "Guilty as charged."

It's true. I'm such a control freak I took full charge of the theme. Charlie just wanted to throw everything on but I made him sort it all into piles by colour and size and then proceeded to craft a vision of perfection. What's more, I enjoyed every minute of it and it's with a huge sense of satisfaction that I sip my mulled wine and congratulate myself on a job well done.

Charlie continues. "Thank you to Santa for delivering the best Christmas gift I could ever wish for and early at that."

He raises his glass and says loudly. "To Victoria Marshall. The most impressive, complex, annoying, infuriating woman I have ever met but also the most beautiful, kind and loving one too. To Victoria."

As the others sip their drinks, I feel myself turn to mush inside. As I look across to Charlie our eyes connect and he smiles sweetly and his eyes twinkle. We share that connection that only two people in love can share. The world fades away as the moment locks us in an understanding. Our lives begin today—together and nobody is happier about that than me.

Evening comes and with it a nightmare. After the Christmas tree lighting ceremony, Charlie and I went for a walk around the amazing gardens and for the first time in years, I fully relaxed. However, as soon as we stepped one foot inside the door, his mother came rushing towards us looking dressed to impress in vintage Chanel and beaming. "Oh my God, there you are. You must be frozen. Why on earth would you want to go outside on a December day?"

She shakes her head as if she's looking at two idiots and smiles happily. "Anyway, get yourselves ready because I have an amazing surprise for you both."

Charlie tenses beside me and the warning bells start ringing loud and clear in my head. She claps her hands and says, "We are having a little get together of just a few local friends to celebrate Christmas. It's taken me all day to arrange, but I had to work fast before you both head back to London and your stuffy jobs."

Charlie says irritably, "You're joking, aren't you? I just wanted a quiet night in with Vick, now I've got to make small talk with people we don't even know."

Linda giggles. "Oh Charlie, you've always been party shy. Never mind, you have Vick beside you now and I bet you can't wait to show her off. Now run along and get changed. The first guest will be here in an hour and there's not a moment to lose. Hey Vick, sorry not to give you long but how was I to know that Charlie would drag you out into the elements?"

She rushes off shaking her head and Charlie looks at me with a pained expression.

"I'm sorry, Vicky. I told you what they're like. Now you're about to see first-hand what I run from all these years. Please be kind and don't react. As soon as we've done our time, we can slip off and leave them to it."

I can see how anxious he feels and just smile brightly. "Listen, it's fine. A little party won't scare me. I mean, how bad can it be."

As it turned out, very bad indeed.

25

Somehow, I have made myself look respectable and we head downstairs to meet the others. Charlie grips my hand tightly and throws me pained looks every so often and I smile reassuringly. As we walk into the living room, I gasp at its transformation.

Candles burn on every surface and fairy lights twinkle in alcoves and around the windows. The fire is burning brightly in the grate and soft music pipes out from goodness only where and creates a warm and inviting atmosphere.

Lila is dressed to impress the guests in her pristine maid's uniform and Harry and Linda are looking every inch the successful people they are as they wear their designer clothes with pride. Emily is sitting on the sofa looking as if she would rather be knife fighting in a prison cell with an axe murderer and I suppress a giggle as I see her pained expression.

Linda says loudly, "There you are, guys. I must say you've done a fab job with the tree. Vick's a good influence on you Charlie, she's even made it look as if we've got a designer in and not just the random dressing you usually do."

Emily smiles and says warmly, "Yes, well done, guys. It looks amazing."

Linda waves towards a table filled with glasses of champagne. "Grab one of those and relax and enjoy yourselves. Work can be forgotten while you enjoy the evening."

Harry beams at his wife. "Same to you, honey. You've worked hard this week and deserve to take it easy."

I smile as Linda looks up at him with total adoration and I feel a warm glow as I see the affection in their eyes. Despite everything, these people obviously love each other very much and I feel privileged to be included in this family scene. This is what I want. To grow old with Charlie and retain that love for each other as we go. I want us to grow together not apart and to share a life of meaning and fulfilment. I don't need everything that money can buy, what does that really get you, anyway? I just want to be happy and if that means giving up everything I always thought I wanted to take a different path, then I would in a heartbeat.

Suddenly, the doorbell rings and Linda beams with excitement. "They're here. Come on guys, let's get this party started."

She rushes off with Harry in tow and Emily groans.

"Oh my god, this is just what I need."

Charlie nods. "Do you know who they invited?"

She shrugs. "No, but you can rest assured they'll be the usual bores and snobs that always come to these things. I wish I'd taken Charlotte up on her offer to go clubbing in Oxford. This will be a disaster."

Charlie nods in agreement. "Never mind, we'll stick together and drink a lot to dull the pain."

We hear voices approaching and Emily sighs. "Well, here goes nothing." Then she downs her drink in one and immediately reaches for another.

The room soon fills up with a variety of Harry and Linda's friends. I look at them with interest and see a well-heeled bunch of people all dressed immaculately and the room hums with the buzz of conversation. I am introduced to many people and find the whole scene fascinating. Emily and Charlie are a credit to their parents as they push aside their own feelings and mingle and interact with the guests. I am pulled from group to group and introduced as the newest addition the family.

Linda is in her element. She chatters incessantly and her loud voice can often be heard ringing over the others. I don't miss the odd raised eyebrow and the smirk on some of the women's faces. I note many hushed conversations and pointed looks as groups of women watch her every move. Linda appears oblivious to it all and I feel angry on her behalf.

I find myself ready to defend her if anyone says one sharp word or hints at their disapproval because, despite everything, I am growing to like

Charlie's family very much. Even though Linda is the total opposite of me, I feel protective of her in a way that has even shocked me.

It's as Charlie and I are chatting to a local councillor that something happens that turns my world upside down. Karren Brady walks into the room.

At first, I think I must be hallucinating. I glance over and then do a double take. Oh. My. God. Karren Brady, entrepreneur businesswoman and personal role model to me in this very same room. She's accompanied by what must be her husband because she is holding his hand as he looks around him with an air of boredom.

Linda shrieks, "Karren, Paul, you made it. Harry, look who's here. Get them a drink and make it a large one."

I must stiffen up because Charlie looks over and whispers, "Do you know them?"

Words fail me as every question I ever wanted to ask her crowd to be the first one from my lips. I yearn to walk across and monopolise her attention all night long and manage to stutter, "No, but I would love to meet her."

Charlie smiles softly. "I'll introduce you."

I look at him in surprise. "Do you know her?"

He nods. "Yeah, they've been to a few of these and she's one of the few women I can tolerate.

She's amazing, you'll like her and her husband's good fun."

I can hardly contain my excitement and then I notice another couple enter the room. I watch Emily turn as white as a sheet as she looks as if Freddy Krueger has come to town. Charlie stiffens beside me and hisses, "What the hell are they doing here?"

Looking with interest, I feel the ice freeze my veins as I recognise Marcus and Sally Adams walking into the room. Marcus looks a little furtive and Sally looks absolutely furious.

As if in slow motion I see her eyes zone in on Emily like an Exocet missile and she starts walking toward her with determination. Linda looks up and shouts excitedly. "Sally, Marcus you made it. Emily will be so happy."

Emily, meanwhile, looks as if she's about to throw up all over the Persian rug and turns as white as a sheet. The noise in the room turns fuzzy as I watch the scene unfolding around us as if I'm dreaming. Everything turns to slow motion in my head as if I'm about to witness a car crash of epic proportions. Then, out of absolutely nowhere, I shriek like a mad woman.

"Oh my God, Sally Adams, is that really you?"

The room turns quiet as I rush towards the couple like a whirlwind, squealing, "It is you! Oh my god, I'm such a fan. I can't believe it. Look,

Charlie, it's Sally Adams from the television! Wow, this is amazing."

I don't even have time to witness the incredulous expressions of Karren Brady and the rest of the guests as I rush over to the toxic couple and almost knock them over in my haste to get to them before they throw their grenade into the room.

Sally looks at me in shock as I reach her and pretend to stumble. As I do, I throw the contents of my glass firmly in her face and cry out in horror, "Oh my god, I'm so sorry, what have I done?"

Blanking out the horrified faces all around me, I shout, "Quickly, come with me, I'll get you cleaned up. I'm such an idiot, always have been always will be. I mean, what must you think of me, and me being your number one fan as well?"

I don't give her any time to react or object and almost carry her from the room, away from Emily and the catastrophic scene she was about to create. I daren't even look at Karren Brady because if I do I'm liable to cry. This is mortifying; what on earth must she think? I'm pretty sure that if they could, all the Botoxed eyebrows in the room would raise in my direction, as I manhandle the danger away to safety.

As we head towards the bathroom, I keep a firm grip on Sally and notice with relief that nobody follows. I was afraid that Linda would feel obliged to lend a helping hand and can only hope that

Charlie has realised what I'm doing and is acting as back up.

The silence hits us as the door closes and Sally says icily, "Let go of me. Don't you think you've done enough damage for one night?"

Shaking my head, I drop the act and spin around to face her with Victoria Matthews definitely in charge. In a cool, hard, voice, I say abruptly. "Just hear me out, Mrs Adams, you will thank me for it later. I have just prevented you from making the biggest mistake of your life."

She looks at me with a shocked expression and I relish it. Like a hunter with its prey in its grasp, I stare at her and enjoy the feeling of power it always gives me. I know something they don't and they have no choice but to hear me out. I am good at what I do and that will become very evident to this woman staring at me through mistrusting, hate-filled eyes. She is on the edge and that makes me madder than ever. However, she will soon replace that look when she hears what I have to say.

I drag her upstairs to Charlie's room and hand her a towel from the bathroom to clean up. The air is filled with unspoken questions and the answers dance around them in delicious anticipation.

She looks at me with a tight expression and says harshly, "I think you have some explaining to do."

Nodding, I motion for her to take a seat on the bed while I stand by the door, ready to rugby tackle her to the floor if she tries to escape. Then I begin.

"Ms Adams. I'm sorry about that, you were about to make a complete fool of yourself and needed removing from the situation."

To her credit, she just stares at me with a blank expression and doesn't try to interrupt. I can see why she's such a good journalist now and a little piece of me relaxes as I contemplate the professional before me.

"I understand that you discovered about your husband's affair with Emily Monroe."

She nods and I paste a blank, professional expression onto my face.

"You will also be aware that this isn't the first time he has strayed."

I see her lips tighten and the hurt in her eyes. She just nods.

"I also know that you would do anything to get out of this marriage and yet you feel trapped by circumstance."

Now I have her full attention as she snaps to attention and snarls, "What are you talking about, you know nothing?"

Shrugging, I continue. "But I do know, Ms Adams. You see, I have a friend who has divulged some very interesting information to me. He told me that for some time you have been planning a way out of this marriage that doesn't compromise your position in the media. He has discovered that you've engineered this whole sorry mess just to extricate yourself from a loveless marriage. You are, in fact, using Emily Monroe to be the match to set this marriage on fire. Your husband will be publicly humiliated and you'll be the woman who will become the example to every woman who has been cheated on over the years. You intend to be a role model to these women and far from harming your position, it will cement it and show you as being strong, courageous and brave."

Sally, to her credit, doesn't react. She just smiles softly. "You're deluded. What proof do you have of any of this? This is just your word against mine and after that stunt you just pulled, I'm quietly confident that you will be perceived as a madwoman. If what you say is true then is it really any business of yours, anyway?"

I smile softly. "But I do have proof, Ms Adams and what's more it's concrete. However, this isn't about what I know and what you want to happen. It's about getting what you want without dragging everyone through the mud. You see, I specialise in getting my clients what they want and more every day of the week. Like you, I'm a professional and not averse to doing the unthinkable to get what I want. You would be wise to do as I say and nobody gets hurt. You avoid a public scandal that would ruin both you, your husband and the family whose house you are sitting in. Instead, you will be free from your hateful prison of a marriage and walk away with everything. Shall I continue, Ms Adams, or have you heard enough?"

To my complete surprise, the tears well up in her eyes and her mask slips. Suddenly, sitting in front of me is a vulnerable woman. I see the years of hurt and desperation line her face and the broken eyes of a woman who has kept it together for far too long. This woman is battle-hardened and weary of the fight. This was her final battle in the hope of winning a long drawn out war. I have seen that look countless times before and move across and sit beside her. Reaching out, I take her shaking hand in mine and say softly, "It's ok, I'm not the mad woman you think I am. As I said, I specialise in helping women like you and my way is a much better one. Let me help you and I promise this will end."

She says in a small voice. "How did you know?"

"I have a friend who does some digging for me from time to time. When Emily told Charlie what was happening he was desperate and confided in me. He loves his sister and despite being angry with her he wanted to help. He will do anything for his family, Sally, as I'm sure you can appreciate. His family are the objects of ridicule and derision in the circles they run in and he is desperate to protect them from the scandal it would cause. Well, once I instructed my friend, he came up with a video from a CCTV camera in a well-known restaurant."

Sally looks worried and I nod.

"Yes, you thought you were being so careful but you should know better than me about this world we live in. People like to protect themselves and when you have a public figure sitting before you asking you to do something that would fetch good money if it fell into the right hands, you take advantage of it."

Sally looks at me angrily and I smile reassuringly.

"It's fine. Luckily for you, the man you met has no interest in taking it further. He swapped your information for another juicy story that will make him far more money. My friend passed everything to me in exchange for my services on a personal matter he has going on, so we are all happy."

She shakes her head. "Not all of us."

I fix her with a hard look. "Not now, but you will be. Firstly, we must agree that you will drop the whole Emily thing. She is just a young girl who was led to believe that your husband was yours in name only. He spun her the usual tale of a loveless marriage, together only for the sake of your public and the children. You know how it goes, he loved her and as soon as he could he would leave you for her. He had to protect his position in the government and the scandal would ruin you both.

Don't blame Emily for the problems with your husband because you know as well I do, she isn't the first and won't be the last."

Sally nods sadly. "I know it's down to him. It always is. When we first met, he was engaged to a powerful Judge. He ended their engagement and moved on to me because I could give him the publicity and social acceptance he needed to get ahead. You see, that's Marcus, always thinking of himself and nobody else. I served a purpose and never realised it until it was too late. Emily is just the last straw. I can't tell you how many Emily's there have been over the years. An endless succession of foolish girls who think they know it all. They look at me with pity in their eyes because they see me as the nagging wife who is trapping him in a loveless marriage."

I say softly, "Is that why you arranged for Emily to work there? You knew that she would prove too tempting and her family association would cause a greater scandal because of it."

She nods. "Taylor-Monroe is big business. It's a family name and Harry and Linda are frequently in the gossip magazines. People are fascinated by their rags to riches story and if the story got out about their daughter with my husband, it would run for months. She is young and impressionable and he is old enough to be her father. I would divorce him and take him for everything and he would be forced to step down."

"This isn't the first time you've tried this, is it Sally?" I say gravely.

She sniffs. "I tried with the daughter of a well-known television personality. I arranged the internship and waited for the inevitable. You see, Marcus likes a young petite blonde with dewy eyes and a vacant mind. However, in that case, looks were deceptive, and she proved to be a strong woman masquerading in a starlet's body. She was having none of it and even threatened him with a sexual harassment suit. We had to brush that one under the carpet pretty quickly and I pretended to believe him when he said it was all in her mind. The trouble is, I've lost count of the number of mistakes he's made and I've had enough. I needed someone prominent to blow this charade out into the open and saw my chance when a friend of mine threw a party. I saw the way Marcus looked at Emily across the room so I did some digging. I found out she was fresh from University and needed a job. So, I engineered the whole thing. I mentioned to her friend's mother that there was an internship available at Marcus's office. She knew that Emily needed a job and suggested it. All I had to do was wait for the inevitable to happen and then cause a public scene. The conversation you saw on the TV footage was with a private detective who I instructed to follow them around and take photos to back up my story. This time I was taking no chances and wanted him gone. I can't be the bad one in all this. Marcus would spin things and make me look like the bad guy. My career would be over because it would be tainted by the whole messy divorce and he is not the sort of man who would go down with his ship. I know he would make out that I was at fault and knows enough people to make the mud stick. So, you see this was the best I had."

As she wipes the tears from her eyes, I smile brightly. "Well, now I'm the best you've got and I never lose. Let me act on your behalf, Sally and we will get you out of this marriage with your dignity intact. Your husband will be given no other choice but to cooperate and in all of your interests, we can end this in a dignified manner that will be yesterday's news by the time it surfaces. Do you trust me, Sally?"

She looks at me and I see the uncertainty driven from her eyes by what I can only describe as hope. Suddenly, she isn't alone anymore. She is vulnerable and in a bad place and looks at me with the relief of someone who now has a burden shared. I see the gratitude and the acceptance and she says with such emotion it even makes me swallow hard. "Thank you....?"

We laugh as I hold out my hand. "Victoria Marshall, rottweiler lawyer at your service."

As she takes my hand in hers and shakes it firmly we share the look of a common purpose and I won't let her down.

26

December 14th

11 Days to Go

Waking up the next morning beside Charlie is one of the best experiences of my life. That is until the events of last night come flooding back and I remember the stunt I pulled in front of my greatest influence.

When Sally and I returned to the party I tried to act as if nothing had happened. Charlie introduced me to Karren, but she was polite and reserved and made a quick escape from my company. By the time the guests left I felt like a complete social pariah.

I must groan as I remember it and Charlie laughs beside me.

"Don't worry, Vick. My family won't think anything about last night. It's the sort of thing my mother has always done and if anything, it makes them love you all the more."

Sitting up, I look at him and wince. "Maybe, but that isn't me, Charlie. I'm not that person and have spent years trying not to be. But never mind, it was all in a good cause and things worked out in the end."

He looks at me gratefully. "Thanks for what you did, Vick. I mean that. Only Emily and I know what a mess you avoided and words can't explain how much that meant to us both."

He looks at me with such a loving look my world stands still. He says softly, "I knew you were the girl for me. I'm not sure why given the fact you obviously couldn't stand the sight of me for most of the time, but I always knew."

I grin. "It's true, you are annoying. You still are but you have worn me down. You have chipped away at every defence I've ever set in place and weakened them forever. I feel a little foolish really, now I come to think of it."

He takes my hand and says softly, "Do you want to tell me the reason for those defences?"

Shaking my head sadly, I take a deep breath.

"The thing is, Emily's story rings true for me too. I was once taken in by a man much like Marcus. He was older than me and everything I thought I wanted. I'd just started university and worked in his office during the holidays. He flattered me, complimented me and made me feel as if I counted in a big way. We started seeing each other, and I never knew he was married. He told me he was separated from his wife and why would I question that?"

Charlie smiles at me reassuringly, "It's ok, carry on."

Sighing heavily, I continue. "It only finished when I took him to a party a friend was having at

Uni. I'd boasted to everyone about my new boyfriend and how mature he was and not like the kids we had to endure during lectures and break. I suppose I was a little supercilious and thought I had it all worked out. So, you can imagine how proud I was to walk into that party holding the hand of what I considered the best catch there. It appears that I was the only one who thought so. I had to endure my own fair share of raised eyebrows and sniggers that night. I couldn't understand why? Surely, they could see what I saw. Apparently not. They saw things for what they really were. A gullible young girl escorting an older man who looked completely out of place at a student party."

Charlie winces. "I know those looks, Vick. I've watched my own parents take their fair share of them over the years and it's not very pleasant. So, what happened next?"

I say quietly. "Much like yesterday as it happens. His wife somehow found out that he was cheating on her and followed us there. We were dancing at the time and I'm embarrassed to admit that wasn't all we were doing. The next thing I knew, I was pulled roughly away from him and she slapped me hard across the face. I think I was in shock because I did nothing but stare at her as she rained blows down upon me. Even her husband did nothing as she well and truly laid into me in front of the entire party. It took a couple of guys to pull her away as

248

she continued to scream names at me as she was pulled from the room."

Charlie looks shocked and I smile weakly. "I suppose I deserved it but I didn't deserve the total idiot that I thought I loved. He didn't even look back as he raced after his wife and I never saw him again. I never returned to work and just hid in my room for the rest of the year."

Charlie pulls me close and his arms caress my back offering a comfort I wish I'd had back then. Sniffing into his chest, I stutter. "I never went to another party again. I couldn't bear the looks, the smirks and the whispers that followed me wherever I went. After a while, people stopped asking me and I became somewhat of a recluse. All I focused on was my studies. I'd show them all. I would make the best of myself and never let my guard down again. Nobody would ever ridicule me or hurt me in that way again and I've done a good job of standing by those values ever since."

To my surprise, Charlie laughs softly and retorts, "You don't say. It does explain a lot though."

Despite myself, I laugh with him. "Yes, I suppose it does. Maybe it explains why I am the way I am, although it doesn't excuse it. I made myself into a machine and I don't like myself most days, let alone expect anyone else to."

Charlie says nothing and just holds me. It doesn't matter because words don't matter. All that does is holding me so tenderly and it feels comforting and natural. I cling onto Charlie like the lifeline he is and only pull back when he says softly, "Well, I like you, Victoria Matthews. I have for quite some time now. You thought you were being so clever hiding from me but I always knew."

I pull away and smile, "Knew what, Charlie Monroe?"

He smiles sweetly. "That you would be the girl I could love."

Tears blind my eyes as I look into his blue ones that are brimming with love. I savour the moment because this moment is one that needs to wrapped up and cherished for the rest of my life. It will keep me warm in the darkest times as the memory wraps me in comfort and chases the bad ones away. Moments like this come but once in a lifetime when you find your true love. As I look into his eyes, I mean every word I say when I say softly, "I love you, Charlie. God only knows how it happened but I do. You are the first man that I ever have and I hope you will be the last."

Charlie just smirks that annoying cheeky grin that used to drive me wild and says, "I love you too, you annoying woman. I'm not sure how it happened but I know it was always meant to. Just don't hold it against me, what can I say, you wore me down."

Laughing, he pulls me close and kisses me so passionately and yet so sweetly I know I'm where I was always meant to be.

We almost forgot about the Advent challenge until I remember as we head down to breakfast. Grabbing my phone, I looked at the little window in the email with excitement.

"What do you think it could be today, Charlie?"

He laughs. "Who knows? Wrestling polar bears in an ice room, perhaps?"

Grinning, I move over to him and we stare at the screen together.

Take two children to a Pantomime.

I look at Charlie and groan. "How on earth are we going to manage that? I think I'd rather the polar bear option."

He shrugs. "I'm sure there are lots of choices around. Do you know any children we could kidnap for the occasion?"

The cold hands of dread clutch my heart and squeeze it tightly as I groan. "Unfortunately, I do and it involves the scariest visit of them all—my sister."

I leave Charlie to organise us four tickets to a nearby Pantomime and take a deep breath as I prepare to make the call I always dread making.

Not that I dislike my sister, I don't. The trouble is, she lives her life very differently to me and I always feel as if she judges me and finds me sorely lacking. Deep inside I know she is right to. I've never been a good sister and always froze her out. The only time I ever visited was when the occasion dictated it. Weddings, births and funerals. Even Christmas day was always spent in a hurry. I would turn up and make polite conversation before inventing an excuse to leave. I'm ashamed to admit that I never wanted to be a part of my family because like everyone else, they look at me as if I am an alien from the planet Zarg. They never understood my drive and ambition. They always thought I was too wrapped up in my own importance and they were probably right. I never offered to help in any way and just found fault with everything they did in life. I raised myself above them and then looked down at my own family. Maybe the shame in me keeps me from witnessing the looks of disappointment they always give me when I do visit.

Seeing how Charlie and Emily accept their own parents, despite not agreeing with the way they do things, makes me feel even worse. I'm a horrible person and I can't think why Charlie appears to like me so much.

Steeling myself, I dial the number and wait with trepidation. As the phone rings, I feel more nervous than I thought possible. Then I hear a terse, "Twice in as many weeks. What's the matter, have you been born again or something?"

Fighting back my usual acid retort I say softly, "Hi, Lisa. How are you?"

"How am I you ask? How am I? Well, let me tell you how I am, totally knackered, fed up with Christmas already and at the end of a very short tether. That's how I am. The kids are out of control and I have a husband who doesn't seem to care. My own mother can't find the time to babysit to give me a break and any friends I have are in the same position as me. Parenthood these days is in crisis. The world is hurtling along taking our children's childhoods with it. I am dealing with miniature adults who think absolutely everything they see on trash TV is real life and demand I give it to them. I am having to sell everything on eBay just to raise funds to buy it all and am very close to eBaying my own family to the highest bidder just to keep my sanity."

I cough nervously. "Um… well, it all sounds… um… difficult, to say the least."

"Difficult you say, I say downright impossible. What happened to me, Vicky? At what point in life did I sign up to all this? I thought life was like Little House on the Prairie and The Brady Bunch. Children were content to skip through meadows and help with the chores. There were no incessant demands and screaming fits if the latest Apple device didn't magically show up in an Amazon box. Children back then made camps and rode their bikes. We played out. *Played out* I tell you, remember that? Nowadays there's no such thing as playing out. In fact, there's no such thing as playing, unless it involves a computer screen and a set of noise reduction headphones. Did our mother see us from one hour to the next? No, she was happy baking and being the mother dreams are made of. How did it get to this hey, Vicky? You tell me."

I feel a bit awkward now. In fact, awkward and worried at the state of my sister's mental health. She is on the edge and I should now be extremely worried about the safety of my niece and nephew. How did I not know she was finding it so hard? My sister Lisa was always so together and assured. She was beautiful and had many friends and boys flocking around her. She could have been anything she wanted to be and yet those dreams fell away with all her ambition when she met and married the first boy that asked her. She never had that amazing career she always promised herself as a buyer in a department store. She was going to travel the world on a shopping spree with somebody else's money and yet here she is now, cleaning offices when the children sleep, while her husband tinkers with his motorbike and pretends to be looking for a job.

She sighs wearily, "Anyway, what can I do you for?"

Fighting back the irritation at her sentence choice, I say brightly, "Yes, well, just call me your Fairy Godmother because you, my dear sister, have earned yourself a night off."

Just for a moment, there is silence and then she says roughly, "Ok, who is this? I know it's not my sister because she wouldn't say any of those words. Who are you because if you are a child abductor, I can have them packed and ready within the hour?"

A small smile moves to my lips and I remember how she always used to make me laugh. "Ok, I deserved that, Lisa. I've been a rubbish Aunt and I want to make it up to you. How about I come by this evening and take Thomas and Sophie off your hands for the evening? I'll even pay for you to go out for a nice meal with Bradley and have a date night."

She laughs out loud. "Make it Justin Timberlake and you have a deal. Where's the fun in going out with Bradley? We would run out of conversation before we even ordered. The last time we had a conversation he asked me for £10 to place on a horse at the Epsom Derby. You know, I always used to think you were gay, Vicky. You never had a boyfriend after that unfortunate incident and I thought it had turned you. I even envied you because nothing can be as bad as putting up with the opposite sex on a daily basis. At least a woman would make conversation and share make up tips. She would sit and watch Love Island without any derogatory comments and be actually interested in what I have to say."

I laugh despite myself and she gasps. "Did you just laugh, Vicky? Wow, I didn't know you could. Have you been on the gin again?"

I can hear Charlie heading back into the room and quickly wrap up the call.

"Anyway, it's been good to chat but we should really get going if we're to make it in time for the panto. Have the children ready by 6.30 and we'll pick them up then."

I quickly hang up before she can ask me who *we* is, and groan. "There, job done. Two children/mini-adults secured for my part of the challenge."

Charlie grins. "Four tickets to see Aladdin at Wimbledon Theatre booked and paid for. Now, all we need is to escape from this place and head back to normality."

I throw him a pained look.

"If you think we are heading back to normality, you are seriously mistaken. I can only apologise for what you are about to experience."

Charlie laughs loudly. "This I can't wait to see."

27

We head back to London and I wish for the umpteenth time that we were spending the night cuddling on the settee watching Christmas films. A night in with Charlie is all I really want but instead, we are heading to Sutton to pick up my family and take them to see a group of people dressed up as the opposite sex.

Women become men and men women. I can't even remember the last time I saw a Panto and wonder if they've changed at all over the years.

I direct Charlie to my sister's house and wonder what he must be thinking. He will never have experienced anything like this in his privileged life and the snob in me is flushed with embarrassment. However, the girl in me feels as if she is coming home. This is familiar to me. I lived here for many years and knew no different. We never had much but at least we had love.

As I think about my childhood, I feel ashamed of myself once again. My mother tried so hard to make up for the fact our father wasn't around. She never had much, but she was always cheerful and interested in everything we did. I can't ever remember her raising her voice or telling us off. She used to reason with us and make us think about things logically. Maybe that's where I learned my craft. I owe it to her for guiding me on the right path and am ashamed that I can't even remember the last time I visited her.

However, I don't have time to dwell on it before the Sat Nav guides us into my sister's road and I steel myself for the night ahead.

We pull up outside a semi-detached house with a garden that's in need of a Gardner's World rescue operation. Bradley's bike dominates the whole front drive and there are broken pots and dirty rags littering the concrete paving that has grass growing up through the cracks. My heart sinks as I see the paint peeling on the front door and the cracks in the step up to it.

Charlie smiles reassuringly as I knock loudly on the door. My heart beats wildly as I hear footsteps and then the light blinds me as it's flung open and my sister stands looking at me with a mixture of emotions on her face. I smile and she looks at me and then Charlie then me again and I say awkwardly, "Aren't you going to ask us in?"

Grinning, she steps aside and smiles sweetly at Charlie. "Hi, I'm Lisa, Vicky's sister. I'm pleased to meet you…?"

Holding out his hand Charlie says, "Charlie. Vicky's boyfriend as of yesterday."

Lisa looks across at me and I see the envy in her eyes. Then she nods her appreciation and shouts, "Bradley, come and say hi to Vicky and Charlie."

We follow her into the living room and see the rest of them looking at us with curiosity. Bradley smiles nervously. "Um… hi, Vicky; long-time no see."

I return his smile and draw Charlie beside me. "Hi, Bradley, children. It's good to see you all. Sorry to land on you like this but we thought it might be fun."

Shaking her head, Lisa says loudly, "Grab your coats kids. Remember to do everything Vicky and Charlie tell you and no answering back."

Two little faces look at us with extremely worried expressions and my heart sinks. I am a stranger to them and they are probably cursing their mother for agreeing to this. Charlie winks at them and says loudly, "This will be fun, guys. I promise to buy as much popcorn as you can eat and if you're good, you can choose where we eat afterwards."

Sophie looks interested. "Can we eat at Frankie and Benny's? My friend Melissa's been there and says it's amazing."

Charlie smiles. "Good choice. I think that could be arranged."

Looking somewhat reassured, the kids head off and Lisa looks worried. "Listen. You don't have to do all this, really. The Panto is more than enough and we wouldn't expect you to put yourselves out."

Once again, I feel bad and look at her guiltily, "Don't be silly. I have many years to make up for and this will be the start of many more nights like this."

Reaching into my purse, I pull out some cash and press it into her hand. "I meant what I said. I want you to get dressed up and go and have a meal on me. You deserve a night out and I should have thought about offering to do this a long time ago."

Just for a moment, I think she's going to refuse. She's always been a proud woman but then her face softens and she steps forward and hugs me, whispering, "Thanks, Sis. This means a lot you know, and it's not just the money."

Choking back the tears, I say quietly. "It means more to me, Lisa. I'm sorry, I've been such a bad sister. I don't know how I'm going to make it up to you but I want to try at least. This is the only way I know how and means more to me than anything."

Leaning back, she fixes me with a determined look. "We're family, Vicky and that will never change. You have worked so hard to get where you are and nothing will ever take that away from you. So what if you've been a little pre-occupied with that? You don't get to be successful without some form of sacrifice. We're proud of you, all of us are and I'm just grateful that at least one of us made it out of this place."

Suddenly, the years melt away and we are back in that bedroom we shared. Two sisters with everything in front of them. I always looked up to my sister and still do. She is the strongest person I've ever met and speaks the most sense. I've missed having her to confide in and it's only my own judgemental ways that have prevented me from sharing her life.

The kids race back into the room as we pull apart and I say awkwardly, "Well, we had better be heading off. Enjoy your evening, guys, we should be back around 10."

Lisa and Bradley walk us to the door and watch as we bundle their kids into the back of Charlie's Porsche. Lisa rolls her eyes as we wave our goodbyes.

28

Well, this is awkward. We travel in silence as I don't know what on earth to say to my own niece and nephew. Any words that come to mind sound stuffy and lacking in any warmth or humanity. I am used to talking to my staff and clients but these children are scaring the hell out of me.

After about ten minutes Charlie says loudly, "Shall we listen to some Christmas songs to get us in the mood?"

Sophie says with no interest, "Only if it's Taylor Swift or Little Mix."

Thomas yells. "No way. I can't stand another minute of listening to that rubbish. Can't you play the new one by Usher?"

Sophie yells, "I asked first, not you. It's my turn, you had your songs on yesterday. You can listen to your rubbish on your headphones."

Thomas yells, "This isn't your car, you don't get to decide."

I look at Charlie in horror and he winks as he blasts out the Christmas playlist, effectively silencing the warring children.

Luckily, Wimbledon isn't that far and we soon find a parking space and I try to relax. I can do this. They are only children and the Panto will soon distract their attention.

We head towards the theatre and Sophie moans. "I'm cold. Is it far?"

I look at her incredulously as the huge neon sign looms before us signifying that it's not far at all.

I say pointedly, "Look up and you'll see it right in front of you."

She whines. "I can see that, but is it far?"

Thomas shouts, "Don't be stupid, Sophie. You can see we're nearly there. You're such an idiot."

She pushes him and yells, "Shut up, You're the idiot, not me. You don't get to call me names. I'll tell mum."

I look at Charlie in utter disbelief and he winks before saying, "Ok, first one there is in charge for the evening. Race you."

He starts to run and is closely followed by the two nightmares. I don't run. In fact, I even briefly consider running in the opposite direction. No wonder Lisa's on the edge. It's been thirty minutes and I'm already craving alcohol to get me through this. I bet that skater family don't have this to contend with. I expect their children are textbook and they talk about educational things and share ideas, not shout and argue over absolutely nothing.

By the time I catch up with them they are queuing for the tickets and appear to be arguing about who won.

"I won, Sophie, didn't I Charlie? You saw I reached the door first."

"Shut up idiot, I won because my glove touched it first."

"Only because you threw it. Your hand wasn't inside it so I won, didn't I, Charlie?"

Charlie looks thoughtful. "That's true. Technically you both won. I mean, Sophie's glove did, in fact, touch the door first but she wasn't in it. Therefore, the glove won but has no say in what we do for the rest of the evening. Thomas's hand did touch the door first, which means he could have a say in it. However, what you are both forgetting is that I was also in the race and actually got there first, so really I won and now get to make all the decisions."

The children groan as Charlie smirks and I say loudly, "So that's decided, Charlie wins. How about we leave him to collect the tickets and you can join me in the line for popcorn? That's one decision you can both make for yourselves."

The children grin and follow me to yet another line filled with extremely loud children, all dressed up in either woolly jumpers or glittering Disney dresses. In fact, even the adults are wearing fancy dress. Some are wearing bright Christmas jumpers with reindeer Antlers on their heads. There are also many bauble earrings and tinsel scarves. The men look around them with resigned expressions and the women chatter excitedly with anyone who will listen. The children demand everything on offer and I look with horror as they brandish weird light sabre plastic wands and use them as weapons on their friends.

Sophie yells, "I want one of those."

Thomas follows. "Me too, Aunty Vicky. Can we?"

I shrug and say for an easy life, "Of course you can."

We soon reach the front of the line and the children ask for huge bags of popcorn and large containers of fizzy drink. The plastic wands are on full display and I ask for one each of those to go with everything else. £30 later and I'm in shock. This is daylight robbery. These toys must have cost pennies to produce and they are charging more mark-up than a pay day loan. The lawyer in me rises for a fight but then I notice the children rushing off as they proceed to hit each other over the head with their new weapons, spilling popcorn as they go.

Thrusting the money at the bored looking assistant, I accompany it with my fiercest glare. That's the only satisfaction I get as I chase after my two charges, praying that the child snatcher doesn't get to them first.

By the time I catch them up, they are stuffing huge handfuls of popcorn in their mouths and having a burping contest.

Charlie soon finds us and I gaze at him helplessly. Is this what parenting is really like? I've seen animals more well behaved and I'm sure if these were my children they would be waiting patiently while sipping on a vegetable smoothie with only a snack box of fresh fruit and nuts to feed their brains.

Feeling slightly calmer at the thought of my own perfect children I smile at Charlie. "So what next?"

He looks at his watch. "Ten minutes until curtain lift off."

Thomas hits him on the back with his wand and yells, "Do you want a sword fight, Charlie?"

Charlie laughs and spins around and rugby tackles Thomas to the ground in a play fight and after a minute I'm not sure who the bigger kid is. Sophie looks at me and raises her eyes, shaking her head as she says, "Boys."

Laughing, I nod in agreement and pull her slightly away from the fighting and say, "So, tell me, Sophie, how are things? Do you have any idea about what you want to do with your life?"

Sophie looks at me as if I'm some sort of moron and says, "I'm only seven, Aunty Vicky. There's plenty of time for all that."

I nod. "True enough but it doesn't hurt to set goals and objectives at a very early age. For instance, it doesn't have to be about a job. It could be to win a competition at school, or achieve high grades in your chosen subject. You may want to win a sports tournament or join a circle of friends who inspire you. There may be that part in the school play you would like to play or you may set your goals closer to home and vow to keep your room tidy."

She thinks about it for a second and then looks at me with an animated gleam in her eye. "There is something I want more than anything."

I smile benevolently, ready to impart my wisdom and devise her a bullet point plan to get there. "Which is?"

"I want an iPhone X for Christmas and an Instagram account. I could post selfies of myself and become famous."

Ok, not what I expected to hear but I give her my best considered look. "So, how will you go about securing the item?"

She shrugs and throws me a pitying look. "I asked Santa for it, so I'll definitely get it."

Once again, I try to look objectively at the problem. "What if he doesn't deal in Adult toys?"

She shrugs. "Then he'll go out of business before the New Year. All the kids want these days are phones and computers. If I was Santa, I would roll with the changes. I mean, you hear about shops closing all the time that don't. Mum was in a really bad mood when Woolworths closed but we never actually shopped there. All she cared about was the pick and mix but they sell that in Tescos. You see, Auntie Vicky, the world is now different to when you were young. My generation demands the best of everything and if you don't keep up, you fall behind in every way. I like to be ahead of the game and if you snooze you lose."

I just stare, I mean, really, I do. Tears spring to my eyes and to both our surprise, I reach over and hug my little niece hard. I feel so proud I could burst and whisper with pure emotion in my voice. "Good for you, Sophie. Don't let anything stand in your way and strive for excellence at all times. You'll be just fine, I just know it."

As we pull apart, I look into my nieces' eyes and we share the same look. I understand her and she does me. Yes, we are from the same family and god only knows how but there is a lot of me inside this tiny child. I was that child too. I saw things in black and white and never saw the boundaries. So, what if what she desires is trivial? She has a purpose and the determination within her to see it through. Maybe I can help alter the perspective on her goals a little and guide her on the right path. Maybe it's time to step up and become the sort of Aunt I should have been from the beginning.

As the bell rings to call us to our seats, I take her little hand in mine and follow the two annoying males in our party to our seats.

It's been more years than I care to remember but it soon all comes flooding back. I love Panto!

Charlie and I laugh louder than the children at what can only be described as the most fun I've had in ages. The popcorn ran out ages ago and I giggle with the rest of the audience as we watch the madness unfold on the stage before our very eyes.

Sophie and Thomas forget they are cool kids and join in with the rest of them. We all shout the usual, 'behind you' and 'Oh no you're not' along with the entire audience. It doesn't matter if you are 2 years old or 90 this appeals to all ages and I vow immediately to make it a yearly tradition from now on.

The only fly in the ointment was when Thomas's wand entangled itself in Sophie's hair. It took the patience of a saint—in this case Charlie, to sort that one out but it didn't take Sophie long to forgive and forget, so it all ended well.

We headed to Frankie and Benny's afterward and enjoyed burgers and fries and replayed every scene in the panto several times over.

By the time we take the children home we are all firm friends.

Lisa is waiting and looks at the excited faces around her with surprise. "Wow, you all look as if you've had the best time ever."

Thomas shouts, "We did, mummy. Charlie's great and Auntie Vicky is nothing like you described her as. She is actually really nice."

Sophie nods as my sister colours up and tries to gloss over the subject. Raising her eyes, she whispers, "Children and their imaginations, whatever am I to do with them?"

I just smile. She was probably right anyway. It's taken what is turning out to be a very clever Advent challenge to make me see myself as others do. Mr Rowanson has worked a miracle here and no matter what happens with the company, I feel as if I have learned a valuable lesson these last couple of weeks.

As Charlie chats with Bradley and the children head off to get changed for bed, Lisa draws me over to one side. "Listen, Vicky, thanks so much for tonight. I can't tell you how much we appreciated it."

I smile and say with interest, "So how was your date?"

She grins. "Great as it happens. We actually made time to have a proper adult conversation. We talked about everything and Bradley even promised to step up his job hunting and help out a bit more around the house. We talked about everything and I was reminded why I married him in the first place."

I breathe a huge sigh of relief as this could have gone the other way. "I'm happy for you, Lisa. You know, anytime you want a babysitter just shout. I didn't think I would, but I loved spending time with Thomas and Sophie. I'm just sorry it took me so long to realise."

Looking over at Charlie, Lisa smiles. "He's a good influence on you, Vicky. He seems really nice too. How did you meet? Was it Tinder?"

Laughing, I just say, "You know me, Lisa. I met him at work."

Rolling her eyes, she says brightly, "Well, maybe you'll have more of a private life now. So, what are your plans for Christmas this year?"

"I'm not sure. Charlie's parents asked me there, but I told them I had to spend it at mums. They told me to ask her to theirs but you know her, she likes to stay near home for Christmas."

Lisa grins. "Then ask them to mine. You can all come, it'll be fun."

Charlie hears her and says loudly, "That sounds like a plan, Lisa. Surely it will be too much for you though."

She shakes her head. "The more the merrier. Run it by your family, Charlie. They may not want to come, but if they do, they would be more than welcome."

I look at Charlie in abject horror. There is no way on God's earth I want Linda and Harry rocking up to Lisa's so I just smile. "Thanks, we'll ask but it might be best if I come here and Charlie goes to his family. Christmas is stressful enough as it is without adding to your burden."

Lisa smiles as Charlie comes over and drapes his arm around my shoulders. "Come on, Vick, let's get you home. It's getting late and if I know you, you'll be up early and ready to take the legal world by storm for another week."

Grateful for the change of subject, I follow him outside. As I turn to leave, I hug my sister and say softly, "Thanks, sis. Listen, let me buy the Christmas food as my contribution. I'll order it from Ocado and have it delivered on the 23rd. My treat."

Lisa laughs. "You'll be lucky. All the slots probably went weeks ago. I doubt you'd get a delivery before the New Year."

I smirk with a great deal of satisfaction as I say airily, "Then it's a good job I'm prepared. I booked my slot as soon as they were released courtesy of a notification on my phone. I'll just swap the delivery address and job done. Email me your preferences and I'll do the rest."

Lisa bursts out laughing and says to Charlie, "Are you sure you know what you're taking on?"

He grins and kisses me on the cheek. "I know very well what I'm taking on and nobody is happier than me about it."

Grinning, we say our goodbyes and for the first time in many years, I am actually looking forward to Christmas with my family.

29

December 18th

7 Days to Go

I'm not sure where this week has gone, but I have loved every minute of it. Despite being extremely busy with work Charlie and I have kept to the deal and completed every challenge set.

Monday's challenge was to organise an office party which we arranged for Christmas Eve. Tuesday was to make a Christmas gift for a loved one. We decided to go to Charlie's and make a variety of sweets courtesy of recipes from the Internet. I think we ate more than we made but for a first attempt, I was pleased with the results.

Wednesday involved writing Christmas cards and mailing them out and today we are going late night shopping for Christmas gifts for our family.

We've decided to go to Oxford Street so we can see the Christmas lights and grab a meal out in Covent Garden.

I'm sure all the staff know that Charlie and I are more than just colleagues. Despite maintaining a professional relationship at work, I can't disguise how happy I am. The fact we have our lunch and arrive and leave together says it all for us.

I am also working on extricating Sally Adams from her marriage and so things are full on at the moment.

For the first time in years, I leave the office at 6 pm ready for some retail therapy. Charlie and I take the Tube to Oxford Circus and stroll hand in hand down the busy street. We stare at the glittering shop windows and appreciate the excitement all around us. London is lit up in all its glory and is a breath-taking sight as we weave our way from shop to shop gathering brightly coloured packages as we go.

Despite the cold, I feel warm inside. Christmas is so magical when shared and far from dreading it this year, I can't wait. The only problem I have is what to buy Charlie. For the man who has everything, this is a hard one. I don't know him well enough to know what he likes and dislikes and there isn't much time left to find out.

However, all I can think of now is spending the most enjoyable evening with the man beside me.

We finish our shopping and head to a great restaurant in Covent Garden that's popular with the city workers. After we've ordered Charlie looks at me with concern.

"You know, Vick, it's only been a few weeks but I feel as if I've known you all my life. Does that make sense?"

I nod in agreement. "Perfect sense. Maybe that's what happens when you meet the person you were always meant to. I'm not sure about you, Charlie but I feel so comfortable around you. There have been none of the usual stilted conversations and worrying about what to say or do to keep the interest alive."

Leaning over, Charlie takes my hand and kisses it gallantly. "Same. Who knows, maybe Donald saw something we never did?"

"Then again, maybe he hasn't seen this coming at all and if he finds out neither of us will get the job. He may not like mixing business with pleasure and take steps to alter things."

"Do you think he will?"

Shaking my head, I smile reassuringly. "If he does object, I'll step down. You can have the job, in fact, the more I think of it the more I think it's an excellent idea."

Looking alarmed, he shakes his head vigorously. "Absolutely not. You deserve this job just as much as me if not more and I would never allow you to do that. It wouldn't be fair."

"What do you mean?"

He grins wickedly. "I want to beat you in a fair fight, Vick. If I win, you'll know I'm superior to you and if you win, we'll both know you just got lucky."

Throwing my serviette at him, I shake my head in pretend anger.

"You're so sure of yourself, aren't you? Well, let me tell you, if I win, I'll make you my PA and expect you to do all the menial jobs. You will have to make me coffee and fetch my dry cleaning. You'll work late and start early and I will insist you accompany me to all my meetings and take notes, leaving only to make the sandwiches. You see, Charlie, when and I mean, *when* I win, your life will become a misery."

We look at each other and burst out laughing. We actually don't care who wins. In fact, I feel as if I've won already. What can be better than winning Charlie's affections? For once in my life work is taking second place, and it feels good. However, we have a bigger problem than the Advent challenge. Leaning over, I whisper, "What on earth are we going to do about Christmas Day? There is no way on earth your parents will want to spend it at my sisters. Shall we just say they couldn't make it?"

Charlie rolls his eyes. "You're such a snob, Vick. Why wouldn't my family enjoy spending time with yours? They don't care about where they spend it, just who with."

I shake my head. "Please, Charlie, don't mention it to them. Maybe next year but I need this year to make my own peace with my family. There's too much going on and it will all be too much."

He smiles sweetly.

"Leave it with me, babe. I'll make sure you have the best Christmas ever."

30

December 19th

6 Days to Go

When the Advent challenge hits my Inbox the next morning, at first my heart sinks and then I think about it differently.

Go Carol singing.

Ok, I am no singer. In fact, I can safely say I should never be entrusted with a microphone in front of any other living being. However, this is a challenge I am very much looking forward to taking on because where I am heading is long overdue.

The phone rings and as I answer it, I hear.

♫ "*Good King Wenceslas last looked out on the feast of Steven!*" ♫

Laughing, I groan, "Enough already. You sound as good as I do."

Sounding hurt, Charlie whines, "What are you saying? For all you know I could have auditioned for the Voice. In fact, I may have even been unanimously selected and got through the six-chair challenge. The battles were won by me and then I subsequently stole the show. It was only because duty called here that I forego a lifetime of sell-out concerts and record deals just to try to win your heart."

I shake my head. "Maybe in your dreams, Charlie but the reality is about to hit you hard. Don't make claims you can't back up because you're about to be sorely tested."

He laughs, "Well, I have this friend on Facebook…"

I interrupt quickly, "Not this time. This time I have a plan and what's more, it's well within the rules of Christmas spirit and will help me accomplish something I've been meaning to do for some time."

Now he's not laughing as he says with interest, "What is it?"

"I'll tell you later. Just meet me after work and you can come home with me this weekend for a change."

I hang up and feel the nerves start to take hold. This could go either way. Either my plan will work, or we will look incredibly stupid. Whatever the outcome I need to try.

Charlie and I manage to grab something quick to eat and then change into warm clothes ready for a night carolling. I have refused to enlighten him until we are in my car and heading to the place I've been meaning to visit for some time—home.

Charlie looks at me in surprise as I tell him where we're going.

"What's the big deal with going home, Vick? To be honest, if I rocked up spilling Christmas carols at my parents' house they wouldn't think twice. Probably just think I'd called into the pub on my way home. Why is this such a big deal?"

I take a deep breath and prepare to divulge yet another snippet of my past.

"When I was at school, I was quite a shy child."

Charlie snorts and I shrug. "I know it's hard to believe, but I had no confidence. Well, I was chosen to sing at one of the school plays and my mum was very proud. She always was of anything we did and I didn't really appreciate that at the time. I spent many nights worrying about it. I must have been Sophie's age at the time and the worry even made me wet the bed. I had nightmares about it but my mum wouldn't let me back out. She told me I had to face my fears in life head on and then they wouldn't have a hold over me. Anything was achievable with a little courage and self-belief. Well, I tried every trick in the book to get out of it but she was firm. I tried to make myself sick and even called The Samaritans for help."

Charlie laughs and then instantly looks contrite as I flash him a pained look. "I'm unburdening the darkest part of my soul to you and you find it funny?"

He tries to look sympathetic but I can still see his mouth twitching. "Anyway, the dreaded day came and with it the concert. Mum had bought me a frilly dress for the occasion and plaited my hair with big pink ribbons. I looked awful and yet it brought tears to her eyes. Despite our poor childhood, we were rich in our mother's love. So, it was for that fact alone that I faced the dreaded ordeal so I didn't let her down. The trouble is, when it came to it, I took one look at the silent audience and lost it. The lights were on my solitary figure on the stage and the silence overwhelmed me. I could feel their eyes on me and it was too scary. The music started, and the teacher was smiling at me with encouragement. I opened my mouth but nothing came out. The music started again and still nothing. There was nothing I could do but stand there like a deer in headlights and stare back at the audience. Then the unthinkable happened, and I had an accident in full view of everyone and my shame was complete."

Charlie gasps, "What, did you fall off the stage or the light fall on your head?"

Shaking my head, I say in a whisper, "No, Charlie. The accident was one of nature. To be blunt, I wet myself."

Charlie looks at me in horror and I wince with remembered mortification.

"So, you see I never did face that particular fear because after that day nobody ever asked me to sing again. I suppose they didn't want to dredge up the bad memories. Well, tonight is my chance to face it and what better way than to knock on my mum's door who I haven't seen in at least three months and sing to the one woman I owe it all to."

Reaching out, Charlie grabs my hand and squeezes it hard. "Good for you, babe. I'll be right beside you so don't worry about a thing."

I say softly, "I know you will. I can count on you, I know that and I wouldn't want it any other way."

It doesn't take us long to reach the place I grew up, which shows how awful I really am because I could pop by most evenings if I wanted to. I'm not sure why I don't, really. It's not as if I dislike my mum but I hate seeing that she still lives in the same place with the same problems. Every time I visit it strikes me how hard her life is and yet she won't accept any help. She has her friends and her belongings as she puts it and doesn't want to move away from that. It angers me so I keep away. For all my ambition she has none, and that is what I find hard to understand. I think I must take after my father who I believe left to emigrate to Australia for a better life.

We turn into Hadrian's Close and the familiar houses rear up out of the darkness. I point to a house we pass and say, "My best friend Annalise lived there. She married a builder and they live in Surbiton now. Oh, and over there was my first boyfriend. Jimmy Miggins from number 2."

Charlie laughs loudly. "Little Jimmy Miggins. I wonder what became of him?"

I grin. "He became big James the Migster and became a professional wrestler."

Charlie goes quiet as I point to the corner shop. "I used to go there to spend my pocket money. Usually on a notebook and a pen or some other stationery related item."

Charlie laughs. "Not pick and mix then?"

"No, that was always Lisa's preference, not mine. I wanted anything I could jot down my goals in."

Charlie smiles and squeezes my hand again. "You're one of a kind, babe."

As we reach the place where my dreams were made, I turn the engine off and take a deep breath. This is the final piece of my life I need to show Charlie. I come from humble beginnings unlike him and he is about to find out how the other half lives.

Charlie looks at me thoughtfully as I sit staring at the house before me. It's a small maisonette that always seemed huge as a child. Now it looks run down and tiny yet will always be home to me.

Charlie says softly, "You ready, Vick?"

Smiling, I take a deep breath and say with determination. "Come on. It's time to face my longest running fear."

Hand in hand, we walk up the small path towards a front door that has seen better days.

Charlie whispers, "What's the plan?"

I look at him thoughtfully. "I think maybe Silent Night. It's fairly easy to remember and I quite like it."

He nods as I take a deep breath and knock loudly on the door.

We hear footsteps and the hall light goes on. Through the net curtains, I see a shape heading towards the door and swallow hard. This is it.

As the door opens, we break out into song.

♫ *Silent night, holy night!*
All is calm, all is bright.
Round yon Virgin, Mother and Child.
Holy infant so tender and mild,
Sleep in heavenly peace,
Sleep in heavenly peace……. ♫

The tears blind me as I see the incredulous expression on my mum's face. At first, she doesn't even realise it's me but as we continue, I see the penny drop and her tears mirror my own.

She looks between us and I feel my soul melt as I stare at the mother I love with all my heart. She looks small and vulnerable, yet has a happiness to her that she wears well. Her eyes sparkle as she holds mine and I see the emotion in them as we carry on singing.

Charlie, to his credit, sings as loudly as he can at a stranger's door and it makes me love him even more. What man would put himself through making a public spectacle of himself in front of his girlfriend's mother that he's meeting for the first time? Charlie would, and now I know how special he really is.

Somehow, we stumble our way to the end of the song and as I face my mother with the tears spilling down my cheeks, I say, "Good to see you, mum."

She holds out her arms and I fall into them as I used to as a child. For a long moment, we hug each other and the years melt away. There is no barrier between us of my own creation. There is no stilted conversation and no judgemental stares. She doesn't look at me in fear as she always does when I come calling. That look always made me feel ashamed of myself for making her feel that way. I hated that look and allowed it to keep me away rather than address the problem—*me*.

After a while, we pull back and she smiles with genuine emotion. "That was the best Christmas present I could ever have wished for."

Smiling hard, I reach out and pull Charlie forward. "Charlie, allow me to introduce you to my mother, Pauline. Mum, this is Charlie, my boyfriend."

Mum's eyes light up and she looks happier than I've seen her look in ages. She hugs Charlie and says happily, "Welcome, Charlie. It's very good to meet you. Now come in from the cold and tell me your news over a nice cup of tea."

We follow her into the small living room that is so familiar to me. All around us is my past. The settee where I used to curl up and watch the documentaries I craved as I was growing up. The table where I sat and did my homework while dreaming of a brighter future. The photographs on the sideboard that was a find in the local Missionary Mart.

As my mum makes the tea, Charlie joins me as I look at the many photographs that have accumulated over the years. He looks at them with interest as I point them out.

"This is me when I was in Junior school. Even then I was pretending it was my photo on the company brochure."

He laughs as we look at the serious face looking back at us. My hair was tied back, and I had a stern look on my face. Even then I was formidable.

"This is me and Lisa when we went to Brownie camp. She hated every minute of it but I was on a mission to get the most badges by the end of it."

Charlie nudges me. "I can just imagine you giving out the orders."

Laughing, I pick up one of my sister's wedding and grin. "Here's Lisa and Bradley. There was also a picture of her first marriage here. Mum diplomatically put it with the other photos that we don't like reminding us of the mistakes we've made."

We are interrupted as mum wheels her hostess trolley into the room. A warm feeling grips me as I see the polished wood of the tray that has wheeled in most of our meals over the years. I begged her to get rid of it because I mean, who uses a hostess trolley these days? But she was adamant and I don't blame her, really. So what if she still uses one? Does it really matter anyway?

She hands Charlie a cup of tea in the cups she reserves for guests, instead of the mugs we all prefer. I can see she has also rustled up some Jammie Dodgers and Wagon Wheels that sit beside the teapot wrapped cosily in its jacket. Charlie smiles as he takes the cup and says warmly, "Sorry to land on you, Mrs Matthews."

She waves her hand. "Call me Pauline, dear. There's no formality here."

She winks as she hands me a cup and I see the approval in her eyes as she nods towards Charlie.

We share a smile that speaks a silent code learned over many years of familiarity. Mum likes him that's obvious and why wouldn't she?

We all sit comfortably in the little living room sharing the moment. Past, present and future sit side by side and merge into one as we talk about anything and everything. She asks Charlie lots of questions about his family and me about my work.

After a while, I say apologetically, "I'm so sorry I've been a stranger, mum."

She looks a little surprised. "Don't worry about it, dear. I know you lead a busy life and don't have time for socialising."

She turns to Charlie. "We're all so proud of Vicky. Marjorie Cousins was only asking about her the other day when I went to Bingo. Her daughter Melanie went to school with Vicky and hasn't done half so well. She works in the local bakers and is on her third live in boyfriend. Marjorie told me she was on the list for one of those new affordable housing in Merton. It's a step up, so fingers crossed she gets on the housing ladder."

She turns to Charlie. "What about you, darling? Have you managed to get one foot on the rung yet?"

Charlie smiles sweetly, "Not yet, Pauline, I still live at home."

She shakes her head. "Never mind, dear. I know how hard it is to get a deposit these days. It's scandalous how much property prices are around here. Melanie's a lucky girl to even get on the list for one. Luckily, Vicky managed to scrape together a deposit for her flat in Worcester Park by sheer hard work and determination. It's why we leave her alone you know. She works all the hours God sends just to pay the mortgage. Like I said, scandalous."

I shrink down in my seat. I feel so bad.
My mum thinks I'm working hard to scrape by. She is so wrong. I work hard just so I can overpay the mortgage and realise the dream of being mortgage free in ten years. I choose to work relentlessly and keep my spending to a minimum because of it. However, I am fast realising that money counts for less than I thought when compared with spending time with family and sharing in their lives. So what if I'll shave a few years off the mortgage? I won't get that time back with the people I should love more than money. I am learning a valuable lesson and vow to turn over a shiny new leaf next year and make more time for my family.

When we stand up to leave for once my mum looks quite sorry to see us go, instead of her usual relieved expression. She walks us to the door and hugs us in turn. "Don't be strangers, both of you. I know it's probably the last thing you want to do but I would love to hear about your fast-paced life. It gives me something to boast about at the Bingo."

I feel a huge wave of affection almost drown me as I turn and hug my mum. It no longer bothers me that she has so little. As it turns out she has a lot more than me. She has friends, a nice home and a family she can be proud of. What right have I to force change on her when she is obviously happy with the life she has?

After assuring her I'll see her on Christmas day at Lisa's, we leave her behind, waving at us until we turn the corner.

31

December 23rd

2 Days to Go

It's the last day of work and I feel as if I've run a marathon. On Saturday the challenge was to go dry-skiing. After my initial worry, I took to it like a natural and by the close of play, Charlie and I were planning a New Year break skiing in the Alps.

Maybe it was my determination to become that skating couple that took the nerves away. Oh, how I've changed.

Sunday was spent making mince pies and drinking mulled wine. Luckily, both were the challenge set which was one we were only too happy to take up. We even went for a walk and picked holly to decorate my apartment. Charlie joked that it was typical of me to decorate with a prickly foliage. However, he didn't object when we discovered a little sprig of mistletoe to bring home and fasten above the kitchen door.

Then on Monday, we took a walk along the South Bank to enjoy the little Christmas market that tempted us with brandy-laced hot chocolate and artisan gifts.

However, today is now the office party, and it's a very different one this year.

Usually, I just show my face for ten minutes and then head back to work. However, this year I have organised it with Charlie and we are now the host and hostess with the mostest. We've ordered large amounts of alcohol and food and devised a secret Santa. The boardroom has been transformed into Santa's grotto and it looks like a scene from Frozen

This year my staff don't look at me with pure horror and dread. For once I see genuine smiles and some of them even take time to speak to me like a normal person. I suppose it's because I no longer speak down to them and rule my domain with fear. No, I've learned that you achieve a much nicer working environment with a few words of praise and a little leniency. For example, I allowed every mother and father time off to watch their children's Nativity plays. I allowed them a bit of freedom if they had errands to run and at our meetings, I tried not to instil fear in my staff but praise and encouragement. I even managed to crack a few jokes, Charlie style, and feel happy that the atmosphere is much more pleasant.

Charlie has also sharpened up his operation. I suppose it's been my influence, but he has adopted a few of my systems and is generally a lot more organised.

So, as we all raise a glass to each other in a toast to another successful year, I am looking forward to the next one in whatever position I end up in.

As the last drop of alcohol is drunk and the last mince pie is eaten, the staff leave for the Christmas break. Charlie and I are the last ones standing and sink back into our seats and smile.

I look at Charlie and say somewhat sadly, "So, this is it. Two more challenges and this will be over."

He nods. "Do you know what you're going to write?"

I think for a moment and smile. "I think so, how about you?"

He nods emphatically. "I've known for some time."

Standing up, he holds out his hand and shakes mine firmly.

"It was a pleasure, Victoria."

I grin. "The pleasure was all mine, Charlie."

As we head back to our respective offices, the challenge of today is forefront in my mind.

Tell me what you have learned in this challenge.

As Charlie said, I have known for some time what I will write.

32

December 24th
Christmas Eve
One Day to Go

As we head through the doors to the office, Charlie smiles sadly. "You know, Vick, I feel a little sad that this is all about to end."

I look around at the sleek, professional space we call home and nod in agreement. "Me too. Although I never thought I'd feel like this four weeks ago."

As we head towards the lift, it strikes me how empty the place feels. It's not just because the staff are now enjoying their Christmas break. No, it's because I wish I was.

Today, Charlie and I have to face Mr Rowanson. The past four weeks are about to count for something and I feel the nerves taking hold. Charlie squeezes my hand reassuringly. "It'll be fine. Whatever happens, I'm with you all the way."

I nod and smile. "Me too, Charlie. I wonder what he's decided."

Charlie leans on the wall by the lift and shrugs. "Whatever it is, will be the right decision. After all, it's still his beloved company and he will do what's best for it."

As we head into the lift, we stand together hand in hand as the doors close and take us the short distance to the man who holds our fate in his hands.

Today, there is no assistant waiting outside his office. The place feels eerie and silent and as if the life has left the building. We are the only ones here and yet it feels right. The last four weeks have taken us on the most incredible journey and one I am loathed to finish. In fact, it has started me on one of my own and I'm impatient to see where that will take me. I am certainly a very different person walking through these doors than I was then. So is Charlie. These last few weeks have changed us both for the better and nobody is more surprised about that than me.

So, we arrive at our destination and stop and share a smile. Charlie nods, "Ready, Vick?"

I smile with a bravery I don't feel and nod. "Ready, Charlie."

He knocks loudly and we wait for the inevitable.

Mr Rowanson smiles as we head inside his office. It strikes me that he also looks a changed man. The tightness to his jaw and the lines around his eyes appear to have softened, and he looks content and happy.

He nods towards the two seats before his desk and leans back watching as we sit. Then he smiles and says warmly, "So, here we are. I must say it only seems like yesterday that you were both sitting here. The month has flown past and I have to say I've enjoyed every second of it. Like you, I have been testing the water."

I look at him curiously. "In what way?"

He grins. "I set myself a challenge every day, much as I did you. Mine were a little different but along the same lines. I wanted to reach outside my comfort zone and push myself. It involved doing things with my family and testing out the new life I want to lead. Well, I'm pleased to report it went well. I've re-discovered things about myself I thought had gone forever. My family have also re-discovered the man they haven't known for some time and now I'm looking forward to a fantastic Christmas surrounded by a family who I believe now want to share my company. After Christmas, Valerie and I are heading off to the Caribbean for a long-awaited holiday and it will be the start of many. During my own personal journey, I've learned things about myself I'd long forgotten and discovered my outlook on the future has changed. It's given me a new lease of life and I'm looking forward to the next chapter with gleeful anticipation. So, that brings me to the two of you and what this month has done for you."

He looks at his computer screen and out of nowhere, the anxiety hits me hard. Oh my God, this is it. The moment we've been leading up to. It's Judgement day and I may not like what I'm about to hear.

I glance across at Charlie who is also looking pensive. He catches my eye and winks and immediately my nerves settle. As he said, we will face the outcome together and whatever it is will be fine by me.

Mr Rowanson turns to Charlie and smiles.

"Charlie. I must say, I'm impressed with how you have handled these challenges. You've given them your full attention and not wavered for a second. I thought you may lose interest after a week but you have proved me wrong."

Charlie looks at him curiously. "I'm sorry to interrupt, Donald but I have a question that has been puzzling me for a while now."

Donald nods. "Go ahead."

"How do you know that we completed the challenges set? For all you know we could have ignored them and carried on with our day. There has been no proof requested, and I was wondering how you would judge our success."

I look at Mr Rowanson with interest. The thought had also crossed my mind on several occasions and yet I never thought to question it. I would always have completed them no matter what.

Mr Rowanson laughs. "I didn't know if you completed them. It was never about that. The challenges were set to make you both see things differently. I guessed that you would approach them in the same manner you do everything you are asked to on a daily basis. I knew that Victoria would make sure you stuck to the plan and you would be so competitive you would give them your all. However, the real indicator is in the letters you emailed me last night. The proof is written between the lines of the words you wrote. I can see if the challenge was completed by those words and don't need any further proof than that."

He smiles at us both and I see a twinkle in his eye as he speaks.

"This is a family business and like I said before, the family element has long disappeared. Somehow it has been edged out by profits and ambition. My brother and I lost sight of what mattered and it only took his death to highlight it. I wanted to prevent you both from making the same mistake. I wanted you to see that there are more important things than the job we do. It's the people we do them for and the world we live in. There is a whole world of extremes outside this panoramic window and you needed to see what that was before you went any further."

He looks at Charlie. "You have lived a charmed life, Charlie. You've always lived well and never had to fight to survive. However, I saw the loneliness inside you. I saw the façade you created to hide the emptiness in your personal life. You made your staff your family and treated them as such. The lines were blurred between work and home and there was a certain chaos surrounding you masking the emptiness."

Turning to me, he smiles. "You, on the other hand, Victoria were all about your profession. There was nothing but ambition in your life and you couldn't see beyond that. These offices were your home, and you cut everyone out of your personal space. You didn't have any. You couldn't see life beyond the job you do and that worried me. It's not natural, and you were storing up a huge amount of problems for yourself in the future. I saw two people who were lost and unsure of how to find themselves. I recognised that look, and I vowed to help you both see things differently."

The emotion hits me as fast as his words. He's so right. The Victoria Marshall that's sitting here is poles apart from the one who was a few weeks ago. My plans have altered and I am happier because of it. I smile at him warmly. "You're right, Mr Rowanson. Every word you say is correct. I've learned things about myself that I've kept buried for years. You have brought out the best in me and it's not in a professional capacity. Whatever your decision, I thank you for that."

Charlie nods in agreement and then Mr Rowanson says loudly. "Anyway, we all agree we have learned valuable lessons these past weeks. Now for the reason for them."

Suddenly, the atmosphere changes and I sit up a little straighter. Charlie looks at me nervously as Mr Rowanson reverts back to business.

"I asked you both what you have learned. I wasn't surprised by what I read. Both of you told me what I hoped to hear and the letters were remarkably similar. Much like we've discussed, you learned things about yourselves that surprised you. You told me how the last few weeks have changed you and how differently you now saw the world. Charlie, you have learned more control. I sense a professionalism in your words that wasn't there before. These challenges have opened your eyes and you see the consequences of your actions and have a more mature outlook on life. Victoria, you have calmed down a lot. There is a warmth to you now that was sorely lacking. You have relaxed and realised that not everything should be approached with a cold, hard, professionalism. You have learned to consider other people's feelings and are now aware of their lives outside these walls. Both of you have learned the value of family and that is the most important thing we have. Like I said before, this is a family business and that was the most important lesson you needed to learn. The office is a happier place and the staff keen to succeed alongside you which means that productivity is up. So, that brings me to the outcome - the prize that you both fought so valiantly to win. The next step where you go forwards and I back. The company."

I think I hold my breath as the last few weeks flash before my eyes. Everything we have done has been heading towards this moment. However, there is something that needs to be said before the decision is delivered, so, I raise my hand and say loudly, "If I may just say something, sir."

Mr Rowanson looks surprised and nods. "Go ahead."

Swallowing hard, I look at him and then at Charlie who looks a little confused. "I must just inform you that things have changed between Charlie and me. We set out on this challenge as colleagues but have ended it as so much more. I need to tell you that I love him. Somehow these challenges brought us together and I can't bear to think of a life without him. I'm not sure how you feel about colleagues dating, you may frown on it and it may change your mind. But I would rather walk away than lose him. I have realised that Charlie means more to me than my job and the only thing that now matters is my future with him. If you need me to look for other employment, I will because out of the two of us he is the one who deserves this job the most."

Charlie interrupts. "No, Vick. I won't let you throw away everything you've worked for. You deserve this much more than me. I would rather be the one to walk away because like you, the only thing that matters is us. We are at the beginning of something life-changing and I'm sorry, Donald but it's not this company. Vicky and I want to make our life together and if that can't be together here then one of us must walk away. I need to be that person because the best person for this company is her."

Mr Rowanson looks at us and nods. "Interesting but nothing I hadn't already worked out."

Once again, the twinkle is back in his eye as he smiles warmly. "I'm happy for you both, really I am. In fact, things have worked out even better than I hoped because now I can see my decision was the right one all along. However, as I said at the beginning, that decision isn't being made today."

We look at him in confusion as he laughs and spins his computer screen around to face us. "There is still one more challenge and the winner will be announced on Christmas day."

We look at the screen and see a picture of the Nativity. He clicks on the image and the challenge is revealed.

Go to midnight mass.

Seeing our shocked faces, he grins. "The reason for Christmas and the perfect way to complete the challenge. Maybe you should both pray hard tonight for what you want to receive on Christmas day. Let's just hope it's what you both really want."

Standing up, he holds out his hand and shakes ours in turn. "Thank you for everything. Now off you go and enjoy your Christmas break. As of the New Year, this office will have a different occupant and only the magic of Christmas will dictate which one of you it is. Happy Christmas to the both of you and good luck with it all."

We return the greeting and as we turn to leave, I wonder what his decision will be.

33

I think we are both a little shell-shocked as we head back to Charlie's. We head back via the River Thames and walk for a while along the Embankment. The air is cold and crisp and yet we walk holding hands with a warmth in our hearts. Every step we take is a shared one and for the first time I have let someone in and discovered that life is a lot better because of it.

We grab some takeout coffees and walk briskly along, enjoying London at its finest. The crowds of people swarm past, heading home to their own Christmas. I hope they have a family to share it with as memories of my own lonely ones over the years come to mind.

Charlie also seems in a reflective mood and says, "You know, I meant what I said back there, Vick. You are the best one for the job and I would step down in a heartbeat for you to succeed."

I squeeze his hand and say jokingly, "You don't get to be the one to make all the sacrifices you know. What if I want to be the greater person in all this? Typical Charlie, so selfish."

We grin at each other and then he spins me around and pulls me hard against him. We stop on the busy path and he looks lovingly into my eyes. "I love you, Victoria Marshall. You annoying, irritating, infuriating, lovely, beautiful woman. I want to say those words to you for the rest of my life but I'm worried that once Christmas is over, you won't be able to stand the sight of me."

Laughing, I pull his face towards mine and whisper, "You don't get to make the grand gestures alone, Charlie. I love you too. You are infuriating, annoying, childish and testing but all of that is pushed away by your kindness, generosity of spirit and warmth. You are everything I always wanted and never thought possible. I love you, Charlie and I want that love to grow into forever."

Our lips meet and I taste the future. I relish the feeling that I have met my match and whatever happens next, nothing will take that away from me.

"You have got to be kidding!"

I look at Charlie in horror as he looks at me sheepishly.

"I'm sorry, Vick. I didn't arrange any of it but you know my mother."

I sit down on the settee in Charlie's house and put my head in my hands. "Please say you're joking. Please say you're winding me up."

He sits down beside me with a thump and says miserably, "I wish I could, babe, but we'll just have to make the best of it."

Before we can say another word, we hear, "Cooee, Charlie, we're here. Is anyone home?"

Groaning, Charlie stands up and shouts, "In here, mum."

I stand beside him as Linda rushes into the room looking as if she's dressed for Siberia in a fur-lined coat and Russian style hat. "There you are. Come and hug your mother."

She races over and hugs each one of us in turn and says excitedly, "Harry, honey, they're in here."

Harry follows her into the room and booms, "It's bloody freezing out there. Get the fire going and I'll crack open the warm stuff."

Our peaceful haven is now full of activity as Harry and Linda fill the place with loud conversation and laughter.

Lila accompanied them and has set to work rustling up warming drinks and delicious food as we all settle around the fire and catch up.

Linda grins and says loudly, "I'm sorry to land on you, guys but we couldn't bear to think of you here alone at Christmas."

Charlie says somewhat disgruntled, "We weren't going to be alone. I was coming to you tomorrow and Vick was going home."

She just shrugs, "Well, it isn't right. Emily will be here soon and we can start celebrating. Now, make sure you're on your best behaviour because we've invited some friends around this evening."

Charlie groans. "You're joking, aren't you? Not again. Why couldn't you have left things as they were?"

Harry booms, "You know your mother, son. Any excuse for a party. Anyway, where's your Christmas spirit? Much better to be surrounded by people at Christmas, hey, Vick?"

Grinning, I nod in agreement. "You're so right, Harry."

As I snuggle next to Charlie with his arm draped around my shoulders, I couldn't care less who they invite. All I want is right next to me.

The rest of the day is spent preparing for Christmas. The last-minute preparations are made and Charlie and I are despatched on tree decorating duty.

We set about transforming this Knightsbridge home into everything Christmas. Fairy lights are strung up everywhere. Decorations are brought down from the loft and tastefully arranged. We work alongside Linda and Harry and when she arrives Emily joins in. Linda makes sure the conversation never runs out and Christmas music fills the usually empty house. I watch it come alive before my very eyes and the usual sterile space is filled with warmth and laughter. The large rooms that usually stay silent are filled with activity that brings them to life. Fires burn in the grates of every fireplace in the house and delicious smells waft out from the designer kitchen as Lila cooks up a storm.

We just have time to change before the first guest arrives.

I watch with interest as a woman heads into the room dressed to impress. She smiles excitedly and Linda shouts, "Nicky, you made it."

The two women shriek and fall into each other's arms as Harry shakes the hand of a jolly looking man who follows her in. "Bill, it's good to see you."

Nicky looks around and shrieks again. "Emily, babe come and give your old Aunt a hug."

Bill smiles over at us and shouts, "Charlie boy. Long-time no see. Who's the babe beside you?"

Charlie laughs. "Uncle Bill, I'd like to introduce you to Vicky, my girlfriend."

His Uncle shakes my hand as his Aunt races over and pulls me into a warm embrace. "Vicky, honey. Pleased to meet you. Linda's told me so much about you."

I feel a little shocked as they babble on asking me everything about myself, as Linda thrusts large gin and tonics in their hands.

The doorbell rings again and again and the normally empty home fills up with various people all much like Linda and Harry and nothing at all like the ones from Oxford.

After a while, I turn to Charlie and say with astonishment, "Are all these people your family, Charlie?"

He grins. "If they're not, they're honorary ones. These are my parents' closest friends and family. They all grew up together and come from all walks of life. Some still live where mum and dad started out and some run hugely successful businesses of their own. Mum's friends that she grew up with are here with their husbands and probably every Aunt and Uncle I have.

I look around me with awe, as I see a very different sight to the one in Oxford. These people are genuine. They are happy to be here and there's a lot of laughter and fun.

There are no polite conversations, just raucous ones full of humour and banter. I'm accepted as a member of the family and everyone is interested to hear about my life and I love hearing about theirs. Not everyone is rich and successful. Some have normal jobs like Casey from the hair salon Linda trained at. When she left school, she trained in hairdressing and I laugh at the stories they tell. There are those who have done well and run successful companies and I'm interested in hearing how they started.

The time passes in a flash as I lap up the lives of this interesting group of people. All the time Charlie is by my side and if he wanders off to chat to another group of people, I catch his eye as I chat happily with another. Our eyes connect across the room and I don't need him standing beside me to feel our connection. For the first time in years, I fully relax and let my guard down around the most delightful of company.

11.30 comes and Charlie takes my hand and whispers, "We have a date, remember?"

Nodding, I follow him from the room where we grab our warmest coats and boots from the cupboard. The party is still going on getting even louder as the alcohol takes effect. Emily follows us out and rolls her eyes. "Room for one more, they are exhausting me. I think I need some spirituality to guide me back on the right path."

Laughing, Charlie thrusts her coat towards her. "Of course, you can come."

As we walk along the now deserted streets to the church nearby, Emily says gratefully. "Vicky, I wanted to thank you for what you did."

I look at her and smile. "I was glad to help. Did you ever hear from Marcus again?"

She shakes her head sadly. "No, but then again I didn't want to. I realised what a fool I'd been and actually wrote and apologised to his wife."

Charlie pulls her against him and hugs her hard. "Good for you, Em."

She nods. "I should have known he was just spinning me a tale. I suppose I was blinded by his charisma and wanted to believe he loved me."

Nodding, I say sadly, "Men like that know how to play the game. They say what you want to hear and reap the rewards."

Then I laugh. "Not this time, though. In the new year, Marcus Adams will be a lot poorer as a result, both financially and publicly. Sally will get the lot in return for her silence and he'll be another divorcee living alone estranged from his family. Don't feel bad for him as I'm sure there will plenty of willing females waiting to keep him company. I feel sorry for him though. He will have lost the one thing we all should protect with everything we've got - family."

The others nod in agreement and then Charlie says, "So what now, Emily?"

She shrugs. "Who knows? I may travel for a bit because I need to get my head straight. I'm not sure what I want to do and just hope I discover it soon. I'm happy that you've both found each other and I want that too. I want to find someone who loves me for who I am and not in the name of desire. It's a rare gift when you do find them and I've recognised it's more important than anything."

As we reach the impressive church, we walk inside three very changed people.
Mr Rowanson said to pray for what we wanted tonight. I have no need. I have everything I want right beside me.

34

Charlie and I are up before everyone like two kids who can't wait to open their presents. This is it. The day of reckoning and the end of the line.

We decided we would open the Advent Calendar together. It doesn't matter who wins the challenge, we will support each other whatever happens.

So, we sit back against the pillows and just stare at our respective phones nervously. It's a little after eight and we see the notifications flash up signifying the end of the challenge. I feel strangely nervous and Charlie appears a little pensive beside me. I feel a little sad as I say as brightly as I can, "So, this is it then."

Charlie nods. "I suppose it is, babe."

We smile at each other. "Ok, but before we end this, Charlie, I just want to say this has been the best time of my life. I never thought I'd be sitting here next to you on Christmas Day when we started this but I'm so happy I am."

His eyes soften and he says huskily, "You know what, Vicky? It's the same for me. I hope this will be the start of the rest of our lives waking up beside each other. I want us to grow old together and look back on a happy life with no regrets."

Just for a moment, we stare at each other and I feel my world right itself around me. There are no more insecurities and shadows to haunt me. Whatever happened before has brought me to this point and now it all makes sense.

Charlie smiles and says ruefully. "Ok, on the count of 3 1-2-3…"

Simultaneously, we open the Advent Calendar and see a picture of Santa with lots of toys around him on his sleigh. The words. "*Happy Christmas!*" fill the screen and I feel the butterflies fluttering inside as I click again and see the words.

Congratulations to the new MD of S & D Rowanson Ltd

Just for a minute, my heart sinks.

I've won.

I suppose the news doesn't really sink in because all I feel is disappointment for Charlie. I almost can't look at him as he says quietly, "What does yours say?"

I show him the screen and a huge smile breaks out across his face. "Congratulations, babe. I'm so happy for you."

I swallow hard as I feel the tears welling up as he hands me his phone. There on his screen is the same message as mine.

Congratulations to the new MD of S & D Rowanson Ltd

The relief hits me as I realise what we dared to hope for has happened and we grin at each other.

Charlie laughs, "Do you think this was always going to be the outcome?"

Nodding, I smile happily. "Yes, I think he knew from the moment he set the challenge. As he said, we both have qualities the other lacks. We need each other to balance the equation and there was never really going to be any other result."

Charlie reaches over and pulls me over to him and says softly, "Congratulations, Vick. You will make an excellent Managing Director. However, I'm getting in first and claiming Donald's office as mine."

Pretending to frown, I say curtly, "In your dreams, Charlie. We both know that office's mine. Donald only gave you joint responsibility because he knew I was the real one in charge."

He pushes me playfully, "You can keep on deluding yourself if you want to, babe, but we all know a woman's place is in the shopping mall and not in the boardroom."

With a strangled cry, I leap on him and we are soon engaged in a huge play fight that only ends when we hear a sharp knock on the door, "Kids are you decent in there? It's Christmas day and Santa's been."

I look at Charlie incredulously and he grins. "Sorry, Vick, there's nothing mum likes more than

Christmas day. I should have warned you about this but you're about to have one of your headaches."

Sinking back on the bed, I pull a pillow over my head and groan. "Finish me off now, Charlie, it will be for the best all round."

He whips the pillow away and grins down at me like the idiot he is. "Sorry, babe, you don't get away from me now, *partner*."

My eyes soften as we share a triumphant look. Partners in every sense of the word.

Charlie wasn't kidding when he said his mother likes Christmas. She must have bought all of Harrods because it takes us all an hour to unwrap the glittering parcels that she has arranged under the tree.

I feel quite ill as I see the huge expense she has gone to and feel embarrassed about my own offerings. However, they open them as if they are the best gifts they have ever received. In the end, I bought them all something quite similar. For Linda a pamper day at a local London spa with one for Emily to keep her company. For Harry, I bought a racing car experience and for Charlie a secret London trip, showing the history of it and places that are not on any tourist map. I didn't forget Lila and bought her a pamper package at the spa of her choice.

You would think I'd given them the world as they totally overreact on opening them. However, it makes me feel warm inside as I recognise the genuine delight in their eyes. So what if they have more money than sense? They have something even more valuable that can't be bought—love.

I'm happy to see they include Lila who sits with us as a valued member of the family. They pile expensive gifts on her and fuss around her making her feel as special as she is.

Breakfast is spent in the fancy dining room that rarely sees the human form. It lies empty for most of the year but is now full of life and laughter.

We feast on bacon and eggs accompanied by the finest champagne. The conversation flows easily and I feel like one of the family as I relax among them.

At one point Linda leans over and whispers, "You know, honey, I'm so happy Charlie found you."

I look across and see him teasing Emily and grin. "Same, Linda. He's very special, you must be very proud."

She nods and I see the proud look of a mother towards her son as she says, "I'm so proud of him, Vick. It's not been easy for either of them having us for parents."

I look at her in surprise. "Why do you say that? You're both amazing ones."

Shaking her head, she looks a little sad. "It wasn't the life I thought it would be when Harry and I married. I thought it would be normal where we lived in a semi-detached and if we were lucky managed to move to a new build in Esher. But things happened and before we knew it we had more money than a lottery winner and I thought we had to spend it. Huge houses, cars, you name it, we had it. I thought I was giving the kids everything they could ever want, and I became the wife that I thought Harry needed. We tried to mix in a world that wasn't ready for us and sometimes I look back and wish we did live in the semi-detached, walking our kids to the local school and joining in with the other mums. I missed out on all that, Vick. I sent my babies away to boarding school because I thought they deserved the best. I followed Harry around the world because I wanted to be the perfect wife. Do you know what though, Vick? My heart has always been in that semi-detached house. All I really wanted was there, so if I can offer you any words of advice for your future, do what makes you happy and not what is expected of you. Don't be afraid to go against expectations because you never get that time back."

As I look at Linda, I see a woman like every other one I grew up with. Strip away the expensive wrapping and we are no different. So, it's either the champagne affecting my brain or my own sense of what's right when I say eagerly, "What are you doing for the rest of the day, Linda?"

She looks surprised. "Nothing, babe. We're staying here for lunch and then may take a nice walk along the river."

"Would you like to come to my sister's for lunch instead and meet my family? Say no if you want to, I would completely understand but you would be most welcome."

Then something happens that takes me by complete surprise. I see Linda's eyes fill with tears and she looks as if I've given her the best gift in the world as she says in a quivering voice. "Do you mean that, Vick? Would you really like us to gate-crash your family Christmas?"

Reaching out, I hug her warmly and whisper, "You are family, Linda and they would love to have you."

She smiles and says softly, "Thanks, babe, we would love to come."

Two hours later and after a few frantic phone calls we are all bundled into the Range Rover and speeding towards my sister's house.

Charlie looked at me as if I was in leave of my senses when I explained what I'd done. However, despite the major anxiety of what is about to happen, I wouldn't have wanted it any other way.

As we near the estate that is worlds away from the type of estate they're used to, I feel anxious about what they are seeing. This place is nothing like Knightsbridge and the smart houses give way to the rather shabby ones nestled together in cramped streets that have little greenery.

Emily looks around with interest, "Is this where you grew up, Vicky?"

I nod. "Not far from here but very similar."

Linda says wistfully, "I grew up in a place like this. We both did. It makes me feel a little nostalgic."

Harry reaches over and squeezes her hand. "Same, honey. Do you remember when we all met up on the rec every night after school?"

She laughs. "Yes, we were a right group of tearaways. We had our first snog on the roundabout in the kiddies play area. It made me feel quite sick, actually."

Charlie laughs. "Great memory, mum. Your first kiss with dad made you feel sick."

Emily giggles as Harry laughs loudly. "It wasn't the kiss that caused the sickness though, was it, Linda?"

She shrieks with laughter. "Harry, you're impossible, not in front of the children, what will Vick be thinking?"

Charlie nudges me and Emily laughs. "Charlie has a habit of making everyone sick."

He grins wickedly, "You all love me and you know it. Even Lila. You all right back there, babe?"

Lila laughs from her place in the seat behind us. "I'm fine thanks."

I turn around and smile at her. "What about you, Lila? Where are your family today?"

She smiles a little sadly. "My mum lives in a nursing home just outside Weybridge. My father died and I have no brothers and sisters. I'll go and visit mum later but she won't remember me."

I feel shocked as I hear her story, I never knew. She smiles reassuringly, "Don't look sad for me, Victoria. Linda and Harry are my family now. They have been for many years and I'm happy with them."

Linda says loudly. "Of course, you're family, babe. We couldn't cope without you."

Leaning towards her, I say quietly, "What about love though, Lila, don't you want to have a family of your own one day?"

She turns a little pink and Charlie nudges me. I look at him in confusion as Linda teases, "I wouldn't worry about Lila, Vick. I think Graham has his eye on her."

Lila shakes her head, "No he doesn't, he's just kind."

Emily snorts. "If it's kindness in his eyes when he sees you then I want some of that. He's besotted,

Lila. You're just never around long enough for him to pluck up the courage to take it further."

Lila is spared from answering as the Sat Nav announces,

You have reached your destination.

My heart lurches as I look at the familiar sight of Lisa's front door hiding behind Bradley's motorbike. Not for the first time, I wonder what on earth Harry and Linda are going to make of all this?

Then I wonder what on earth my family are going to make of them?

35

We bundle out of the car and the door opens and we see my sister's anxious face looking out. Her eyes widen as she sees the six of us standing there carrying large bags of food and everything Christmas.

Stepping forward, I hug her warmly and whisper, "Thanks for having us, sis."

She steps back and smiles. "Hi, I'm Lisa, Vicky's sister. It's a pleasure to meet you."

Linda steps forward and hugs her hard, "I'm Linda and this is Harry. Thanks for having us, love. We've brought some food and drinks to help out. I hope you don't mind."

Lisa shakes her head as we all carry something into the small house that looks even smaller now we are all crowding inside. Linda says excitedly, "Harry, this reminds me of my house in Sherman Street."

He nods. "Good little house that one. The council certainly knew how to build a good solid house."

He turns to Bradley. "When would you say this one was built?"

He looks surprised. "Just after the war, I think."

Harry looks thoughtful. "Yes, same age, babe. Not many built like this these days, Linda. Shame really, I'm betting these houses will outlive most of the rubbish they throw up now."

Emily rolls her eyes, "You should know, dad, you build most of that rubbish."

Harry laughs loudly. "You're right there, Emily."

I see the wide eyes of Sophie and Thomas looking at us all as if royalty has visited. Laughing, I head over to them and say with interest "So, what did Santa bring you?"

Sophie looks excited, "Why, the iPhone of course, Aunty Vicky. Look, it's set up already and I've already taken fifty photos and opened an Instagram account under a false name."

I look at her phone and my heart sinks. "Are you sure about this, Sophie? There's plenty of time for all of that when you're older."

She shrugs. "You might be right. Mum has made the settings private and I only have one friend on it because no one else has one."

I feel myself relax a little. "So, who's your friend?"

She smiles. "Mummy."

Lisa comes over and says softly, "Always will be, baby girl. Remember, your best friend is always your mum."

Smiling, I reach for my phone. "Maybe you should show me how to set up one of those Instagram accounts, then we can be friends too."

Sophie grins and sets about showing me how to join the rest of the world on the virtual highway.

About half an hour later my mum arrives and I see her eyes widen as she sees the large number of people sitting in Lisa's living room. Racing over to her, I hug her warmly and say, "Happy Christmas, mum."

She laughs as she looks around at the chaos. "Well, this is unusual."

As Lisa takes her coat, I introduce her to everyone and then watch with interest as she sits down next to Linda and they start chatting as if they are long-lost friends. I see Bradley chatting to Harry over a couple of beers and watch Charlie building some sort of mechanical monster with Thomas on the carpet. Lila and Emily are giggling in the corner and Lisa turns to me and smiles. "They seem nice, Vick. You seem really happy."

I look around and say happily, "I am, Lisa. I never realised the importance of family until I met Charlie. It doesn't matter how much money someone has, or what they do for a living, all that matters is spending time with the people you love and who love you."

She nods. "I'm glad you're happy, Vicky. You deserve it more than anyone I know."

Shaking my head, I say firmly, "Everyone deserves happiness, Lisa. It doesn't matter where you come from or where you end up, family matters more than any of it."

Christmas dinner this year is a strange affair. Lisa has brought out the decorating table and created one huge table that runs the length of the living room. Somehow, she has managed to rustle up enough chairs by raiding the garden shed and bringing in the plastic ones that only needed a wipe down. A bed sheet makes a brilliant tablecloth, and the table is soon set with an array of mismatched china and cutlery. The food that we brought with us is added to the Ocado delivery and the table is soon groaning under the weight of it.

As we all sit huddled together in the small room, the laughter is loud and genuine. The sound of cheap crackers fills the air with their snaps and the jokes are read out accompanied by loud groans and laughter. We all sit wearing paper hats and smiles bigger than usual as we chat among ourselves. In fact, as I look around, I notice there is only one face missing and turn to my mother and say, "Have you heard from, Eddie?"

She looks a little sad. "He's had to stay in Scotland and man the bar. He skyped me earlier and seems happy but I thought he looked tired."

Linda says with interest. "Who's Eddie?"

Mum smiles proudly. "My son. He lives in Scotland and manages a bar there with his girlfriend. We don't see much of him and especially not at Christmas. They are so busy all the time."

Linda looks sympathetic. "Shame. That must hurt not seeing him. When are you going to see him next?"

Mum smiles bravely. "Oh, who knows? Maybe in a few months when things are less busy."

Linda looks excited. "Why don't you come to Scotland with us, Pauline? We always head there for Hogmanay and you can visit Eddie at the same time?"

She looks across to Harry and says loudly, "Honey, we could fit one more person in the helicopter, couldn't we?"

I think my mum is about to faint as Harry booms, "Course, babe. Sounds a great idea."

My mum looks a little shell-shocked and says in bewilderment, "What do you mean?"

Linda smiles. "We always go to Scotland for the New Year. The Scots certainly know how to party and we meet up with friends there. There's always room for more and we could visit your son at the same time. Normally we only go for a few days because Harry always has to head back to the office a couple of days later but it would be good to have someone to chat to."

Mum's eyes fill with tears as she looks at Linda as if she's her fairy godmother. She whispers, "Are you sure it's not too much trouble?"

Shaking her head, Linda smiles warmly. "Of course not, it will be great having someone I can chat to and if your son is as amazing as your daughters, I can't wait to meet him."

I look across at Lisa and she smiles wistfully. We all miss Eddie. As big brothers go, he's the best and when he moved to Scotland it meant we see less of him than we would like. Mum misses him so I'm glad she is getting this chance.

Blinking away the tears, I start to help tidy away the dishes but as I do Linda says loudly, "Listen, guys, we have a family tradition that I hope you won't mind me mentioning."

I sit down and see Emily roll her eyes at Charlie and giggle. I look at Linda with curiosity as she beams around the table at everyone.

"Well, it's something we used to do in my house when I was a child. We never had the sort of Christmas's that I do now and money was always tight. However, as the years have gone on, I realised more and more that it wasn't about the money at all. We always went around the table after dinner and gave each other gifts. Not the gifts that cost money but the gifts of a promise."

The room falls silent and I laugh at the confusion on the children's faces. They must be wondering what other types of gift there could be other than the tangible kind.

Linda carries on. "So, I'll start." She turns to mum and says, "My gift to you, Pauline, is the trip to Scotland. I promise to take you to see your son and bring you back home again. Our house will be yours for the entire stay and I promise to show you a good time."

Mum looks quite taken aback but I see the emotion in her eyes as she stutters, "Thank you, Linda. That's a very generous gift and one I can't easily match. However, my gift to you is to take you to the Bingo with me as my guest and show you how we party there."

Lisa groans as Linda looks excited. "Party - at the Bingo?"

Mum laughs. "Yes, it's called Bongo Bingo. It's amazing, Linda. It's like one big party and they have music and a DJ and everything. The prizes are hilarious and quite honestly you can't move in there because it's the hottest place to go in town."

Linda claps her hands excitedly. "I love Bingo. I used to go with my mum and it became a regular treat that I'd look forward to."

She turns to Harry. "You hear that, Harry, Pauline's taking me to Bongo Bingo and I can't wait."

Harry smiles happily at his wife and says in his loud voice. "Well, I guess it's my turn now."

He looks at Bradley and says loudly, "Brad, a little bird told me you were in the market for a job. Well, I happen to have lots of them so, my promise to you is a job on one of my sites. I'll sort out something for you in the New Year and if you report to my office on the 4th of January, I'll have them fix you up with something you like."

Lisa gasps as Bradley looks shell-shocked. I see the emotion on both of their faces as I realise what this means to them. I swallow the huge lump in my throat as Bradley says emotionally, "Thanks, Harry. I really mean that, it means a lot."

Harry smiles happily as Bradley turns to Lisa. "My promise is to you, Lisa. I promise to become the husband I should have been and do more around the house. I'll fix that skirting board in the kitchen and paint the hallway."

Lisa rolls her eyes, "I'll believe that when I see it." Everyone laughs as she turns to Emily. "Emily, I promise I'll take you to see that film you mentioned. It's a bit of a selfish one because I've been wanting to see it for ages and had nobody to go with."

Emily looks at her gratefully and turns to me.

"Vicky, I promise to make you dinner twice a week for a month. You work so hard and the ready meals you eat aren't fit for the purpose."

Laughing, I smile my thanks and turn to Sophie.

"Sophie, my promise to you is that I will be the sort of Aunt I should have always been. Every last Saturday in the month we will do something together, a girl's day out that you can choose."

She squeals loudly, "Can we go to a spa, Aunty Vicky?" Lisa rolls her eyes as I laugh. "I'm not sure you're allowed to a spa but I'm sure we could get our nails done and go swimming if you like."

Nodding her head vigorously, Sophie turns to Thomas. "I promise to make your bed for one week, Thomas."

Thomas looks a little unimpressed and whines. "I don't make it anyway, how is that a good promise?"

Sophie frowns. "It's a great promise you idiot."

She turns to Lisa. "Tell him, mum. He's so ungrateful, isn't he? Take that back and say it's a good promise otherwise I'll tell Sally Barnes you fancy her."

Thomas yells. "Shut up. Tell her, dad. She can't go around telling lies. I'll put spiders in her bed."

Sophie shrieks. "Gross, tell him, mum. He can't put spiders in my bed if he does I'll...."

"ENOUGH!" Lisa shouts while reaching for her wine. "One more word out of either of you and I promise you both you'll be washing up for the whole of next year."

Everyone laughs as Thomas looks at her sulkily and then turns to Charlie. "Charlie, I promise to teach you how to play Fortnight."

Charlie looks excited and this time I roll my eyes. Then he turns to me and says sweetly, "Vicky, I promise to annoy you every day for the rest of your life and treat you so well you will never want to let me go."

Linda pipes in, "And take her shopping. I'm sorry, Vick but I still can't get my head around the shopping aversion thing. If I promise you anything and I know it's not my turn, I'm going to make a shopper out of you."

Lisa giggles. "Good luck with that."

I interrupt and turn to Harry and say, "I know I've already had my turn but Harry, I promise you that when I ask about your business, I'm genuinely interested. I promise that I'll badger you constantly throughout the year for tips on how to succeed and because that's not a great promise for you, I also promise to be your caddy when you need one when you play golf."

Harry laughs. "Anytime, Vick. This old man could use some help getting around the golf course these days."

Linda buts in, "You've no problem with stamina, babe." She winks as Emily and Charlie groan.

Then she turns to Lila and says, "I promise to get you and Graham together, babe. I've always considered myself a bit of a matchmaker and will enjoy playing cupid."

We all laugh as Lila blushes and giggles. "I promise you all that I'll wash up while you let your dinner go down."

We all shout, "No!" Then Linda says, "We promise you a night off, babe. Pauline and I will wash up and Harry can dry." Harry groans and looks around him with a resigned look.

Then Charlie holds up his hand and says loudly, "One more thing, Vicky and I have some exciting news."

There's a sudden hush as everyone looks at us expectantly. I see Linda grip my mother's arm and say excitedly, "Oh my God, please say you're getting married, please say I'm getting my grandchildren at long last, oh my god, please, please, please!"

Charlie laughs and looks at her apologetically, "Sorry mum, not so fast."

He smiles and I grin as he says, "Vicky and I, as of today, are joint Managing Directors of S&D Rowanson Ltd. We have both been promoted and in the new year will work together in charge of the biggest Law firm in Canary Wharf."

The noise is deafening as everyone congratulates us but I don't miss Linda's disappointed expression as she catches my eye and shakes her head sadly.

When the noise subsides, she says, "You poor thing, Vick. It's not right you know. How is that good news? You'll be busier than ever and it's no fun working all the time. Charl, babe, make sure you let Vick have lots of shopping time. A girl needs the distraction you know, and it's not right thinking of her working so hard and missing out on the good stuff."

She turns to my mum and looks so upset I get a fit of the giggles. "Your poor daughter, Pauline. Don't worry, I'll make her take some time out."

Mum laughs. "Good luck with that, Linda. Vicky does what she wants and nothing will ever change that."

As I catch her eye, I smile. Yes, I've always been the same. Relentless and driven and set on a plan. No room in my life for frivolities and with one aim in mind - getting ahead. But as I look around the table, I realise my priorities have changed. Work is still an important part of who I am and always will be but now my home life is more important.

As I catch Charlie's eye, I smile happily. The most important thing in my life is now an annoying, childish, infuriating package that will drive me mad with frustration. However, he is also the most loving, sexy, gorgeous man, I've ever met and above everything, I will always put him first.

So, I make a silent promise to him - he will get the girlfriend he deserves. Someone who will walk side by side with him through life and always be there. Team Charia is about to take the legal world by storm but more important than that, we are now a family and will never lose sight of how important that is.

The End

Have you checked out my website? There are free
books and giveaways on offer there.

sjcrabb.com

Have You read?

sjcrabb.com

19164176R00186

Made in the USA
Lexington, KY
26 November 2018